# What Happened to Karisma?

By: Joanne Monteiro

Published by Joanne Monteiro in Partnership with
The Literary Revolutionary

THE LITERARY REVOLUTIONARY & Co.

www.theliteraryrevolutionary.com

Editing By: Anjé McLish
Cover Design By: Opeyemi Ikuborije

**Manufactured in the United States of America**

ISBN #: 978-1-950279-34-0

Joanne Monteiro

# What Happened to Karisma?

# What Happened to Karisma?

# Table of Contents

# Chapter One

Welcome on a journey which has no end. Still many bricks not laid, still many friends not paid the price of redemption. The journey will be steadfast, so try to keep up. Fresh out of high school Mercedes Rollins was her name. Not any ordinary young woman. A heart made of steel, never wanting for anything except the love of her father. Never needing anything, because she always took it. Her body was curvy, her hair shoulder length, her complexion indescribable, her trademark, a tattoo across her belly.

The tattoo was in her father's legacy. She felt as though if she had this design, her father would understand how much love she had for him. The tattoo had so many colors. So bright and vibrant that it caught all men's attention except the one that she wanted it to. Mercedes described it as a combination of a white dove showing the peace that she wanted to overwhelm her, and the broken rainbow to symbolize the great feeling she would never achieve; because she could never mend the fence with her dad. Men loved her; women loathed her. She had no shame. If your man was fine, there was a possibility he would not be yours for long.

Mercedes lives in Las Vegas. The city of lights is what it was called. Las Vegas was possibly the most racist place that Mercedes could escape to when she looked for somewhere new to start her life. Her first visit was amazing. Mercedes walked down the strip in awe. She stood on the streets and watched all the attractions. She stayed up all night wondering to herself how much fun she could have in a city like this. As she stood in front of Treasure Island and watched the pirate show, she thought, hey, I could dance better than these chicks.

That first night, Mercedes made up her mind and decided that she was going to make a life change. She was going to leave her past behind, move to sin city where no one knew her, and make a fresh start. Mercedes didn't want to take this journey all alone though; she was still a little nervous about that. As she flew back home and watched the lights of Las Vegas fade away, she thought about the one friend she knew she could count on would be the person she would throw the idea out to and maybe, just maybe, Jasmine would be down.

Mercedes was an exotic dancer. The club she worked in was a high-class establishment. It was a very dark club located off the strip, which kind of disappointed Mercedes. The windows were covered in expensive drapes. This reminded her of the casino. Every table had fresh lavender carnations with a black vase. Every tablecloth was purple and black. The candles on the table were scented which added to the décor.

Mercedes was a hoe to everyone who thought they knew her, a misunderstood woman and an unguided soul. Mercedes was a woman who lacked the warmth of a real man. She spent her days sleeping and her nights filled with sweaty hands on her thighs and a stiff penis on her backside. Whenever someone would pay for a lap dance, she would even go as far as masturbating for them for the right price. She didn't need the money; she enjoyed the reaction that she would get every single time. It was the very same. The sexuality of it all was a turn on. It would get her juices flowing. No man could turn Mercedes on, only Mercedes was fit for that job. She learned about self-gratification early in life. Night after night Mercedes managed to have all the attention at the club. Sometimes, her co-workers got upset because all the men would wait for her. Mercedes would walk around the club strutting her stuff just to make them upset. She knew it wasn't right, but she didn't really care. She had a really fucked up way of treating people and once you treated her wrong, it was a wrap.

They would call her a bitch underneath their breath and sometimes, Mercedes would hear them and just laugh it off because she thrived off jealousy. This made her feel more important and even more confident. Her boss loved her. She was the money maker and she knew it. As much as her bosses hated when she needed time off, he would give it to her because he knew that once she came back to work, she would go hard. She basically made up the money that the club lost when she was gone. At the end of every night, Mercedes would take out all her money and count it in front of the other girls just to piss them off. Then she would go over to any guy, mostly her regulars, and they would escort her to her ride. Just as she got to the door, she would lift up her skirt and point to her basically bare ass, except for her G-string which was barely showing, bend over, and walk out telling the other females to kiss her ass.

At home Mercedes had a roommate, a best friend, a soul mate to guide her, but she would never know. Mercedes had convinced her friend to move with her. To her, she was a plain Jane, smart-ass who knew too much at an early age. She worked at the phone company and went to school at night. She was also amazed at the Las Vegas lights. It didn't take much convincing her to make the move. Mercedes had arranged a quick weekend trip out to Las Vegas and the next thing you know, her friend was asking her to move to sin city. Her soul mate's name was Jasmine. Jasmine spent most of her time daydreaming, telling Mercedes that she didn't have to live the life she did. She watched over her buddy like a hawk. She was the voice of reason for Mercedes. Jasmine was a chocolate sister, much more attractive than she portrayed herself. She lacked the charisma and spirit of ever becoming a real diva.

Her ass was flat as a pancake, but her breasts were as supple and beautiful as a porn star. She wore her hair in a ponytail most of the time. If you caught her with her hair out, people would be amazed just how long and beautiful it was. When she did wear it out, she would look in the mirror in amazement, almost thinking that it wasn't really her. Thinking *what is wrong with me?* when there wasn't a thing wrong except that she didn't believe in herself as much as she should.

She admired Mercedes for having the courage for doing things, but she loathed her for destroying her temple. She knew it would not be long before it all fell apart, before Mercedes world would come crumbling around her. Who would be there to help pick up the pieces? Not any of those scum sucking men. Speaking of men, who in Jasmine's life were few, she would find wounded souls to become involved with. People she could take care of. She never wanted anybody to help her. That is where her weakness really lied. It wasn't her lack of confidence which played a big role, but the fact that she would seek out all of the helpless men that she thought she could save. It would wind up hurting her to the core. In her heart, Jasmine knew it wasn't the right way, but it was her only way.

Mercedes would say to her girl, "You're not going to get anywhere in life always paying other people's way." Jasmine would always respond the same, "Shut up bitch". In her mind, she was thinking people pay your way because you fuck them for free. They should give something back in return. Sometimes it would be food, jewelry, and sometimes they paid her car note.

Mercedes drove a Durango, Jasmine a Civic. Two totally different people, rarely going anywhere together; though, on January 18, 1989 something changed. Two new people were born, two caterpillars changing into butterflies, or maybe I could say two beautiful girls changing into women; or so they thought.

"For once Jasmine, let's go to a club together and not do our own thing but hang together," Mercedes belted.

Jasmine didn't respond at first. She felt a little bloated. She just got over her period, thinking maybe she could use one more day of solitude before going out and facing rejection, or so she thought. Mercedes kept hounding her,

"Jasmine put your skimpiest skirt on and let's bounce," Mercedes said.

Jasmine stayed quiet thinking this is pointless, also thinking that if she went this one night, Mercedes would get off her back.

So, she replied, "Yes, yes, yes, now shut-up bitch."

Mercedes smiled, hoping this could be the beginning of a new Jasmine. Little did she know that it was the end of the old Mercedes, for a while at least. As they got dressed to go out Mercedes was torn between two outfits, both which Jasmine felt were tasteless. She thought that they should never be worn in the public, unless you were walking the streets of Hollywood Boulevard. One was a black dress that stopped underneath the ass. It had hundreds of little holes in it. Mercedes thought this was sexy. Jasmine thought it was trampy.

Jasmine said, "Girl you are not wearing that shit out with me. People are going to think you are a hooker and maybe me too just because we are together."

Mercedes grinned, "Good fuck them, now I have my mind made up. And I am not wearing panties."

Jasmine was disgusted. Mercedes pubic hairs came through the holes. She would constantly be touching herself all night. Jasmine wore a gray pantsuit with a leopard shirt underneath. Mercedes looked and just said "corny", thinking to herself, *this girl will never figure out that sexy is good to catch a man when you are going to the club.*

Jasmine would drive that night, but not her car because in case Mercedes decided to bring a man home, she didn't want them in her car. You know, the whack Honda Civic.

As they got in the car, Jasmine reminded Mercedes "together all night"

"Yes," replied Mercedes.

Jasmine was concerned by Mercedes' choice of outfits and the potential danger this could bring. She would not voice her concerns out loud to Mercedes, but in her mind, she thought nothing could not turn out good with her buddy dressed like a slut. Jasmine just shook it off trying to keep as positive as possible.

11:30pm.

They ended up at the Ambassador, Mercedes choice of course. A cover charge of $5.00. As they walked through the door, Jasmine saw two men. One guy stood with a metal detector, the other one with a walkie-talkie.

"Open your bag," one said as the other patted Jasmine down.

"You can go," he said.

Jasmine stood on the side as they did the same to Mercedes, except the one with the walkie talkie's fingers got stuck right in front of the many holes by her vagina. Jasmine watched him go in and out with his index finger, and the look of enjoyment on Mercedes' face. I mean after all he was fine; about 5' 9" around 170 pounds of muscle, brown skin complexion, almost looked as if he may have been Spanish mixed.

"Mercedes!" Jasmine screamed.

It startled them both. He removed his hand, her opening her eyes, "Can we go please, together?" she emphasized with a look of disgust. Mercedes sighed as if she was interrupted and strutted inside, glancing back at this man, as she glided her tongue across her lips.

"Listen," Jasmine said sternly, "if it's going to be that type of party you can count me out. I do not get down like this shit and if you ever pull any shit like this, you are on your own."

Mercedes, knowing she was wrong, nodded in agreement. But in the front of her mind she was thinking about this guy, Felix. He had softly whispered his name to her, letting her to look him up later. In her head she was grinning, but she was hoping that Jasmine didn't see it.

1:30am

The music was pumping and both Jasmine and Mercedes had already indulged in several of their favorite cocktails. Mercedes, gin and cranberry, Jasmine, white Russian. For the first time ever, Mercedes saw a side of Jasmine never seen before. Guys were flocking towards her. She danced the night away with numerous partners. Some grabbing her big supple breast and others groping her small ass. She didn't seem to mind though. She was into the music and drinks. Mercedes was very happy that Jasmine was having a good time. She had almost forgot that Jasmine wasn't that tight stiff check she acted like most of the time,

As Mercedes was dancing and admiring the attention Jasmine was getting a man, that same man from the door, walked up behind her and placed his arms around her thin waist. She turned around and gazed into his eyes.

"Hi," said the chiseled man. "I'm not sure if you heard me whisper my name at the door. Do I need to reintroduce myself?"

With sweat pouring down her face she replied, "Mercedes."

Felix looked her up and down as if he was a doctor examining his patient. "Would you like to go somewhere where we could talk? Where the music is not so loud?" She looked around to make sure Jasmine was okay, and nodded yes. He grabbed her hand and guided her back through the entrance door, down a long corridor, and through another door. It was quiet in this room. You could actually hear yourself think. For a flash Mercedes did think, was she crazy? But that quickly passed. Felix pulled Mercedes close to him. Her chest touching his, his hands on her large round ass, moving it ever so gently up and down. He started kissing her neck, lips moist, and then he moved up and kissed her chin then her mouth. Her pussy became extremely wet, her mind becoming blank. He stuck his tongue feverishly in her mouth; his hands were now touching her bare ass. He had slipped them up her dress. His hands were kind of sweaty but soft and tender. He laid her on the couch and slowly removed her dress. Felix now had his moist mouth on her breast, licking her around the nipples. He made his way down to her belly button as she massaged her breast. He noticed the tattoo "Mercedes" across her belly. He then gently spread open her legs and let out a deep breath, her body trembling.

"Only if you want," Felix said.

She then, in response, pushed his head between her moist thighs. He began a journey that would feel like it would last a lifetime.

2:55am

Back on the dance floor, Jasmine finally noticed that her partner was missing. Panic struck her as she searched the dark room. Floor pumping from the music, she couldn't hear herself think. Jasmine began feeling nauseated, so she went outside for some air. While walking out the door she saw a man. *Perfect*, she thought, body toned, fudge, muscular and tall, about 6'3", but she had other things to worry about like throwing up right there.

He rushed to her and asked, "Is everything okay?" his voice husky yet tender.

She looked up and replied "yes."

Jasmine was starting to feel better and a burst of confidence came over her. "Excuse Me," she stated. "Your name would be?"

"Alston," he replied with a grin. "Yours would be Jasmine I presume."

She looked startled and confused. "And how would you know that?" she sternly asked as she looked both intrigued, yet concerned.

"UNLV" he replied. "You do take classes, there don't you?"

She smiled and started to walk away. As he watched her hips flow and her tiny ass fade away, he yelled," Can I call you?"

She replied "yes" and walked out of sight thinking, *could I have just let the most beautiful specimen of a male slip through my fingers?* but she dismissed the thought.

4:22am

Jasmine and Mercedes met back up on the dance floor, drinks in hand, both replaying the evening over in their minds. Neither said a word on the way back home. Jasmine was so deep into her thoughts she ran right through a red light, not even noticing the police car on the corner. Suddenly, Mercedes noticed the flashing lights behind them. Alcohol instantly popped into her mind. They had both been drinking quite a bit, but she also realized the time. It was 6:05 am, hours since they had been drinking.

"Jasmine, Jasmine," Mercedes screamed. "Pull over don't you see the cops behind us".

"Oh shit," Jasmine replied. "I didn't even notice."

"Really?" Mercedes sighed.

Jasmine pulled over and got out her wallet. She cracked her window to be able to slip through everything, license and registration.

"Ma'am," the officer said. Jasmine didn't even look at him and just slid them out.

"Did you know ma'am-" before he could even finish, she stated, "I know, I know" As the officer shined the flashlight on her license, he saw her name, Jasmine Black.

"Can you step out of the car Ms. Black?" he stated in a firm, intimidating voice. She was hesitant at first, but something about that voice sounded familiar, husky yet tender. She rolled down her window completely and saw the 6'3', dark brown man with a goatee. Something she didn't even notice before.

The same man that not even a few hours ago was concerned about her. Except this time, he didn't have on black slacks and a gray button up shirt. He had on a uniform looking even sexier than before.

"Do I really have to get out?" Jasmine said.

"Yes," he replied.

Jasmine proceeded to get out of the car. The officer watched like a hawk stalking his prey.

"Maybe if you weren't such a smart ass, I would have let you off with just a warning. But now I must punish you, or we could make a fair trade."

"Maybe," she replied.

"I won't write this ticket if you write down your phone number." He hesitated and then said, "your real number." He could sense that Jasmine played games.

"Can I have a pen?" she requested, then began to write her number down and then stopped, looked over into his eyes and just kissed him, not even understanding why. As she pulled away, she could feel the moisture in her panties. She jumped back into her car, handed him the number, and said goodnight.

# Chapter Two

If time was of the essence, Imani was running out. It was 8:45am and her interview was at 9:30am. Imani Jackson is her name. She is at the point in her life where every chapter was closing. It was winter and living in a big city like New York, she could not keep up with the hustle and bustle. Not a clue on what was next. Imani was a borderline alcoholic; her life revolved around liquor and men.

Never the right choices, she was a short, stubby, and mainly breasts. She scurried to the bathroom and turned on the shower. She stood in front of the mirror as she took her clothes off, "FAT!" she shouted. Just then the phone rang, and she paused for a minute debating if she was going to answer it. On the fourth ring she picked it up.

"Bitch," said the other voice on the line. "Why are you even home?" The voice continued, "Because people like you keep interrupting me."

It was Imani's best friend, probably the most self-centered person that exists. A person that surrounds herself with people that can only make her look better. Precious Gray is her name. Precious is a beautician. She is tall and slender, hair always fabulous and she knew it. No man was ever good enough for her. She was a dick tease to most. Time would be her undoing, because eventually she would run into the wrong man.

By the time Imani hung up the phone, they had already made plans for the night. They would be doing the usual thing: bar hopping. It was now 9:10am and to Imani, getting dressed was pointless. She cut off the shower and proceeded to the kitchen. As she opened the cabinet to see what there was to eat she pulled out the bread, cut on the frying pan, and put some butter in it. *Grilled cheese,* she thought. She went into the refrigerator and pulled out the cheese and a beer. She opened the beer and sat down.

Before she knew it, it was 12:30, she cut back on the shower and got in it. As she ran her hands across her body, she started to remember a part of her life which she couldn't forget. No matter how hard she tried she couldn't forget.

Lonely and vulnerable Imani sat on her couch laughing and drinking with her friend Leslie. In the background the music was playing, "Sexual Healing" by Marvin Gaye. At first, Imani thought that she could control the one feeling she had felt whenever Leslie was around. But on this night, there would be no denying her attraction. Leslie sat with her pj's on, which included a black camisole. As Leslie stood up to get another beer, Imani noticed that she had on thongs. For some unknown reason this was a turn on to her. The feeling was strong yet, Imani tried to fight it. When Leslie sat back down, her round bouncy ass grazed Imani's hand. She thought about pulling it away but she didn't, instead she caressed it, rubbing her hand all around it. Not to push things, Leslie just let her do what she wanted. As Imani began to move up the inside of the camisole, Leslie stopped her. Her friendship with Imani was more important than one night of ecstasy.

"This may not be something you will be pleased with in the morning," Leslie stated, looking directly in Imani's eyes hoping to see some regret. "Please be sure that you understand that your friendship means everything to me," Leslie said.

Imani leaned over and gently kissed her. The smell of Leslie's perfume consumed her. She put her left hand between Leslie's thighs. Leslie was a very frail girl and she wasn't attractive. She had a shape like a scarecrow and her hair was wiry, but her ass stood out. She always felt women understood her more than men. The sensual touch of a woman always made her feel wanted.

The passion that Imani and Leslie shared that one night was never to be spoken of again. The understanding and warmth between them was phenomenal. To Imani, this experience could never compare to any with the many men she had slept with. No one touched her, kissed her, or spoke to her the way Leslie did. Just then, the shower had gotten cold and Imani had snapped back to the present. Her hands were wet with vaginal secretions. She realized without even knowing that she made herself have an orgasm. The first one since that night. She wondered to herself, maybe this experience soured her to men because now a man's touch skived her. The only pleasure she got from lovemaking was oral sex.

Imani got out of the shower with a grin of satisfaction, thinking maybe she should give Leslie a call. She quickly shrugged that thought off. Leslie and Imani had a falling out over money. Leslie owed Imani money and didn't attempt to pay her back, but that didn't really bother Imani. What the real deal was, Precious didn't approve. If one day she ever found out what Imani did, she would never look at her the same way.

At 10pm Precious called her best friend to see if she was making any progress and that she was just about ready to go. Precious drove a Lexus of course. Precious drove wherever they went. She got her car cleaned and waxed once a week. Imani was ready to go.

Their first stop would be Sapphires, a bar that had a dance floor. They would always make that their first stop because it closed a 2am, and to them the night was just getting started. Sapphires had two rooms, Reggae and Hip Hop. Hip Hop was both their things. Precious was very popular and as soon as she walked in, everybody knew her. This never bothered Imani because she always latched on to her best friends. Almost stealing them in a sense, but Precious would never notice something like that. The bass of the music was thumping. They had guys buying them drinks all night long, one right after another. Whenever they would sit down to breathe, here comes someone else. Before they knew it, it was 12am and time to bounce.

The Palace was next and would turn out to be the final stop of the night. As they pulled up to park, Imani noticed a very familiar face, it was Leslie.

"Look," Imani said while she pointed into the crowd. Imani could sense the resentment coming from Precious. They both looked at Leslie and said hi. Leslie smiled and nodded her head.

"See you inside Imani," Leslie stated as she walked through the doors.

Inside the club was packed, maybe 200 people inside, all dressed up like it was a fashion show. Imani informed Precious she was going to the bar to get a drink. Precious stayed behind. As Imani walked through the crowd, she felt a hand touch on her ass. She immediately turned thinking it was one of those ghetto guys being disrespectful, but to her surprise it was Leslie.

At first Imani panicked thinking someone may have seen her but once she looked around, she realized everyone was so into what they were doing, why would they care.

Leslie said, "I'm leaving at about 5:30. What time are you staying until?"

Imani replied, "When Precious is ready to go."

Imani immediately flashed back to the shower this morning as she thought to herself it could never happen again.

"What about an early morning breakfast?" Leslie said. She paused and continued "on me," which Imani wasn't sure how to take. On her body, or was she treating?

"Not tonight," Imani replied. "I'll take a rain check." She proceeded to the bar.

As the evening began to bore them Precious decided it was time to go.

"Would you like to grab a bite to eat Imani?" Precious asked. Imani looked and felt bad.

"No thanks," Imani replied. "Just take me home."

It was about 6:15am now. When Imani arrived at the house, she had 6 messages on her answering machine. She cut it on and went to the bathroom. As she listened, she heard two messages from her mom, two from some guys she had met out before, and two from Leslie. *"I'll be up for a while,"* the message said, *"so give me a call back if you want."* Imani was hesitant but said what the hell. She wiped herself, flushed the toilet, and went to the phonebook to look for Leslie's number. She remembered that she tore it out when she first got angry with her. *Oh well.* At that same moment the phone rang. She quickly picked it up and didn't say a word. She just listened. Imani the female voice on the other end said, "Are you up?" It was Precious. She wanted to remind her that tomorrow was ladies' night at Club Gizmo and to be ready early. It kind of was a disappointment to Imani, and in the back of her mind she had wished it were Leslie.

As she sat there dozing off, she heard a strange sound at her door, was someone knocking? She tiptoed to the door and looked out at the peep hole it was Leslie. She opened the door and said, "What in the hell are you doing here, are you crazy?!"

"Can I come in?" Leslie said. "Or do I have to talk to you in this cold hallway."

Imani grabbed her hand and pulled her inside.

"What's up Leslie? I told you I would get with you later."

Leslie proceeded to tell her that she missed their friendship and threw all the money on the floor that she had owed her. She explained that her life had been messed up, and she is now making it right. She apologized for the aggravation she had caused, and stood up to leave. Imani knew the best thing was to let her walk out of the door. She said thank you, and opened the door. Imani's heart was racing and she knew that she didn't want to let Leslie never make it out of the door. Leslie could feel the attraction.

Imani said, "Stay for a while and we can talk." As much as Leslie wanted her, her conscience knew better. It would only be a matter of time before they would have another fallout, and that would take the beauty out of their newfound friendship. Leslie said goodnight and left.

Imani was resting for about twenty minutes when she heard tapping at her door. She jumped up, not expecting anyone at her home. She noticed that it was beginning to get light outside. Imani went to the door and asked who it was. She didn't hear a reply. Imani then asked again.

Leslie was the voice on the other side of the door. Imani opened the door looking a little stunned. "What's up?"

"I would like to talk if that's okay with you," Leslie said.

Imani noticed a very sincere look on her face. "Okay," she replied.

As Leslie walked into the door her body brushed up against Imani. Imani quickly jumped back in fear, fear that it was going to happen again and make her think that this is really all she wants.

Leslie apologized and advised her it wasn't intentional. It didn't matter though, because Imani was already sucked in. She grabbed Leslie tight and started kissing her. She grabbed her ass and held it like she didn't want to let it go. Not this time. Imani was no longer scared. She knew that this is what she wanted and she wanted it now. Imani dropped her robe, revealing she was naked. Making Imani think that she knew why she never put anything on. She knew or hoped that Leslie would be back. She led Leslie over to the couch and sat down on the edge. Imani spread her legs wide and without resistance, Leslie stuck her head between Imani's legs and began licking her clit, her favorite flavor. Sucking it until Imani began to moan and groan.

Leslie was a little shocked about how aggressive Imani was being. The one and only time this had happened, Imani was very cautious and not seeming to be pleased enough to want to ever do this again.

Imani got her voice to stop quivering and said sixty-nine. Leslie was again shocked, but didn't hesitate to flip her body around. She continued to not miss a beat by sucking the clit oh so gently, pleasing Imani to the fullest. Imani began to kiss Leslie's pussy lips. Leslie was a very clean shaved woman and took extreme care of herself. Almost as though she knew that it was going to get some action. Imani also followed the lead by beginning to suck on Leslie's clit, but not as gently which turned Leslie on. Imani took two of her fingers and began to stick them in and out of her pussy. Leslie was moaning louder than Imani. Leslie was enjoying this exchange as much or even more than Imani. Both women reached their peak at about the same time. Imani didn't want it to stop but she could barely move as they both went to sleep.

It was the next day and it was dark and dank outside. The rain was pouring down Precious' window as she stared out of it. Precious wasn't sure if she still wanted to go out. The decision would be left up to Imani. Precious called her to see what the deal was, and Imani still wanted to go out. She needed to get her drink on, especially after what had just gone on. She could still smell Leslie's perfume lingering around the living room. Imani knew she needed to forget about what happened, but she could only think about how much she enjoyed it. She had a grin on her face that could light up the dark night sky.

At 11:20pm Precious pulled up to Imani's home. She didn't even need to beep the horn; Imani was outside waiting. They decided to stay local because of the weather. They went to a local place called the Sound Bar, and by one o' clock they both were stoned. Precious was busy flirting with a male she had just met and Imani was talking to the DJ.

John was the guy who Precious had met. He was dark skinned, about 6 ft. 4 and had a physique of a God. He acted like he was all that. Challenging Precious, taunting her, telling her that she couldn't handle this. Normally, Precious would never entertain people like this, but tonight she was feeling bold and this coupled with alcohol, was going to make for a crazy night.

John asked if they could go to the car and talk. Precious dismissed the question, practically ignoring him. He decided he would try a new approach by buying her another drink and whispering in her ear. His hot breath gave her the chills. She felt a sensation that she hadn't felt in a longtime. She closed her eyes and enjoyed his touch, by now his hand on her inner thigh. She trembled in anticipation. He whispered let's go to the car. She shook her head in agreement, and then said she had to go on talk to her friend.

Precious went to Imani who was still conversing with the DJ. She pulled her to the side and said, "I think I want to go and get my swerve on." Imani looked at her in disbelief. Precious had always been a flirt, but never actually went through with it. "You have my blessing if you're okay with it." Precious told her that she would make sure she came back to pick her up within two hours. She walked back up to the bar, grabbed John's hand, and led him away. Imani watched and hoped that everything would be okay.

Imani continued drinking and talking with the DJ. The bar continued to empty out. She was so drunk that she didn't even realize that she was the only female left there besides the barmaids. As Precious and John rode to their destination, they laughed and giggled like high school kids out on their first date. They went to the three-star motel. It was $20 an hour or $100 for six hours. He paid for one hour, because he knew she had to get back to the bar by 3:30 AM. If they ran a little over, he would pay the balance. At first it was a little awkward for the both of them. Believe it or not, John didn't do this most of the time and Precious never did. He began by kissing her hands then moving up to her arm. As he did this, she could see his penis becoming erect. She could see how large he was. Precious began to rub his chest, which reminded her of one of her clients' hair she used to do every week. The type of hair that when you rubbed it gently it just moved in that direction. The type of chest hair a woman desires to touch. There were no tangling or kinks in it, and she liked this. He removed her blouse, which was a little uncomfortable for her. She always had a problem with this because her breasts were very small. John didn't seem to mind. He caressed them, licked them, and sucked them. Every move so gentle. She then unbuckled his pants cautiously, but with confidence that she would be able to handle this.

John pulled out a condom and Precious was very pleased; she didn't even have to ask. Once John put it on, at first John had trouble penetrating. So, he decided to go a new route. He took his hand and put it between Precious' vagina, rubbing her clit until she was extremely wet. He then thrusted inside her. She received him like a perfect strike. The next forty-five minutes would be the most passionate of both of their lives. It was pure seduction till the end. Precious realized that the idea of a tease wasn't only a waste of time, she picked the right time to put a stop to it.

Meanwhile, Imani found herself in the opposite of situations. The DJ was coming on hot and heavy, and she was completely turned off. Not interested in the least bit. She kept trying to laugh it off. In her mind, she was wishing Precious had never left. The DJ said, "I'm having a private party and you're the only one invited. Would you like to come?"

"No," Imani responded. She kept glancing at her watch wishing Precious would walk in. The next half an hour would be the most hideous experience in Imani's life.

She watched as the gate went down around the bar. The door was just locked. Imani went to the bartender and said,

"My girlfriend is coming back to get me and I would like to wait outside." She ended her sentence with "please," almost sounding desperate.

"It's much safer in here," the bartender replied. She wasn't sure about this, but didn't leave praying that Precious would come. She sat on the stool in front of the bar. It was quiet, the music that was playing was no longer playing. The bartender handed her a beer and said, "on the house." Imani drank the beer slowly as she watched the three males' cleanup. She no longer saw the bar maids. She felt an arm wrap around her waist, the DJ's. He hugged her like she was his favorite teddy bear. The last words she would say were "no" over and over again.

He pulled her off the chair in one fell swoop. The two other guys didn't even need to assist. They just looked on as if this was a frequent occurrence. He grabbed her shirt trying to yank it off, ripping all the buttons off. She screamed no over and over again. It fell on deaf ears. One of the other guys went over to help hold her arms down. The bra was next. Her big breasts were now exposed. Imani felt as though they could take her life because what was about to happen felt as though they already did. The DJ pulled down her pants and then panties. Practically tearing her flesh, she just kept saying in her head just where a condom.

The other guy was called over by name but she was barely coherent to understand. The two guys pulled open her legs and just that moment she felt something cold pushed insider of her. She let out such a scream that broke glass. It went in and out over and over again hitting her insides so hard she knew the damage would be irreversible. She could hear nothing around her. Imani could only feel pain. To her it lasted forever. When the punishment stopped, the pain didn't go away. She could feel moisture running down her legs like a lake where the dam was broken. A second later, she was barely standing up, her body so limp. One of the men pushed her out of the door with the trail of blood intact. She was now outside naked, going nowhere. She was barely conscious. She prayed and prayed that God would take her quickly, that the nightmare would be over. That maybe some crazy person would just come by and take for life because she knew the longer she stayed out there, the more suffering she would have to endure.

Bright lights further blinded her from the little bit of vision she had left. It was a car, Precious'. Too little too late. Before the car even stopped, John jumped out of the car with the car coming to a screeching halt. Precious jumped out and tears were running down her face, screaming in contempt. She screamed at John to call 911 on her cell phone, and he did it expeditiously.

The police and ambulance were there even faster.

"What happened?" one policeman asked.

"Fuck what happened!" Precious replied. "Take her to the hospital now!"

The policeman didn't like her reply but understood. "Call down, calm down," he said. The paramedic had just put Imani in the ambulance.

"Can I ride?" Precious said, anxiously awaiting an answer and she was told yes She gave John her car keys and asked him to follow. Of course, he would, and did.

They quickly arrived at the hospital, and Precious tried to go to the back but the nurse stopped her. John came in after. "Isn't there someone you should call, her parents? somebody?" John said. Precious hadn't even thought that far. She asked John to hand her her cell and dialed Imani's parents. It was now about 5 AM. The phone rang and rang, finally her mother answered, hello. This is "Precious," she replied as her voice quivered. Imani's family knew her well. "Please come to New Rochelle hospital as fast as you can, Imani is hurt bad, really bad." The next thing Precious heard was a dial tone. Precious dialed another number, a male answered this time. It was Al. Al was a very dear friend of

Imani's family and the person that kept the group together. Precious explained to him the situation and he said he would be there as soon as possible. Before Al left home, he knew that he had to make one phone call. He knew that he had to make sure Imani and Precious' childhood friends were contacted. Even though they didn't live in the same state anymore, they still all had an unbreakable bond and distance wasn't going to change this. He had to call Mercedes, but when he did Jasmine answered. He explained everything to her, letting her know he would call back as soon as he knew more details. Jasmine promised to give Mercedes the details as soon she got home.

It was 7am and everyone was at the hospital. They waited and waited until a doctor appeared. He asked to see only Imani's parents, and informed them that she had lost a lot of blood and was in critical condition. They asked if anyone could donate blood, and that it would be appreciated. They both agreed. The last detail he informed them was that she had slipped into a coma, and the next twenty-four hours would be crucial. Mr. and Mrs. Jackson explained the situation to Precious and Al. Precious cried and cried, blaming herself, wishing she had never left Imani by herself. Mrs. Jackson finally got herself together to find out what happened. She went over to Precious and asked, "Please tell me there wasn't a thing you can do but you tried your best." Precious couldn't even answer. Sobbing, she replied, "I wasn't there. She was alone." Mrs. Jackson smacked her, not being able to control her anger and pain. Precious just cried. She understood her pain. She thought of Imani like a sister. She just went into the corner and kept looking up to ask why.

The policemen were back now taking statements. They wanted to get these people as much as the family did. They interviewed Precious and John, who stayed with her the whole time. He comforted and held her the entire time. He wiped the tears whenever she cried, and this was quite often. Hours had passed and Al suggested that everyone go to the cafeteria to get some food. There wasn't a thing they could do for now. Mr. and Mrs. Jackson didn't want to leave, but they finally convinced them. None of them really had an appetite, but Al forced them to eat. Al took this time to call Mercedes and Jasmine to update them about the situation. This time, he spoke with Mercedes who sounded like she was a wreck. He summarized that Imani is in a coma and she's in bad shape. Everyone is giving blood just in case she needs a transfusion. By the time Al finished speaking to Mercedes, she was in tears.

"Do you know exactly what happened yet?"

"No one knows what happened except Imani, and right now she can't tell us."

"Are the cops trying to get to the bottom of this?"

"Yes," Al replied. "I have to go now; the doctors are coming. I will phone you back if there is anything to tell." He hung up the phone.

They watched as it appeared that the doctor was walking down the hall in a slow pace. By the way his brows were furrowed, they could tell that he was concerned. In turn, it made them all have an uncomfortable feeling.

"She is out of the coma," the doctor. informed them. "But be aware, she looks hideous." He didn't want to use a word like that but they needed to know the truth.

"Will she ever fully recover?" Mr. and Mrs. Jackson asked.

"We will have to wait and see. Right now, she's asking for Precious, is she here?"

Precious stepped up. "That's me. Can I go in and see her?"

"Yes", the doctor answered, "but not for very long."

To Precious, the corridor appeared very long. The walk felt like walking through the desert with no water. Her mouth was dry. By the time she stepped into the room, she could hardly speak. She just went to Imani's bedside and began to cry. The one thing she promised herself that she would not do. Partly because of how her best friend looked, but even more for her own guilt. Imani looked like she was knocking on death's door. Her face was swollen like she was an air balloon that had been inflated too much and popped. Her body lay their limp, numerous tubes hooked up to her.

Finally, the words were spoken. "I'm sorry, Imani. I should have never left you there by yourself. If one day you ever find it in your heart to forgive me, I still will never be able to forgive myself."

Tears streamed down out of both of their eyes. It took all her strength, for Imani to speak. "I have already forgiven you." Taking several deep breaths in between each word. "I want you to go on and continue to live your life without blame. There is no one to blame except those people that did this to me. Don't let anyone make you believe otherwise, my parents, Al, no one. Do you hear me Precious? That's what will make me mad at you."

Precious shook her head in agreement knowing that this would not change her feelings. She wondered how she ever made a friend like Imani and how lucky she was to just be a part of her life. Their friendship had been through many tests over the years they'd known each other but none like this. Precious kissed Imani and left the room.

Back in Vegas, Mercedes and Jasmine were packing their clothes for another trip to New York. They didn't care if they had to wait standby. Just as they were walking out of the door, the phone rang. Jasmine ran and picked it up. It was Al, and he wanted to give them the news. He had no idea they were on their way to New York. Al told Jasmine that Imani was out of the coma. He mentioned that she is speaking, she looks bad, and is very weak. Jasmine told Al they would be there by mourning, possibly sooner. It was

7am when the plane landed. They still needed to get a rental car.

By 8:30am they had arrived at the hospital. Neither of them truly prepared for the site they would witness. As they walked down the corridor looking for room 421 there was complete silence. Mercedes walked in first, with Jasmine following behind. The tears welled up in both their eyes as they tried to hold them back.

"Come over here," a soft voice said. It was Precious. She had been sitting vigil with Iman while she was asleep. Everyone said their hellos. Jasmine walked over to Precious to give her a much-needed hug. Jasmine asked her how she was doing and if she needed a break. Now that they were there, she could go and grab a bite to eat, or make any phone calls she might need to make. Precious thanked Jasmine, but assured her that she was okay and wasn't leaving Imani's side.

Mercedes didn't waste any time to dig into Precious. "Can we go out of the hallway?" she demanded not really giving Precious a choice.

They both went out the door while Jasmine stayed with Imani. Mercedes wasn't really sure if she was doing the right thing, but her blood was boiling. She couldn't shake the feeling that her friend Precious was showing her selfish side, and that was why Imani was in the shape she was in.

Mercedes immediately spoke. "What in the hell is wrong with you leaving her in the bar by herself? Was your pussy that thirsty you couldn't use your brain huh huh?!" Mercedes didn't even realize she was screaming.

"Calm down," Precious said. "We are in the hospital."

"I know I made a huge mistake and you can't make me feel any worse than I already do. Imani told me she was OK with me going and if I thought she would have been in any danger; I would've never left her. "

"If you would have even thought it through one bit, you wouldn't have left. You were local for god sakes; you could have taken her home first. Imani doesn't deserve a friend like you. You have always taken her for granted. She will probably forgive you, but I never will." Mercedes brought out another side of Precious she hadn't seen in longtime.

Precious thought about it before she started to speak, but she knew that she wasn't going to be able to control herself. She just kept thinking to herself *don't do it,* but she could not refrain. She had already pretty much beaten herself up, she wasn't about to let Mercedes do it.

"Let me tell you something bitch, where have you been for the past few years. How many phone calls have you returned, how many letters did you write? What kind of friend have you been to anyone? All you have ever cared about was Mercedes." Precious blurted out. Just as Precious was about to finish ripping into her, Precious felt a hard slap across her face.

First Precious was in disbelief. She stood still; her blood was boiling in her veins. She balled up her fist to strike back but she felt another blow to her face. Amazingly, so did Mercedes. It was Jasmine, who had heard and seen enough. She was heated. What the hell was wrong with her two friends?

"When you selfish bitches finish with your shit, remember why we're here. Not for you, Mercedes, not for you either Precious. We're here for Imani, remember her. The woman in the room, badly bruised, face damaged so bad it may never look the same." Jasmine paused to wipe the tears dripping from her eyes. She needs everyone's strength right now. "I don't give a fuck what you do to each other when she is better but for now, please, for her sake cut the shit," Jasmine stated, walking back into the room with a look of disgust on her face.

Imani was awake when Jasmine walked back in. She asked Jasmine if everything was all right. Jasmine looked at her and said, "It is now. Are you feeling any better girl?"

"Not really," Imani replied. "But I am starving. I am not sure what I can eat, can you find out and have someone get me some food?

"Sure," Jasmine stated. "What would you like?"

"Just bring me anything," Imani said, sounding almost desperate. Jasmine walked out of the room not saying bye to Precious or Mercedes, neither questioning where she was going.

# Chapter Three

Fifteen days later, Imani was released from the hospital. Everyone was relieved. Her spirits were much better. Her face was still swollen. The doctor said everyone would just have to wait and see. It was possible that if necessary, she would have cosmetic surgery. Her parents wanted her to come stay with them, but she insisted on going home. When she arrived at her house, she found roses, carnations, balloons, and streamers. It was a welcome home party. Imani was elated. All her friends and family had gathered together just for her. Too bad it had to be a tragedy for something like this to take place. Usually if there is a happy occasion, it would be like pulling teeth to get people to come out and support. The music was blasting and everyone was getting their drink on. You could still feel the tension between Precious and Mercedes. Their problems with each other continued to grow the whole time Imani was in the hospital. Every time a disagreement would break out, Jasmine was right there to break it up.

Today would be different though, Jasmine could not get involved this time. Probably because she had too much to drink. Precious was hanging all over her friend John, laughing and joking as if she didn't have a care in the world. So, Mercedes decided to say "breaking out tonight to get some dick? It would be safe because she is home and all her real friends are here."

Everyone looked as if their high had just worn off.

"Bitch I know you hear me talking to you."

Finally, Precious stood up to address Mercedes. First, she grabbed her arm and took her into another room. She pointed her finger in Mercedes' face. "If you have issues with me take it up with me not with everyone else. Don't ever as long as you live call me a bitch and disrespect me. I respect and understand that you didn't agree with what I did but my friend, Imani, loves me and forgave me so chill the fuck out and relax. Are you jealous because you and Jasmine don't have the same kind of friendship as me and Imani?"

"Well Mercedes," Precious' voice was trembling uncontrollably now as she continued, "maybe if you knew what a friend was, you would know how to treat one. Jasmine has been a dedicated friend to you forever. She moved to Vegas because she knew what kind of shit you would get yourself into, and she wanted to be there to make sure you were not alone when shit happened. All you have ever done is shit on her but she still continues being your friend and she stood by your side the whole time."

For the first-time Mercedes was speechless. Could it be that some of the things Precious said were true? Mercedes felt her blood start to boil. Suddenly Mercedes and Precious were fighting and everything was flying everywhere. Precious was picking up bottles and throwing them all over the room. Al walked in the room but decided not to break it up at first. Al then realized he must try to break it up, because Imani's room was looking like a volcano had erupted and she didn't have the strength to clean it up. He didn't want to spend the night cleaning it up for her.

By the time they had finished beating each other silly, both out of breath, neither being able to throw another punch or one more thing, everyone was just staring at them. The room was wrecked. There was glass all over the floor. All the bottles that were on the dresser, were now on the floor and the bed. There were trickles of blood all over, both of them had blood on them. There would be no winners this day. They had ruined Imani's party for their own selfish reasons. Imani had seen enough and threw them both out of the house. Mercedes tried to apologize to Imani, but still made excuses that she was asking for it. Precious told Imani simply "we'll talk tomorrow," not taking any responsibility at this time. Imani sat back down and just looked around the room, shaking her head thinking what the hell just happened. She was heartbroken, but quickly snapped out of the funk because she knew she was blessed from what she recently survived. She then continued to enjoy her party.

As the following days passed, Jasmine tried to get Mercedes to reach out to Precious. She would not hear any of this. Jasmine would remind her that they had plans coming up in a little over a week and it would be uncomfortable and unfair to Imani to not have tried to fix this issue. Mercedes deep down knew that Jasmine was right, but what would she say? Mercedes didn't really feel bad about what happened. She knew it wasn't the ideal place and time, but she would not have taken one punch back. In her mind, Precious always walked around like she was bullet proof, and she needed to make sure she knew she wasn't.

Meanwhile, Imani and Precious had begun to mend fences with each other. Imani also felt that Precious should reach out to Mercedes. She tried to explain that history runs deep between them and they need to have a sit down as adults and make it right. How were they going to all hang out together as adults if they couldn't be mature enough to fix this? This conversation was one that took place many times before they had gotten together again. Imani and Jasmine would get together and update each other like every other day saying how stubborn these women were.

They had all made plans to go out two weeks later. Mercedes and Precious had not really pieced it up, but they would do anything to make Imani happy at this time. They would be going to the hottest club in New York, Total was its name, and it was totally hard to get inside. You had to have a hookup to get inside, and of course that is what

Mercedes was good at. Even though she now lived in Las Vegas, her professional times went far. If they were lucky, they might even run into some stars. The idea of them all going out the two weeks after Imani getting released from the hospital seemed like a big leap to Imani. She wasn't 100% comfortable with it, but because of the person that she was and with the support of Jasmine, she thought that she might be able to still make it happen. She would fight through the fact that her face still wasn't back to normal but she knew it may never go back. She knew that her confidence was already shaky, but now it would be even less. Every morning she would wake up, look in the mirror, and think one day she would really recognize the person that was looking back at her. Unfortunately, that day would not be today. She wasn't excited that she would get a taste of how it would be when people saw her so soon.

That day, Mercedes and Jasmine ran around getting their nails and hair done up. Mercedes knew the place where Jasmine could get a nice weave for length. Good thing they started early because they were in the beauty parlor for hours. Next, they went to see if they could find some hot outfits to wear to the spot. Jasmine wanted a pair of wedge heel boots. They stopped and grabbed a bite to eat and talked. Jasmine asked Mercedes to tell her more about Imani and Precious, and what she should expect. Jasmine felt as though since she had moved down to Vegas, she had not kept in touch with them as much and it had appeared a lot of things had changed.

"Well, as I told you before, Imani has gotten more laid back and started drinking a lot more," Mercedes said.

"Precious has not changed much. She still has a nasty disposition but is mostly kinda cool."

Mercedes continued. "Just be you and it will be like old times. You know like when he used to have sleepovers on the weekends at Imani or my house and you would ask why we don't ever stay at Precious' house? She would lie and say because her parents didn't allow it when the truth we all knew was she didn't want us to come over and hang out because she didn't want us to see how her family lived. We tried to make her understand that we didn't care about that, but it was all about appearances for her."

The time had finally arrived. It was 10:15pm and Al's bell rang, revealing Precious and Imani. They walked in the door and Imani quickly said, "I hope you guys are ready, because we have to hurry up if we are going to catch that train." They had all agreed on taking the train because they all were going to drink and no one would be in any condition to drive. Everyone rushed to grab their jackets and bags and jetted.

Precious and Imani talked to Jasmine on the way to the train station. Imani and Jasmine paired off as the rest of the gang walked together. As they arrived, the train was pulling in. They stepped on the train laughing and joking. Jasmine and Imani were picking up right where they left off, on their way to picking up on their beautiful friendship. Jasmine and Imani were very close before Jasmine started to leave to watch out for Mercedes. Their families were close and they spent their weekends as children taking turns sleeping over each other's homes. There was no secret that wasn't safe between them. Even Precious knew that they shared a bond that was sacred. They talked about sports and sex. Imani told Jasmine how she could never keep a man. Jasmine told Imani she was never interested in keeping one.

Finally, Imani asked, "Has anyone ever had a three-way?"

Mercedes quickly replied, "Of course. Hasn't everyone?"

Now, two of the three others replied. "What is it like?" Precious asked.

"It was the best orgasm I ever had. One in your pussy and the other sticking his big fat juicy dick up your ass. Then sucking your tits while you suck his stuff. I must have come three times. Then one just fucks your pussy so hard you can hardly breathe. Is that how it was for you Imani?"

"Not quite that exciting. I did have one fondling my breast while the other moved oh so carefully in an out of my vagina. I didn't suck their stuff. That's whack!"

Mercedes quickly jumped in cutting off Imani. "You have to give head. It's best when you feel his head get so hard and you know he's about to explode. He comes all over your face and you lick it off. You know they say sperm is great for protein."

Everyone was silent for a minute before Mercedes continued. "What the hell is wrong with y'all? All of you must be corny in bed. No wonder you can't keep lovers. Mine constantly comes back for more."

By the time the sex conversation was over they were at Grand Central station. They got off the train, all still thinking about the conversation. They went outside and hailed a cab. Ten minutes later they had pulled up to the club. The line was long but luckily not only did Mercedes have the hookup, Al was a regular and phoned ahead of time. They knew that they were coming. They went directly in the side door, all paying half-price. When they stepped inside, the music totally consumed them. The base was so loud they could barely hear each other. The club had two floors. The bottom floor had strobe lights all over, and there was dry ice coming from the floor and rising up to the ceiling. They had a few tables around the exterior of the floor, but there was plenty of room to dance. They went straight to the bar to get some drinks. Precious immediately saw a fellow she knew from another club. He said he would pay for her drink and of course she let him. Jasmine was more amazed at the whole scene. She hadn't seen so many fine men in one room since she moved to Vegas. Mercedes came by Jasmine making jokes. "Stop drooling on yourself, girl," wiping the corner of her mouth. Jasmine replied, "I see Precious talking to one of her friends, have you seen any of your people from back in the days here?"

Just then, some cute guys walked up where they were standing and were looking Mercedes in the face.

"Don't I know you miss?"

Mercedes looked at them, but didn't seem to recognize them. "Sorry," she said, "you must have the wrong person. I'm not from around here."

"Sorry," he replied, then they walked away.

Mercedes and Jasmine just looked at each other and busted out laughing. By now, Al was standing with them. He had broken out in a heavy sweat in such a short time.

"You ladies come to shake your ass or just in here to profile?" Al said.

"We're coming," they said as if they were joined at the hips.

Mercedes was dancing with some old brother, but he was annoying her because he kept stepping or her feet. She finally got fed up with it and walked away. As she walked through the crowd she ran into the same cutie again, but this time she called him by name.

"Hey Cory," she said with this huge smile on her face.

"Why did you act like you didn't know me before? I knew it was you Mercedes," he said. Cory appeared to be a little agitated by the whole situation, but at the same time he had what you would call a Kool-Aid smile on his face.

"I wanted to see if I could fool you, and I certainly did."

"No," he paused as he replied. "You didn't fool me. I just figured I would play your game. I thought maybe you were lesbian now and didn't want your lover to see you with the best lover you ever had."

"Ha! Things have definitely changed from back then. I have had better lovers than you."

"I'm hurt," he joked. "How long have you been here?  Do we have time for someone for us to catch up with each other, both mentally and physically?"

"We will see.  I am staying at my friend Al's house. You might remember him.  No, I wasn't fucking him, he is legitimately my friend.  Speaking of friends, you see my friend that I was standing with?  You have any friends that might be interested in her?"  Mercedes asked hesitantly, knowing more than likely Jasmine would not be down for that.

"Let me see what I can figure out.  She is not bad looking at all.  Think she may be in for a three some, me, you and her.  Just joking."

Jasmine was at the bar getting another drink.  A young guy walked up and asked the bartender for a drink.  He pulled out his money and asked if he could get her something.  He reached out his hand and introduced himself as Mark Grant, as she introduced herself as Jasmine and asked if he'd like to dance.  He quickly grabbed her drink and led her to the dance floor. *He was a great dancer*, she thought. *If he could dance like that what could he do in the bedroom.*  She quickly tried to erase those thoughts.  She didn't even know him.  Nothing except his name, that he was a great dancer, and he was fine. They danced and danced and it seemed like hours until they exchanged numbers.  Jasmine did let him know that Vegas was her home and she would only be here for a short time. Marc didn't really seem to care about that part.  He made her aware that he would like to see her again, do some more dancing, and see where that would leave.  Jasmine just smiled as she walked away from him.

It was getting late and they all agreed to meet at the bar at 3:30am.  Everyone was accounted for except Precious.  Al decided he would go see if he could find her.  The place was still very crowded.  It was about five minutes before Al came dashing back in a panic.  "I think Precious is about to get into some shit.  We should get over there, like yesterday."  Al said. They followed Al out to her. She was dancing with some ugly muscle guy, flinging her hands back and forth, and watching her very closely were four other girls. These were the same girls Jasmine remembered eyeing Precious down when she was chatting with the same muscle guy. At that time, Jasmine didn't think anything of it because women always stared at her. But this time the way the girls were looking at Precious was different. Jasmine looked at Mercedes and said sternly, "There is going to be some shit." Mercedes gave her a look that could kill. Mercedes walked up to Precious and said let's go. Precious just kept dancing. One of the females just walked up to Precious from the back then proceeded to punch her in the face. Before you knew it a fight had ensued. The four girls were right in the middle of everything. All hell had broken loose. The fight lasted about ten minutes before security could break it up. The music had stopped and there was a dead silence. The bouncer told everyone to get out except Precious, Imani, Mercedes, Al, and Jasmine. The bouncer had them standing next to the bar. As the other girls were exiting, Mercedes got to an argument with one of them. The bouncer that was holding Precious went to break up the argument, and Precious went behind the bar. She started throwing liquor bottles across the bar, bottle after bottle barely missing Jasmine. Everyone was trying to grab her without getting hit. Finally, they got her under control. By then, the owner had caught wind of what was going on and he was pissed. He advised the bouncer to throw Precious out the door on her ass. They did, and following behind her was Mercedes. No one even realized that Imani had gotten pushed outside with the crowd. The owner closed the gate and locked the door with Jasmine and Al still inside. Jasmine begged to be let out but the owner refused to open the door. He stated that he tried to do the right thing and let us stay inside, but their dumb ass friend got out of control and now they all have to pay. She then finally demanded him to call the cops. Within seconds, the cops were outside and the crowd was gone. Apparently, someone had already called the police. With all the chaos, no one even noticed that Precious was back inside. The door and gate was now open. Jasmine went outside to find Mercedes with no shirt or bra on, and even worse Imani badly beaten and lying on the ground. She quickly covered Mercedes up. Mercedes had a busted knee but she was okay. She went to tend to Imani. As Imani looked up at Jasmine, tears began to swell up in her eyes. Imani looked like the elephant man. Her face was black and blue and so swollen her eyes barely opened. It was like the nightmare all over again. She had just begun to recover from a tragic situation and here she was going through it all over again. This time though, Imani felt as though this was Precious's fault. Mercedes and Jasmine lifted Imani up and brought her back inside the bar. Imani was unaware of the damage the people had done to her.

Meanwhile, Precious was in the club looking for her missing jewelry not really concerned about what was going on. The cops questioned each one of them. After, Al told them he had called for a driver to take them home. The whole ride back home, they all argued with each other, blaming each other for what had transpired. Jasmine was trying to focus on getting Imani to the hospital.

"This is not the time for us to accuse anyone!" Jasmine finally said. "We need to stick together because this is going to be another rough time for Imani."

Arriving in Larchmont it was light outside, and you could really see the damage to Imani's face. As they all went inside Al's house, all you could hear was yelling and screaming. Mercedes was very upset. She had run outside the club to help Precious and somehow she had wound up back inside. Imani was quiet the whole time. She knew that she had gone all out for her friend. Jasmine and Al felt guilty because they could not help. Their main focus had to be getting Imani to the hospital. Mercedes went outside to get the car. Everyone else helped Imani up as she was very weak. They arrived at Lawrence hospital, and there was no wait. Al called Imani's family to let them know what was happening. They took x-rays of multiple body parts including her skull and luckily they were all negative. Mercedes asked if there was anything they could do about the facial swelling and bruises. They told her they would just have to be patient. As they were about to release her, Imani's parents arrived. They took one look at her face and went berserk. Mr. and Mrs. Jackson went to the front desk and asked to see the doctor. She wanted to know if it was anything she needed to get for Imani. The doctor informed her to put cold compresses on her face and she should take aspirins for the headache. That night, Imani stayed with her parents.

When Imani arrived at her parents' home, she began to explain the scenario. It was different this time, Imani wasn't saying not to blame Precious. She wasn't really saying to blame her either. Imani was keeping a big secret from all her friends, that her first hospital visit changed her life forever. She will never be able to have kids. The pipe that the pushed into her vagina numerous times ripped her insides so bad that she would never be the same. Her mother asked her if she ever told any of them about the situation and Imani advised them no. She wasn't ready to give that information up yet. Now, the fact is that Precious would have been the one she would have entrusted her secret with, but now she is doubting their friendship. Two incidents she was involved in and one that Imani knew for a fact that could have been avoided. Imani knew that Precious made a huge mistake not listening to Mercedes when she said lets go, and then getting kicked out of the club. How was Imani going to pick up the pieces and move on? She had to find a way to put all of this behind her, and she had no clue how she was going to go about it. She would sometimes have nightmares about what she had been through with her dear old friend Precious. Sometimes, she felt like if she let the friendship go, she would be able to sleep better at night. Hell, maybe she would be able to just sleep. She decided tomorrow was a blessing because again, she would be alive. So, she would think about it then.

The next day in Al, Jasmine, and Mercedes woke up talking about the incident. Mercedes asked if anybody was hungry because she was going to the kitchen to cook some food. As they sat at the kitchen table eating Jasmine said solemnly, "Sorry about last night. I wished it had never happened. I wish I could have helped more, to be honest with you I was scared. I never thought I would say this out loud but I was honestly scared." Jasmine admitted that she does not think that she was built for that type of action. Mercedes respected that fact that she admitted it. Mercedes had to put her two cents in by making sure Jasmine knew that she knew that she wasn't built for it, but also she advised her of the security she felt when Jasmine was around because she knew that she would not leave her. At least she would call 911 to help.

Al jumped into the conversation and advised them both that maybe it was time for them to come back to New York to live. He hoped they would consider it. If not today or tomorrow but in the near future. He admitted that he truly missed them a lot and in order to try to make things right, it would benefit all of them for them to be close. Al just looked at them and thought about all the times he had to intervene in some mess they always made. He remembered when they were kids and Mercedes had a big mouth back then. She would tell him to go away, but he just saw something special in her. He smiled at Jasmine thinking that she was the same old little girl. Yes, she was older now and a little more confident, but nothing really had changed. He felt that she was always a loyal friend to all of them. He advised that if they went back to Vegas things would never get fully resolved and Imani's safety would not be guaranteed, even if they didn't want to admit it. Those chickens at the club may not forget and if something goes down the flight from Vegas is way too long. Both Jasmine and Mercedes looked at each other and agreed to consider it. They were not making any promises to Al.

Time went on and everyday things became a little more difficult for the four friends. Things were not the same. Jasmine realized that her life in Vegas didn't seem as important anymore. She felt as though being around her friends again, even with all the craziness, was where she thought she should be. She felt that her relationship with Imani was getting back on a good page. Even though Mercedes knew being her crazy self wasn't healthy, she was doing it for the right reasons and it made her feel good. It was time for Jasmine and Mercedes to make a decision if they were going to stay or go back to Vegas.

Jasmine thought that they had overstayed their welcome at Al's house. Mercedes wasn't really ready to make that decision, but left it up to Jasmine. Jasmine was the one who had the legitimate job and was completing school, but she didn't feel that it was fair to make such a big decision for the two of them. She asked Mercedes if it was okay for her to sleep on it before making up her mind. Mercedes agreed.

Before Jasmine would make a decision, she went to Al to see how much more time they could stay with him, and how much money it would take for Jasmine to find a decent apartment. She wasn't really too concerned with Mercedes as she had money in the bank and men to pay her way. Al advised Jasmine that they had as much time as needed. He was totally okay with them staying there for the rest of their lives.

Jasmine's next step was to call her job at the phone company to see if it was possible for an emergency transfer. She checked into possibly transferring to a school in New York that would accept the majority of her credits. Jasmine took the entire day looking into her options. Mercedes spent the day on the telephone making arrangements just in case a move was going to be made. She called a bunch of her male friends to see what they could help her out with. She checked the phone book and talked to Al about a great strip club to visit to see where she could bring a lot of cash in. Al informed her that her best bet was in Rockland County where the white men paid well. Mercedes decided she would go and visit once Jasmine made up her mind. Mercedes also called to find out how much it would cost to have their vehicles shipped up to New York. She thought about getting two of her male friends to drive them up, but she wasn't sure if Jasmine was okay with that idea. She kind of chuckled to herself that Jasmine would never go for that because she never wants anybody to drive her ride.

Precious and Imani were not hanging out on a regular basis. Imani still continued to let Precious do her hair every week, but as far as going out to have drinks all the time? NOT! You could see that Precious and Imani's friendship had also changed. It was making Imani depressed, and also she was gaining a great amount of weight. She could no longer fit into the clothes that she struggled to stay in. Precious just watched as she saw her best friend unwinding. Precious knew in her heart that she needed to figure out how to make things right but she didn't know where to begin. She agonized during the day and night about what would be the right approach, but she was clueless. She didn't even know how to show the pain because she always tried to hide the important things. She didn't ever want anyone to know that she was hurting. This time wasn't an exception. Precious knew that Imani had not gotten over the fact that she was beat down really bad, and the fact that she was molested with an object that should not be used on the human body. Yet, Precious still didn't do a thing. She didn't even try to reach out to her. Imani wasn't sure if it was guilt or she just didn't care but it was wrong, way wrong. It hurt her soul and made her question her judgement. Imani knew that she would have laid her life down for her friend Precious, and now she was starting to question her judgement. Could she have been wrong all these years? Was her friendship made up of falsities? She was constantly questioning herself and wondered why her dear friend wasn't providing the answers.

Jasmine sat down with Mercedes and told her that she would definitely have a decision by tomorrow afternoon. Mercedes was curious which way she was leading, but didn't want to put any pressure on her so she just left it alone. That night, Jasmine could barely sleep, tossing and turning. She got out of the bed and decided that she needed to release some tension. She needed to clear her mind. Jasmine went into the hallway and just listened. She was trying to hear if anyone was up. It was about 2am and it was silent. She went into the bathroom and cut the water on in the bathtub. She let the water run over her hands until it was just right. She removed the bubble bath that she bought out of the bedroom from her pocket, pouring the entire remainder of the contents into the water. The bubbles began to fill the tub. She stood and watched for a minute and then went back into the bedroom. With a sense of urgency, she moved through her bag searching for something. She located her vibrator in seconds.

She put it in her robe and rushed back to the bathroom. She got there just in time before the water was almost at the top. Jasmine quickly cut it off and then realized it was the bubbles that were making it seem like it was full. She put her hand in the water to make sure it was just right and it was. Jasmine removed her robe and was bare underneath. She looked down at her toes thinking, *I just got a pedicure and my feet look like this.* Jasmine put a half as grin on her face and got into the water. She still had the bag with her vibrator in it. Jasmine laid back and relaxed for a while, still thinking about what she was going to do. Should she stay or should she go? It would be very easy for her to walk away from the mess here in New York and leave her two friends behind, but could she do this? Jasmine lived by a set of rules that not everyone else did. Her faith was now being tested. She would need to make sure she would let God make the decision for her. But first she thought, pleasure.

Jasmine took her little friend out of the bag and waved it around her wet body. She was trying to decide if she needed any lubricant but why would she as she was already wet. Jasmine put her hand on her left breast and started to massage it slowly caressing the nipple. She could feel a different wetness and warmth between her legs. Jasmine started to lick her nipples. She was going to have an orgasm tonight and she would enjoy it. She cut the vibrator on and ran it across her clit. At first, the sensation was very mild. She started thinking that she wasn't relaxed. Jasmine sat back up and took a couple of deep breaths and thought, *why am I making this so difficult for myself? Clear your head* she kept repeating over and over and over again until finally she started feeling her body tingle. Just as she began to insert the vibrator into her now wet pussy a knock came on the door. It took a minute for Jasmine to get her mind right. She cleared her voice and asked who it was. Al answered asking, "Is everything okay?" "Yes," Jasmine replied. Jasmine listened while Al walked away down the hallway. Jasmine just figured her moment had ended so she just started washing up and let the water out of the tub. By the time she finished rinsing off, she laid down on the bed without putting her clothes on and dozed off.

The next day Jasmine woke up with Mercedes standing over her. Jasmine took a moment to focus her eyes. Mercedes just laughed and said, "You are an ugly bitch when you first wake up in the morning." Jasmine didn't really know what to say at first. She was kind of embarrassed because she had no clothes on and the covers were only partially covering her private parts. She slid the covers over her bare body and cleared her voice.

"Ha, Ha" Jasmine replied. "I am glad you woke up with the jokes."

"Well bitch, it is 2 o'clock in the afternoon and you said you would have a decision for me today. I thought we could go out and have a bite to eat and discuss the decision that you have come up with. You got half an hour to get yourself ready bitch." Jasmine just looked up and nodded her head in compliance.

Jasmine got up out of the bed and looked around to locate her robe that was laying on the side of the bed. She put it on and went into the bathroom. She washed her face and her private areas. She brushed her teeth and smiled in the mirror. Jasmine had her insecurities, but she was content with where she was in her life at the moment. She knew that even though she was going to be able to transfer her job, she would have to deal with a lot of new people. Jasmine was used to autonomy at work in Vegas, and now she had to build that back up in a totally different environment. At least she was confident that her friends would have her back when things go crazy, and she knew they always did. She went back into the bedroom and picked out a pair of jeans and shirt she could find that didn't need ironing. She put on her favorite sneakers and yelled out to Mercedes, "I'm ready".

"Where should we go out to eat?" Jasmine asked. "It is not like we have a ride and we could go anywhere."

Mercedes smiled. "I have arranged everything. Put on your jacket and let's go." They walked out the door together to see a car parked in front of the crib.

"Don't say a word, Mercedes. "Just get in the car and let's go".

They jumped into the car and Mercedes pulled off. Jasmine didn't even ask where they were headed. She was hungry and just wanted to make her decision known. They arrived at Red Lobster, and Jasmine was pleased with Mercedes' decision. She was already planning on what she was going to order. They walked inside and sat right down.

Hell, it was the middle of the day. *Thank goodness* Jasmine thought, as she knew that she had to be on a big budget for a while. They sat for a minute waiting for the waitress to come over. They didn't really do much talking the first few minutes even though Mercedes was anxiously awaiting Jasmine's decision. Mercedes felt that if Jasmine had declined to stay in New York, she would be okay with her decision. Instead, both of them just looked around the diner. Neither of them wanted to start the conversation. The atmosphere seemed a little tense and neither really expected this.

Finally, Mercedes blurted out, "Come on girl, let the cat out of the bag. I have been waiting patiently and cannot wait anymore." Even though she felt a relief by breaking the ice, she still was sort of uneasy about what she was about to hear. She wanted to believe that Jasmine wanted to stay, but it could have just been how she felt, more like wishful thinking.

"Okay, okay," Jasmine replied. "Let's do it, let's move back to New York for good. I may require your assistance for a while, do you think that would be possible." It didn't even take a second for Mercedes to reply. She answered with an emphatic YES. It was all said and done. For some reason Jasmine felt a relief come over her body. She had just figured out that she made the right decision.

The entire next week was full for both Mercedes and Jasmine. They waited to call Imani to let her know about their decision until everything was in place. They apartment hunted together because they both made a decision for them to be on their own. It made financial sense to live together, but as far as them getting on with their lives individually it would be best for them to live alone. Mercedes had a certain way about her and she loved to entertain. Meanwhile, Jasmine was more low key and she knew that if she wanted to go back to school she would need quiet time at night, and if Mercedes wasn't working it would be impossible to study.

It took about two full weeks for them both to find something that they felt was to their satisfaction. They would live close but not too close. Mercedes made the arrangements for both vehicles to be driven from Vegas to New York, and surprisingly Jasmine agreed.

The tension between everyone had finally simmered down. Jasmine felt that the news that they were staying made things a little better because they all knew they could now start to mend fences. Mercedes had stopped concentrating on the rifts she had with the group and focused on her own life and what she needed to put herself in the best position possible in New York. They all felt like time was healing some of the open wounds. Jasmine was starting to feel like a family. She thought that it was the perfect opportunity to go out and celebrate their friendship. Jasmine thought that a girls night out was in order, but she always thought in the back of her mind that a girls night out always turned into a disaster. That morning, Jasmine woke up with a positive outlook. She checked the weather and saw that there was no rain in the forecast. Jasmine looked at the five-day forecast and began making her plans. Jasmine thought of a surprise. A gathering at her house would be a safe plan; she could not go wrong there. A few friends together, having a few drinks and good food, maybe getting a nice friendly card game going and just some reminiscing. Jasmine picked up the phone and called Mercedes first because she was always the busiest, always finding things to do on the weekend. If not going to the club or shaking her ass, just having a male friend come over and keep her company. Mercedes was immediately down for the shenanigans. Mercedes was so amped she said she would contribute by making some food. Jasmine laughed and told her whatever floats your boat. Any and everything is welcome. Jasmine then picked up the phone and called Imani. She explained that situation again and asked if she was down. Imani already had plans but was willing to cancel since it was like a family get together. Imani asked how long it would last because she might want to extend her plans to later in the night. This kind of annoyed Jasmine, almost making her feel like she was cutting into her personal time. Jasmine left it like this with Imani, "Come if you want, or don't come. It is all up to you." Jasmine was now a little pissed and thought about taking a break before calling Precious. Precious wasn't always the easiest person to sell an idea of staying in. So, Jasmine just sat back on her couch and cut on the TV. She flipped through the channels for about five minutes and then picked up the phone. She called Precious' cell first. The voice mail came on.

She then called the house number and Precious answered the phone. "What's up?" she said enthusiastically.

"Hey girl, it's Jasmine. Just wanted to know if you wanted to stop by my place this weekend for a girl's night in. Nothing crazy. Just time to bond."

"I am already aware," Precious said. "Imani surprisingly called me a few minutes ago. It was strange to hear from here since we haven't been speaking that much, but I'm down. Just give me that time and I'm there."

"That's what's up," Jasmine replied. "See you this weekend."

The weekend rolled around pretty quickly. Jasmine was all ready for the fun. Her new place was nicely decorated and so snazzy, at least to Jasmine. Most of the colors in the apartment were a different shade of purple. She had impressed herself. She knew that everyone needed a big, big break. She thought that maybe she would think of some fun games they could play beside just playing cards. But she thought, what could she do? Jasmine sat down on the couch to pick her brain. She got up and went to the frig and began pouring herself a glass of wine. Jasmine didn't realize it was still so early, she thought for a moment, *should I be having a drink?* She paused and was like really. Jasmine thought that she needed extra inspiration. Jasmine went back and sat on the couch. She thought and thought and thought. Finally, after drinking the entire glass of wine, the idea came to her. *We will play a little game to see who really knows who.* But in the same thought she knew this could cause some problems. She picked up a pen to write down the questions she could think of. Jasmine thought about the most fucked up questions that she could for everyone to answer, everything and anything she already knew the answers to, or thought that she did. Things that would expose the true feeling that everyone really had for each other. The only problem was Jasmine had to put questions in about her, and she wasn't too comfortable about this. But in the same token, she knew that this would patch their friendships back up or totally destroy them. She thought long and hard to just throw the questions in the garbage and stick to a game of spades only. As she walked to the garbage to chuck the entire idea, she thought to herself *if our friendships can't survive this, why did we move back to New York?*

It was midafternoon when Jasmine's phone rang for the first time since Imani called her back. She looked at her call id to see who it was. She looked down and smiled, it was Mercedes. Jasmine cut on the speaker and said, "What's up dog?"

Mercedes laughed and began speaking, "Nothing much girl. I am so looking forward to tonight, just wanted to know what you needed me to bring. You need any food or alcohol? Just let me know because I will pick it up."

Jasmine replied by saying for Mercedes to get some beer, chips and dip. "Food is not an issue because Imani is making some fried chicken and ziti. It was really weird though," Jasmine stated. "At first, Imani acted like she wasn't even down with the festivities, but then she called back and started naming all the things she would make or bring." Mercedes was quiet for a minute. Jasmine had to ask her if she was still there. It was like Mercedes had just zoned out. "Hello," Jasmine said.

"Finally. Guess what girl," Mercedes said. "It is kind of funny you say that Imani acted a little funny. She has been acting very weird for a minute, but maybe this little get together will make her snap out of it. I am not sure what has been going through her mind, but it is something big. I guess until she is ready to talk about it, we will never know. I just hope that everything is okay and that she does not let it get too deep before she talks about it."

"Good point," Jasmine replied. "I know that Imani knows that I love her, but sometimes she puts all her stock into the word of her great friend Precious when sometimes I don't think that Precious does not take the same stock into her. Hey, I guess I just want her to be okay." Just as Jasmine was finishing her thought out loud, her phone beeped. She looked at her Caller ID box again and it was Imani. "Speaking of the devil," Jasmine said. "I guess we talked her up. Mercedes get here when you get here, I am not going out, but if I do I will holler at you and let you know, later."

Jasmine clicked over and spoke with Imani for about twenty minutes before she hung up the phone and thought about another glass of wine. Jasmine was in heaven drinking the cheapest bottle in the store. She only liked the sweet stuff, and Harbor Mist was it. Jasmine went into the bathroom and decided to take a nice hot bath. She pulled out her smell good for the tub and began running the water. Her phone rang again, but this time she didn't even look at the Caller ID. she didn't even walk over by the phone. She just thought it was her time before the quiet house got loud. Jasmine loved her quiet time, and this was the last opportunity to get it for the rest of the night. Jasmine stuck her hand into the tub to see how hot it was, and when she found it was perfect she went into her bedroom to pull out her favorite vibrator and lubricant. All the ideas just started flashing through her mind. It was like she was getting moist without even doing anything. Jasmine didn't have to touch herself to get turned on. It was almost like she hopped and skipped on her way back to the bathroom. Jasmine stuck her hand back into the water to make sure it was still warm enough. It was, so she quickly took her clothes off and hopped in the tub. Jasmine thought about all the things that she was going to do and laid back in the tub and put her legs up. She pulled out the vibrator and made sure that the batteries were working. Jasmine felt as if her pussy was all wet and not from the water. She took out her lube and started stroking the vibrator. She cut the speed on low because she always got the best sensation when it moved slowly. She started rubbing the lubricant up and down, stroking it like it was the real thing. This really turned Jasmine on. She began licking her lips because that made it more sensual. She took the vibrator and sat it on the side of the tub and started caressing her breast. She picked up the left breast and made sure that the nipple was hard. Jasmine's breast was so big she could take it and put the nipple inside her mouth, and massage it around the edges. It was where her heart was at. If there was anything that a man should know about Jasmine was that her breast was the key. He could lick it and stroke it lightly that it would make the juices run out her pussy and down her leg. She would shake before the dick was inside her.

After Jasmine finished rubbing and sucking her breast, she began to massage her clit. First at a nice slow steady pace, and then at a much faster pace. She laid her head back like she couldn't take it anymore and thrusted the vibrator inside her pussy, arching her back like there was a man behind the vibrator. Jasmine pumped her hips like she was in heaven. The vibrator had a suction bottom, so she stuck it on the bottom of the bathtub and jumped on the tip like she was riding a bull. She rode that vibrator and sucked her breasts like she had not been fucked in months. She was in a place that she loved to be in. Jasmine felt that she needed multiple orgasms today, because tonight was going to be a piece of work. She felt herself begin to shake and she yelled out "yes" without even realizing that she was going to do it. This didn't stop Jasmine though. She kept pumping hard, over and over again. She pulled out the vibrator and started sucking on it like it was a dick that just came and she needed to suck the rest of the juices out. She rubbed the vibrator between her breast breathing heavier and heavier. At that moment, she realized she needed to start this personal party again.

She began to grab the lubricant and this time she put it between her breasts. She rubbed the vibrator in between them. Jasmine was still gyrating her hips like she still had the dick inside her. It was the best high she could have. All the great feelings of sex without the entanglements. She put the lube back onto the vibrator and started to massage it on her clit. Her clit was hard and ripe and ready to be teased. She teased it until her legs started shaking again. She quickly stuck the vibrator into her pussy and again started pumping. She pumped and pumped until she could not pump anymore. This was it. The second big orgasm. This time though the pussy juice felt like it ran through her body. She felt like she had just hit the jackpot. She was rich and connected if not for long but for that moment. Jasmine was in tune with her body and loving it. Unfortunately, she knew that this had to come to an end. Jasmine pulled the vibrator out of her pussy very slowly to make sure she maximized the feeling. She then put it on the side of the tub and stood up. She started letting the water out of the tub so she could take a shower. Jasmine could not even touch her body because it was so sensitive, but damn she loved it.

After Jasmine got out of the shower she looked into her closet to see what she was going to wear. She figured it was a casual night, no need to look fancy. It was girl's night in. She pulled out some baggy jeans and a tee shirt because it was always hot in the crib. She went over to the radio and put in her Prince tape. Jasmine was always surprised when the tape played, because it was so old and she played it every opportunity she got. As she vibed to the beat she just laughed to herself, thinking what kind of night this could be.

She finished ironing and got dressed. She didn't put on any socks or shoes. She had carpet on the floor and liked to feel the texture on her feet. Jasmine thought to herself how life was so strange. Everything around her was so beautiful but not. She had such a great outlook on life most of the time. In her dreamy world, everything was perfect, but in reality everything was always the same. She went into the kitchen to make sure everything was cleaned up. She took a wet rag and went over the stove to make sure it was perfect. This was a rarity because she wasn't the cleanest person in the world. The fridge was semi full, but she wasn't concerned about this because the grub was coming. She finished in the kitchen and went into the living room and finished listening to the tape. Jasmine was so into the music playing she didn't even hear her bell ringing. Somehow Mercedes and Imani got inside the building and were banging on the door. Finally, Jasmine heard the banging at the door. She quickly ran over to the radio and shut off the tape. She yelled, "I'm coming" as she scurried over to answer the door. She didn't even look to see who it was; she already knew. Jasmine opened the door with her simple smile and opened her arms to give her peeps a hug. Both Mercedes and Imani walked right past Jasmine as she wasn't even there.

"Stupid!" Mercedes blurted out. "You're so into your music you didn't even hear us out there."

"Was it long?" Jasmine asked. They both continued their walk into the kitchen.

"Long enough." Mercedes replied. "It's not as if you didn't know we were on our way to your house and you should have been listening out."

"Just get your ass in here and help us out. You got us carrying the food and drinks and you chillin."

"Why are you always so hostile? Mercedes and Imani, why are you so quiet?" Imani, finally opened her mouth and asked did I have a cold beer waiting for her.

Jasmine just smiled. "By the way, how long before Precious gets here? I am ready to get this party started." Nobody answered her question right away. Nobody really appeared to care what time she was coming. They were more interested in getting the party started right this minute.

Imani turned to Jasmine and said again "Beer. Cold. Now. Precious is always late. I guess she will be here when she gets here. We don't need her here to get the party started. Let's do the damn thing."

"What are we going to do, play three handed spades until she gets here?" Mercedes asked.

"It's not the first time or the last time we will play three handed spades. It's nice to start out like this because you know once she gets here the tension of winning will be intense," Jasmine replied.

"I guess so," Imani replied unsure.

They played spades for over an hour before the bell rang. Precious had finally arrived. As usual in grand fashion. She was the only one dressed up to go out. She had in her hands some chips and dip. That was the only bright spot Mercedes felt. She apologized for being late with some bullshit story. Everyone knew she was busy running her mouth on the phone and wasn't dressed when she got off and so she was late. "Do you think we can get a spades game going now?" Mercedes asked. Jasmine went over to the radio and cut it on. The party was really about to start. Jasmine then went into the kitchen and pulled out two big bowls and two small ones for the dip. She poured the chips and dip in and brought them out into the living room. They sat around the table and Imani started shuffling the cards. "It's on and popping" Jasmine blurted out.

They played spades for over three hours and they all drank like a fish. All but Jasmine, as she was never a real big drinker. She felt it would be better to keep her wits about her. They talked shit and talked shit until there was really nothing left to say until Mercedes said, "I have this kind of to tell the truth type of game that they are playing at my job but you have to tell the truth for real. Are y'all down for a game like this tonight? Heck we all are, well not all, but mostly all fucked up so what difference would it make?" Everyone nodded their head in agreement except Precious. She wanted to know exactly what kind of game this was, a full explanation before she committed to anything. Mercedes broke it down to its simplest form. Basically, she told them they would ask each other a series of questions and they must answer them honestly. It was blind faith that each one of them would tell the truth, because most of the questions were very personal and only they would know if they were telling the truth. If any lies were told and found out, they would have to drink a whole bottle of wine without throwing it up. If they did throw up, they would have to do it all over again. Finally, they all agreed. Now they just needed to figure out who was going to get asked first and who was going to be doing the asking. They agreed to draw cards from the deck. The first high card was safe. She got to ask the first set of questions. The low card was the first victim.

They all picked a card and left them faced down so the other could not see it. They themselves didn't look at them. Mercedes then told them to turn them face up. First, Jasmine turned hers up and it was the Queen of Clubs. Next, Imani turned hers up and it was the Four of Spades. "Not looking too good for you," Jasmine said with a stupid smirk on her face. Imani didn't reply. Mercedes was next. She turned over the Ace of Hearts. She smiled. Precious waited until last. She waited for a minute extra as she had to be extra in everything that she did. She flipped her card and didn't look down. It was a Five of Diamonds. She just escaped from being first. Now they knew the order and the game was about to begin. Mercedes got up from the table and went into the fridge. She pulled out a bottle of wine and sat it back on the table. She looked at Imani and let her know this was her prize for lying. Mercedes was first to ask Imani a question. She had to think about it for a minute. Just then, Precious thought about the questions she thought about and had written down. She thought they would be perfect for the game and then she paused and thought better. She just relaxed and waited to see what they would ask. Mercedes sat quietly for a few more seconds because she wanted Imani to sweat a little bit more.

"Come on!" Imai yelled.

Mercedes looked up and smiled. "I got one for you. I will start out nice with your ass because the night is still young. How do you really feel about your friendship with Precious?"

Imani asked if she had time to think about her answer or did she have to answer right away. "Right away" Mercedes replied. "If you take time to think about it most likely you will throw some lies in there. You are probably thinking about it right now."

"Fine, Precious is like my best friend. I feel like I can count on her whenever I need something. Most of the time she comes through for me. We have a special bond."

"Good answer," Mercedes replied. "I believe you. Is there anyone here who does not?" Nobody shook their heads.

Jasmine was up next with the questioning. She also waited a minute before she asked, but not because she wanted Imani to sweat. She wasn't sure if she really wanted to put Imani on the spot. Instead of asking about her first thought, she went right to the second one.

"So, what do you think about Mercedes?" Jasmine asked. Imani, didn't hesitate to reply.

"Bitch, that is what I think. She is a great friend and in the same token she is a bitch. She thinks she is always right. But she stands up for what she believes in. Oh, by the way, did I forget to mention she is a slut. But she is not ashamed of that either. That does not mean I don't love her." Jasmine looked at everyone and asked if anyone thought she was lying. Everyone thought she was telling the truth again. Imani felt a sign of release.

Precious was the only one left and she didn't think that she would put her on the spot. Precious looked at each one of them and asked "It's my turn now right? Well, Imani, I am not going to take it easy with you like they did. I guess you expected me to ask you how you feel about Jasmine, but that would be a waste of time." Jasmine wasn't sure how she was supposed to take that remark but she just brushed it off. "My question to you Imani, are you bisexual?"

Imani looked stunned. In her head, she was thinking *how could, of all people, Precious ask me this?* If anything, she would have expected that from Mercedes. Jasmine thought to herself *that was the question I was going to ask,* but didn't really want to put her on the spot. Mercedes thought, *wow what a fucked-up friend Precious was to Imani who worshiped her.*

Imani really didn't take long to reply. "If you are asking me if I ever slept with a female, yes. I have not done it on a regular basis and do not consider myself a lesbian. I like dick as much as y'all do. I tried it and yes I enjoyed it, but it didn't change my life. I don't want to discuss it any further. Thanks. Precious wait until it's your turn. Oh, that's next right?"

Mercedes was up to ask Precious a question and she wasn't sure what to ask her. She thought about it as everyone was in the kitchen getting something to drink. Finally, it came to her. She wanted to know the truth so she was going to ask. Everyone came back to the table and sat down. Imani still looked a little pissed but she was taking it in stride.

"Okay, Precious, what do you really feel about me?" Mercedes said.

Precious looked around the table and didn't take a minute more, "I can't stand you bitch. I put up with you because you are friends with everyone else. I think that you are manipulative, a user, selfish, and a hoe. And that is the polite way to say it. If we never talked again, I probably would not give a fuck. How is that for an answer for you?

Mercedes just smiled, but deep in her heart she knew that was how she felt already. She just wanted to see if she was going to have the balls to say it out loud. Jasmine had a look on her face which was puzzling. She thought that maybe Precious had those feelings but not to that degree. Imani wasn't surprised at all.

Next up was Jasmine. "My question is simple; how do you feel about me?"

"Easy," Precious replied. "I think that you are weak. Not weak in the mind but weak in how you act. You don't have any kind of back bone and you don't stand up for yourself when Mercedes talks shit. You are a very nice person and I do like you. I just wish you would stand up for yourself more often. I definitely like you more than Mercedes if that means much." Everyone again looked like they were satisfied with the answer. Jasmine was going to say something, but she knew it would be pointless. She felt like Precious was just trying to treat her like she treats Mercedes, but knew she could get away from saying it. Mercedes nudged Jasmine to try to get her to speak up but it didn't work, and as usual Imani remained silent. Next up was Imani. She thought that since everyone was asking about themselves, heck why wouldn't she? Imani wished that she had a down and dirty question to ask Precious like she did to her, but she could not think of one.

"Well," Imani started. "How do you feel about me?" This time though, Precious paused as she was thinking about an answer.

"Come on now!" Mercedes blurted out.

"Fuck you Mercedes," Precious yelled. "Imani, you are different from anybody I know. I had a feeling you were a lesbo though. I just needed confirmation. It's not like you ever tried to hit on me or anything, but I just knew. I love you girl. You are the one person I can count on. You will do anything with me and for me. I believe you are the one person here who can be used very easily and yes I have used you before, but not to hurt you. I needed something and I knew you would do it. I have nothing but love for you so I hope you got the answer you wanted." Imani got up and told everyone she was going to get a beer. She quickly went into the kitchen and stuck her head in the fridge to cool off, and also block the tears streaming down her face. She didn't want anyone to see how hurt she was by Precious' statement. She grabbed the beer, wiped her face, and came and sat back down, hoping nobody knew that she was upset. Next up was Jasmine in the hot seat and she was ready. There wasn't a thing that she really hid anyway. She felt that she was taking on all questions with a vengeance.

Mercedes started it off. "Have you ever been with a female?

It didn't take Jasmine two seconds to answer. "Hell, to the no. Never. Not even a thought in my mind. I don't even like to watch two bitches together in a porno. I am strictly dickly. I don't think I can answer that question any better than that. And if anyone thinks I am lying kiss my ass. No offense Imani." Everyone including Imani laughed.

Precious jumped right in and followed suit. "So, what do you think about me?"

"Hmm, that is an interesting question that requires an interesting answer. I think that you are selfish. You treat Imani like shit most of the time, but I think in your own sick way you really care about her. I think that you are an okay person most of the time. Would you be my first choice if I needed someone to hang out with? No. But I don't think that

I would be yours so we are kind of even. We have found a way to co-exist without any incidents. You are an okay person but not someone that I would really consider my friend, not even half the time. That is an honest answer for you. Does anyone have a problem with that?" Precious put on a half ass grin and looked up at Jasmine. "That's fair." There was the only reply so Jasmine felt good. She knew she was telling the truth and wasn't worried. She even thought that her question didn't even put her in an uncomfortable position.

Finally, it was all about Mercedes and everyone knew that this could get very interesting. Jasmine wondered the type of questions that Precious and Imani would ask. Would this start a big argument and make the night a total bust? Was there a reason why Mercedes was last. Her attitude could be unpredictable and if someone pissed her off there could be a fight. This game was her idea, so hopefully she would remember this and it would not get out of hand.

First up was Jasmine. She thought for a while and looked at Mercedes and asked. "Have you ever been with a woman?"

Mercedes put a sneaky grin on her face and, to everyone's surprise, she nodded yes. "I have been with a female or two. It was an experiment the first time and I realized I enjoyed it. It was a threesome and was great. So great that I exchanged numbers with the female and she called. I called back and we did it again. The second time was even better because the man this time was hung and he was way into watching than participating. We did things that night that were unbelievable. It was like my own porno. I felt like a superstar, a sex goddess. I never did it again because I thought maybe I loved it too much. It made me think that with one false move I could turn into a lesbian. Now that is what this game was about, honesty. How do you like me now? Who's next."

Mercedes was ready for all questions. Precious had only one question. "What do you think of me?"

"Ha!" Mercedes blurted. "I knew you were going to ask me that. What do I think of the all mighty Precious? I really don't. How is that? I don't really think about you. Mostly because you are phony to me. You are a user. All you think of is yourself and I don't blame you for that. It's because of your fucked-up upbringing. You grew up in a household where everyone had to do what they needed to do to survive. You had a big family with not a lot of money. I'm sure your struggles were real and I get that part. It's just that I don't understand how long you are going to use that as an excuse. I guess only you can answer that." Sometimes people are pathetic because of what they have seen. You have not seen any kind of quality things in your life so how would you really know how to know when something is quality. You have a best friend like Imani that you are willing to risk that friendship at a drop of a dime. You could care less whose feelings you hurt. You had no business asking Imani if she had sex with a female. You had already known the answer and you wanted all of us to know. Why? To take the spotlight off of yourself tonight. Precious you, think you are the prettiest and sexiest person on earth, and most of the time you love being around Imani because she makes you look like that. No offense Imani, because you are beautiful. The answer, like I stated in the beginning of this, stays that same. What do I think of good old Precious? I don't." "We all grew up together watching how our friendship grew and some of them separated. Maybe it's because we were so young and didn't know how to deal with our feelings back then. Or maybe we just didn't want to. Now we are adults and maybe we should start acting like them. Maybe we should ask each other why we would have to ask each other these questions, instead of having adult conversations about our issues. I know it's strange for you to hear me say this, but I do love

Joanne Monteiro

each and every one of you guys despite what has gone on here tonight."

Last but not least was Imani. She was drained from the entire night and all the questions. She felt like this night didn't go the way she thought it was supposed to go. How did this night get so out of hand? She had other plans, and if she had gone she knew it would have gone a lot better. Hearing all the answers made her feel like maybe she really needed to re-evaluate her friendships, hell maybe everyone did. But she knew it was about to be over and she was happy to get it over with. Her question was a relief from all the bullshit that had gone on.

"Mercedes, do you want to go out now?" Mercedes smiled at Imani and stated, "You want an honest answer, huh? Yeah, after all this talking I think it is time for us to go out and shake our asses. I know we said we were going to stay in tonight, but I think after all this true confession stuff we need to get out of here. I hope there are no hard feelings in this room. Let's not even discuss if we are going out. Let's just talk about where we are going."

Everyone thought about going out for a quick minute and then agreed that no one but Precious was dressed to go out. They would have to go home and change and then meet back up and by the time they did all that it would be way too late.

So Precious thought about it and said, "Why don't we call it a night tonight and regroup tomorrow to go and shake our asses. There is supposed to be a hot party tomorrow night. Ladies free before midnight. We can meet up here at Jasmine's house again, if that is okay with you, and go out and party hard." Everyone seemed to be okay with this idea. Mercedes and Precious left together, which surprised both Jasmine and Imani. They just hoped that they didn't go outside and try to kill each other. Imani stayed behind to help Jasmine pick up. Jasmine continued to drink her wine and Imani her beers as they cleaned and talked.

Imani finally said something about the bisexual issues. "Are you a little shell shocked about my woman experience?"

"No," Jasmine replied honestly. "But I thought you said that you didn't want to talk about it anymore."

"Well, I feel comfortable talking to you about it. I know you would not judge me. I was very shocked that it was Precious who asked me about it though. That is something I would expect from Mercedes."

"Yeah, me too. It just makes me wonder why she did it. But I guess that is not what is important. I am comfortable with any lifestyle you decide on. It is not my choice to make and it is not right for me to judge. I still love you wholeheartedly." Imani felt a huge sense of relief. She was happy to hear that she and Jasmine were on the same page. She didn't even feel the need to explain any further about the experience itself because she felt the acceptance of the entire situation.

They both plopped down on the couch and Jasmine told Imani she might as well stay over, and she would take her home in the morning. Imani agreed and Jasmine gave Imani a tee shirt and some sweats to sleep in. Jasmine cut off the radio and they got into the bed and went to sleep.

The next day both Jasmine and Imani were up at the crack of dawn, more Imani than Jasmine. As soon as Imani cut on the radio, that woke Jasmine up. Jasmine rolled over and saw Imani walking out of the room. She asked her if she was trying to sneak out. Imani looked back and shook her head no. Jasmine got out of the bed and went into the bathroom. She brushed her teeth and washed her face. She then proceeded into the kitchen where Imani was cooking. That made Jasmine very happy because she was starving. What didn't make Jasmine happy was the fact that Imani was guzzling on a beer. She felt that she was drinking beer way too early. "I know, I know," Imani spoke. "But I have a hangover and the only way to get over that is to have a beer and knock it out. I am making some eggs and home fries for us and then you can take me home. I know you have some things to do before we go out tonight. I think you need to visit the hairdresser." They both laughed.

They both ate a nice breakfast and threw on some clothes. Jasmine drove Imani home and then continued to the hairdresser to get her hair done not because they were going out, but because her hair really did look like shit. It was shedding a whole lot and was hard to comb. It was a plus she was getting it done before they were going out. Jasmine was relieved that it wasn't crowded and she would not have to wait a long time to get started, because there was nothing worse than needing a perm and waiting then scratching your head right before they called you to the seat. Jasmine brought her laptop with her so that she could play some games online while she was getting permed and sitting under the drying. That just helped to make the time go faster.

Everyone was getting ready for their night out. It was supposed to be a great night with the intention of patching all the friendships up. After the last outing or home get together, this is what they needed.

As the night rolled around, everyone was ready on time for the first time in a long time. Jasmine called Imani, who then called Mercedes, who then called Precious to set their clocks as they were leaving in 1 hour. It was the usual conversation on the telephone. What are you wearing and do you think I need a jacket? How are you wearing your hair? By the time they all hung up the phone, it was about 30 minutes left. They decided that they were going to meet at Jasmine's house.

Jasmine left her door unlocked as she put the finishing touches on her outfit and hair. She was very proud of her accomplishments as she paraded around the bedroom looking in the mirror. Imani and Precious watched her and laughed as they finally interrupted her moment asking if they could leave now.

Since Mercedes had the new whip and always liked to drive, they took her car. Off to Manhattan they went. The first stop was the best club in the city where of course, Mercedes was a VIP. They were immediately let in. The crowd seemed to be a little annoyed by this, but this didn't stop Mercedes from flaunting her stuff. They were led upstairs where it was semiprivate. The waiter immediately came over and asked them what they wanted to drink, and they all placed their orders. Imani, as in her usual fashion ordered two beers.

As the night continued to pass by, all of the women shook their asses. They didn't stop dancing and drinking all night long. Precious was on fire as all the men flocked to her unique look and the mystique she gave off. The men loved her goddess like long straight hair and her thin frame. Her movement was like a graceful dancer. She was dancing with two or three men at one time. She was living on the top of the world. Jasmine went back upstairs in the VIP section to take a break. As she was walking upstairs, she ran into Mercedes who was on the staircase tonguing down a fine black man. She just smiled at her and kept it moving. This was something that she was used to seeing. In her mind, Jasmine wished she was like this. Maybe if she was more out there she could find a good man, but she just shook that thought out of her head and thought *not like this*.

It was about 2am and the gang was all back upstairs. Imani was on her eighth beer, and Precious was way past that. Mercedes and Jasmine were about halfway to their point as they were taking it easy. Mercedes knew there would be more stops, and she had to keep her head to drive. Jasmine asked everyone if they were ready to hit another spot as this one to her was played out. Imani concurred. Precious and Mercedes wanted to stay for a little while longer as they were the men magnets this night. Jasmine and

Imani agreed to hang out for another hour and go dance. Precious was sitting in VIP with one of the men she had met. It appeared that they were having friendly conversation. Jasmine could see her laughing. Jasmine thought to herself that the dude was kind of cute, but not all that. He was dressed in an Armani suit and had a lot of ice on his wrist. *Most likely a player,* Jasmine thought.

Just as she took her eyes off the VIP section Imani said to her, "Do you see what I see?" Jasmine didn't know what she was talking about. She glanced over at Imani with a puzzling look on her face.

"What?" she asked.

"I think Mercedes was going to go over and check out the guy that Precious was chilling with, but now I don't see her." Imani said. Jasmine looked around the room but it was really too crowded and she didn't see Mercedes but when she looked up at the VIP section she no longer saw Precious either.

"Both Precious and Mercedes are gone." *That quick* Jasmine thought. *How did that happen?* She wasn't really concerned about Mercedes because she wasn't in the VIP section when she was looking up there. *But* she thought, *where could Precious have gone that quick without telling them?*

Jasmine grabbed Imani's arm and dragged her to the VIP section. All that was left up there was a burning cigarette. Imani pulled out her phone and called Mercedes while Jasmine phoned Precious. Mercedes picked up and asked where they were. Imani asked her if she was with Precious. Mercedes let her know that she wasn't with Precious. She was on her way up the stairs as she was coming back from the bathroom. Before Imani hung up the phone Mercedes was back with them. Jasmine hung up the phone and let them both know that she got her voicemail.

"Did you see Precious in the bathroom?" Imani asked Mercedes.

"No, why? You can't find her?"

"No," Jasmine replied. "She was just sitting up here with some guy and then she was gone. This is not like her to disappear without telling anybody where she was going. I have an uneasy feeling about this."

"Let's not jump the gun here, Jasmine. She may have just gone outside to get some air," Mercedes quickly replied.

"Then why did she not answer her?" Imani asked.

"Let's just take a moment to think. Let's not panic until there is something to panic about. Jasmine, call her again." Jasmine did so with no answer again.

Mercedes decided to go downstairs and talk to some of her buddies who ran the club to see if there was anything they may have heard or if there has been anything funky going on is the club in the VIP section. Jasmine and Imani chose to stay put. It took about five minutes before Mercedes returned. Jasmine and Imani could not wait to hear what, if anything, she had to say. Jasmine could tell that something was wrong by the look on Mercedes' face. "I think that you should sit down. One of my buddies told me that he saw Precious and that fellow leave together. What disturbs me is he stated that Precious appeared to be drunk, but not putting up a fight. I'm not sure what we should do or if we should do anything at this point but pray." Jasmine asked if she thought that we should stay at the club and wait to see if Precious was going to come back, or should they leave and just try to keep calling her on the telephone. Nobody really had an answer for that. Mercedes was really sore to the entire idea. At first she was thinking it very typical of Precious to flat leave them without an explanation. She was starting to get angry. Imani was in sheer panic. She felt in her heart that something was wrong. Precious would not just do this. Not after all the talks they had. How everyone was calling her selfish, this was the opportunity to prove everyone wrong. Jasmine was just praying that everything was going to be okay, trying to keep a level head.

Jasmine did suggest that they say a prayer for her. She asked God to watch over her tonight. All said "amen" at the same time. They wound up staying at the club until it closed. No signs of Precious the entire night. Both Jasmine and Imani called over and over again with no answer. Their worry now had turned to fear and panic. All of them wondered if they should call the police, but she was grown and there wasn't a thing they could do at this point. Finally, Mercedes told them that they should go home. The first stop would be to check and see if Precious was there. If she wasn't, they would go get some food and think up a plan B. Due to the hour, it didn't take them long to get back to Westchester. They arrived at Precious' home before the sun was up. Imani jumped out of the car to go upstairs. Imani had a set of keys to get inside of her apartment, and went upstairs. She knocked on the door first with no answer. She took out her keys and opened the door. The house was quiet. Imani yelled for Precious with no reply. She walked around the house but it was empty. Imani went over to the telephone to see if Precious had any voice messages. She had three messages. Imani paused, debating if she would listen to them or not, but maybe one of them would give her an idea of where Precious was. The first and second message was just from her family. Nothing important, but the third message made Imani think. It was a message from a female voice, one that Imani didn't recognize. The message read, "*I hope that you made it home safely. If at any time you need someone to talk to, just give me a call. You have my number.*" Imani replayed the message over and over again trying to pick up the voice, but she couldn't. She then looked at the Caller ID to see if she recognized the phone number, but one of the numbers was private which made her think that was the number from the message. What made Imani even more curious was that the call had come in at 4:30am, making her believe that Precious had spoken to someone but not one of them.

Imani went back downstairs to the car. She got in and immediately told them what she had found. This had made all of them a little uneasy. Mercedes felt that something was wrong, but they would not find out until they spoke with Precious. She knew that twenty-four hours had not passed so they could not call the police. Mercedes suggested that they go to the diner to get some food, and while they were eating they would continue to try to contact Precious. Mercedes would call her friends from the club to see if they had heard anything.

When Mercedes hung up the phone at the dinner she advised them that her club friends had not heard anything. She thought that no news from them is good news. Imani informed everyone that Precious was still not answering the phone. Jasmine was very quiet, trying to put the entire pieces together, and to her it looked very grim. She didn't want to believe that Precious was in big trouble, but based on everything that was going on, she couldn't stop herself from feeling anything else. Mercedes kept praying in her head because despite their differences, she didn't want anything bad to happen to her. She needed her to be okay. Imani felt nothing. In her head, she knew that anything bad would be disastrous for her. It was like a piece of her was missing and she knew that Precious was the only one who could put the piece back. There was no reason that Precious would have left the club without telling them. She has not called anyone just to say she was okay, and she had a strange message on her answering machine at home. Jasmine knew that all wasn't well. Jasmine told them that maybe they should go home and wait for Precious to call. They all agreed this was a good idea, and if anyone heard from her to call each other right away.

They waited all night and heard nothing. Jasmine finally three-way called Imani and Mercedes, and they all agreed to call Precious' mother. Imani spoke to her and asked if she had heard from Precious. Janet informed her that she had not spoken to her today. Janet asked if anything was wrong, but Imani acted as if everything was okay as she didn't want to alert Janet for no reason. They then all agreed to call the police. Jasmine asked if they should have told Janet what was going on, but hell they didn't even know themselves.

Jasmine spoke with the police. They asked a lot of questions over the phone and then informed them all to come down to the station to make a statement in the morning if they didn't hear from her. Imani told Jasmine and Mercedes to come over to her house. She would cook some food and they could talk about what they should do next. They agreed and were on their way.

As the night continued to pass, they ladies still didn't have an idea of what they were going to do. There was a sadness in the air. They knew something was wrong, and what made it worse was that they just didn't know what. It was hard to deal with the reality that they could not reach out and touch something, anything that would give them answers. There was no trail that they could follow that could lead them to the end of the road. It was like everything that a human would use to help them figure things out went stale. There was no sense they could utilize to make it better. It was late and they all agreed to stay over Imani's house. Imani set her alarm to get up early so they could go to the police station. None of them could really sleep. Jasmine and Mercedes stayed up smoking cigarettes, but not really talking.

At about 3am the phone rang and woke everyone up out of there sleep. Imani picked the phone up and Precious was on the other line. Imani could not contain her feelings. "Where the hell have you been?!" she shouted. Precious apologized for getting everyone all crazy. She stated that she wound up hooking up with the guy and had to sleep off her hangover. She wanted to wait until she got home to call and take the tongue lashing she knew that she was going to get. To Imani, the story was believable. She told Imani to tell the rest of the guys, and told her that she would holler at her in the A.M. Imani hung the phone up and told both Mercedes and Jasmine that Precious was okay. She was home and she was safe. She didn't have the details, but she was ecstatic that she was fine. She wanted to go outside and scream at the top of her lungs. The relief she was feeling, words could not describe. Imani still had a lot of questions, she wanted to know details about everything that happened, but she knew that would have to wait.

Back at Precious' house she was in the bathroom trying to wash her body. She cut on the shower and the water was steaming hot. Precious didn't even check the temperature she just pulled her clothes off and jumped in. She was washing it like she was trying to take her skin off. She didn't appear that everything was okay like she said on the phone to Imani. Precious scrubbed over and over again. Precious knew that the tears coming out of her eyes showed that something had happened and she wasn't telling anyone about it. The water was so hot it was making her skin red, but it didn't faze her. She just scrubbed and scrubbed until her body was red. Precious then took the scissors out of the medicine cabinet and started cutting off her pubic hairs. She cut until she could not cut anymore, then began to shave the remaining hairs. Precious could not hold back the tears in her eyes. She could barely see what she was doing. After she finished, she cut off the water and got out of the shower. She dried off, picked up the clothes she had on, and went into the kitchen. Precious pulled out a garbage bag and threw the clothes in the bag, tied the bag in a knot, and flung it across the room in anger. Precious even threw out her shoes she was wearing. Then she laid on the kitchen floor and just cried until her throat felt irritated.

# Chapter Four

Two weeks went by and Precious still really never talked much about what had happened. Jasmine wasn't sure if anyone had picked up on it like she did. She noticed that Precious wasn't the same. She wasn't as much of a smart ass and her dress wasn't as neat. Imani and Mercedes didn't discuss the situation much. Every now and then one of them would ask, "Where is Precious? When are we going out?" but that was about it. Precious had basically given up the party scene.

Finally, Jasmine was compelled to ask. Jasmine, Mercedes and Imani were sitting at the diner after hanging out all night. Jasmine felt that this was the best time. She looked across the table and said, "Can I ask y'all a question?" The other two shook their heads up and down. "What's up with Precious?" Both Imani and Mercedes looked back at each other and shrugged their shoulders. "Did anyone even think about asking her about what really went on the night she was MIA?" Jasmine continued. "I think it is really strange that she does not hang out with us much anymore. She has not been to a club since then and she does not appear to care as much about her appearance. I really find strange." Jasmine looked over at both the ladies waiting for a reply.

Mercedes took a moment and finally spoke. "Yeah, I know what you mean. I was waiting for someone to bring it up before I did. When she calls me, which we all know is very rare in the first place, she just makes ideal chit chat. She just acts like everything is all good. I don't want to ask her about it because heck we have never gotten down like that. Not that intimate shit. I just thought that she was most likely talking to Imani about it and Imani chose not to share."

Imani quickly jumped in and let them know it wasn't like that. "Precious has been very secretive with me too. She calls me every day like usual, but she keeps the conversation short and to the point of whatever she wants to discuss. It is almost like she is guiding the conversation. When I tell her we're going out, she says she is busy and cannot go. If I tell her that I will come over and bring the drinks, she just says she is tired. I don't push the issue because I feel that sooner or later she will come around and talk about it. I just hope that she is talking about it with someone. Unfortunately, that someone is not me." The three continued to eat their food like they didn't just have that little discussion. Jasmine thought to herself that there was nothing left to be said. They basically all agreed that if and when Precious wanted to discuss whatever went on, she would.

Two days later, Mercedes was driving down the block. It was pretty early in the morning and she saw Precious. She beeped her horn and pulled over. She rolled down the window and told Precious to hop in. Precious told her that she was on her way to take care of something, but she would catch up with her later. Mercedes asked if she needed a ride but Precious declined. What Mercedes did notice though was the Precious looked a little disheveled. Her clothes, to Mercedes, were not only out of place but big. Precious' clothes were always bigger than her normal size, but this time it looked like she was filling them out. This made Mercedes immediately hop on the horn and call Jasmine.

Jasmine picked up the phone and Mercedes was almost screaming. "I figured it out, I figured it out. That bitch is pregnant!" Jasmine told her to slow down because she didn't know what the fuck she was talking about. "Precious is pregnant. That would explain why she has not been partying or drinking. I can't believe she would not share something so important like this with us. That is kind of fucked up don't you think?" Jasmine was at a loss of words. This thought had not ever crossed her mind. Could Mercedes be right? Most likely not as Jasmine knew that Mercedes was always stretching shit to fit her imagination.

"You are bugging," Jasmine replied. "There is no way on God's green earth that Precious would hide her pregnancy from us. If it was all possible, who the fuck was Precious fucking on a regular basis that she would have a baby? It is not like she had a steady man and shit. I can't believe this one, Mercedes." Jasmine wasn't a believer. Mercedes told her to check it out herself if she didn't believe her. Jasmine decided that is just what she would do. She would find out for herself if Precious was with child. "Okay, that is what I will do..." she informed Mercedes.

After Jasmine hung up the phone she knew she would need a plan. How could she find out the truth without arousing anybody else's suspicion? She could go to Imani, but if Imani knew she would not tell the truth because she had not told them. If she didn't know she would immediately call Precious and ask her and that would blow her chances of uncovering the truth. The big question was, if Precious was pregnant who was the father and did he know? Did Janet know that her daughter was going to have a baby? Jasmine was so miffed by the situation that she just sat on the couch and smiled. She would not let this little situation defeat her. Jasmine thought of herself as a super sleuth and nothing like this would stop her. Only a minor setback.

Jasmine woke up the next morning and drove over to see Precious. As she pulled up to her crib, Precious was walking out the door. Jasmine beeped her horn thinking that she was going to need a ride wherever she was going, so her timing was perfect. Precious came over to the car and asked her what she was doing there. Jasmine let her know that it seemed like ages since they sat down and chilled so she was just stopping by to see if they could grab a bite to eat.

Precious informed Jasmine that she was on her out, but they could catch up with each other later. Jasmine offered to drop her off wherever she was going but Precious passed. *Wow,* Jasmine thought. *She may be trying to avoid us.* "Okay," she said to Precious. "Just make sure you holler when you finish whatever you doin'."

Jasmine went back home and immediately got on her phone. She called up Mercedes to let her know that she may believe what she told her. Unfortunately, Mercedes didn't answer the phone. Jasmine was tempted to call Imani but she thought better of it. Jasmine just kept thinking over and over again could she be pregnant or could it be something else? Jasmine also thought that if she was pregnant she could not hide it forever. Maybe she would just keep it to herself and just watch.

Time had passed and no one had discussed what was going on with Precious, yet it still weighed heavy on everyone's mind. Precious had not been coming around and she had not been out with them since that one night she went missing. She still hadn't given anyone an explanation, or at least no one has admitted that she has.

Mercedes was at home chillin and watching television for once on a Saturday. She was kind of bored, but wasn't sure what she was going to do. She didn't have to go to the club tonight and she didn't feel like sitting inside. She decided she would call Imani and Jasmine to see if they had something planned for the day. As Mercedes started to pick up the phone, it rang. This time she decided to look at the call id to see who it was. She didn't feel like talking to any bill collectors. Mercedes was surprised as it was Precious was on the phone. She picked up the phone stating "Hello, stranger."

Precious took a second to answer and then replied, "What are you doing tonight, girl?"

"Nothing," Mercedes replied emphatically.

"Do you want to come over to my crib?"

"What time?"

"How about right now." It didn't take but a second for Mercedes to agree. She quickly hung up the phone with Precious and immediately started dialing Jasmine. Jasmine picked up the phone laughing, "I will meet you there."

It wasn't a half hour before everyone was at Precious' door. Everyone arrived around the same time. Jasmine didn't want all of them to go in at the same time, so she sat in her car and waited for both Imani and Mercedes to go inside. Once she saw them go inside, she got out of the car. She took her time walking across the street thinking what the hell was going on. Jasmine could not wait any longer to find out. She quickly put pep in her step and got to the door. The door was unlocked so she tapped on the door and walked in. As she was walking inside the house, she could see the frame of Precious' body. It looked bigger than normal. Her body was no longer that frail looking body with the bump from behind; even her butt had spread out. It really wasn't a surprise to Jasmine, but more like conformation. Precious was pregnant. Not just a little pregnant, but big time pregnant. As Jasmine looked back at the amount of time that had passed from when the incident occurred, everything was adding up. There was no other explanation except something sexual happened that night. Jasmine walked into the living room where she saw Imani, Mercedes, and Janet sitting. She was kind of surprised that Janet was there. They all were sitting around laughing together like they were not shocked about Precious being pregnant. That made Jasmine think that maybe she was the only one who didn't know, but of course she knew that Mercedes definitely didn't know.

Precious sat down next to her mother and started speaking. "I know that y'all are a little shocked about this. I probably should have told y'all a long time ago. I just didn't know how. First, I had to make a decision for myself like if I was going to keep the baby. Was I ready to have everyone talking about who her baby's daddy is? I know that is what my best friend right here is thinking. I don't really want to have a big discussion about this but I felt that I owed y'all some kind of explanation. I don't expect y'all to understand, but I hope that you will respect my decision to have this baby." The tears started to run down the side of Precious' face. She was still having an internal fight with herself about the decision that she had made. Precious knew that her friends really didn't have a clue about what had happened to her. They didn't know what turmoil she was feeling. Every day of this pregnancy, she had to come to terms with the choices she made. Precious thought that she had finally made peace with her decision until this day. She continued to tell her story. "The night when we went out to have a great time. It turned out to be the worst night of my life. I drank way too much and thought I could handle it. I was chillin in the VIP section with that guy. Can you believe that I don't even remember his name? At this point I wish I could forget what he looked like. But to this day, I still can remember what he smelled like. How his hot breath felt on my neck. Going down my breast and on my back. He continued to breathe heavy on my stomach and my legs. I tried to fight him but I was too weak. Probably due to being so damn drunk. At first, I thought I wanted him to do it, but I realized that I didn't but the time I tried to stop him it was too late. He had taken all my clothes off and was standing in front of me. I kept looking up at him trying to speak. I think the only word I can remember saying was no over and over again." Precious looked around the room and broke down sobbing. She was crying so hard she started choking. Janet jumped up and helped Precious put her arms up like she was a little kid.

"It's okay baby. We are here for you." Precious stood straight up again and continued speaking.

"He would not stop. He took his hands and pulled my legs apart. He pushed them so hard and far he bruised my inner thigh. That was another memory that I can't forget. He took out his dick and waived it around in my face. He tried to stick it inside my mouth several times but I would not open my mouth. Finally, he grabbed my chin so hard that I could not keep it shut and when I released my jaws in my mouth his dick went. The first thing I thought of was to try to bite it off but he quickly made me change my mind by letting me know saying 'bitch, put those teeth on my dick and you will not leave here today.' I just sat there crying and dying inside. By the time he took his dick out of my mouth I was numb. I could not even tell you if he came. What I can tell you though is that when he fucked me over and over again he enjoyed it. All I can remember him saying is 'this is some good pussy bitch and I knew I had to have it tonight. You invited me to take it. You wanted it just as much as I wanted to give it to you.' When he was finished, he took my clothes and put them in my arms as gentle as if he was holding a baby. He stroked my hair as if he really believed that we made love. He then told me to get dressed and he would drive me home. I knew I was no longer drunk and had to make some decisions. I wasn't sure what I was going to do. Should I let this animal drive me home and know where I lived? Or would I just run out of there taking the chance that he would catch me and kill my ass? I put my clothes on slowly as my body ached so badly. When I finished he reminded me that if I was to ever open my fuckin mouth and told anyone what happened, he would make sure I paid for it. The pain I would endure would be ten times worse than the enjoyment that I had felt tonight. I walked out the door and got into his car. I am ashamed to even say that. I let him drop me off around the corner from my house. I waited to make sure he pulled off and walked around the corner and went inside the house. When I got inside, I thought over and over to call 911 and let someone know what had happened to me, but I was too ashamed. I scrubbed my body until I could not feel the skin. I crawled up into a ball and cried over and over again until I threw up. I thought that I could forget about it. I didn't think or want to have to explain this to anyone ever." Precious sat down like a weight was just lifted from her shoulders. She felt as though her faith had pulled her through this time and guided her to make the decisions that she had made. Precious felt talking about the incident had purged her guilt, guilt that she had trouble shaking in the beginning. She blamed herself for months for what happened to her.

Imani came and sat next to her and put her arms around her. Jasmine and Mercedes followed and they had the tightest group huge in a very long time. Everyone's heart was broken for Precious, what kind of pain she endured, and the amount of time that she had held this in before coming clean to them.

It was so quiet in the room you could hear a pin drop. No one knew what to say or if they were going to say anything. Nobody ever thought it was anything like this. As much as they all had their difference, they never would wish anything like this on her.

"By the way," Precious started. "On a lighter note, I am pregnant." She ended the statement with a grin on her face, and nobody knew how to take that. Was she saying that to be sarcastic, or was she trying to lighten up the mood?

Mercedes was thinking to herself but couldn't hold it in. "Is this man the father?" Precious' eyes sunk in the back of her head. She took a deep breath and cleared her throat.

She looked at Mercedes and admitted, "Yes. I made the decision to keep this baby. It took me a while to make the decision, but decided that my child should not pay the price due to my stupidity. I love this baby that is growing inside my stomach. I hope that everyone here will also grow to love this little baby too." Imani shook her head up and down as if to say she would love that baby.

Jasmine got up and put her arms around Precious. Jasmine spoke in a calm tone trying not to get Precious any more upset than she was. "I am here for you girl through thick and thin. I respect and admire your decision. It truly shows your strength which I never knew that you had to this degree. I love you girl and don't forget it." Precious hugged Jasmine so hard it hurt, but Jasmine didn't mind. Next Mercedes stood up and joined in the hug. She whispered in Precious' ear letting her know how crazy she was. The decision that she made would not have been Mercedes first choice and she let her know how mad she was that she just was finding out, but she still loved her in her own strange way. It turned into a group hug. It was a somber but satisfying moment for all of them. There was a sense of something fresh and new coming down the pipe. There was going to be a new baby in their tight knit family, and they needed to make some changes. All of them decided they would make a vow to do things differently, to make sure they tell the truth all the time to each other no matter how much it would hurt the other. To bond with this baby and help out whenever needed and to always try to respect and love one another. After all was said and done, they cut on the radio and enjoyed some old school jams, dancing around like they were having a celebration.

# Chapter Five

Precious slowly got closer to her due date. The ladies' friendships had been the strongest it ever had been. Everyone rallied around Precious like they were having a baby. Every week each of them took time out of their schedules to run around with Precious to the stores and pick out the cutest outfits. Everyone was trying to outdo the other. The time leading up to the big day was almost like all the things that surrounded how it happened almost faded away. Almost. It made Precious' decision that much harder. She was almost ready to deliver, and she needed to decide who was going to go into the delivery room. She weighed her options long and hard. She knew that Jasmine wasn't an option. She could not stomach the sight of blood and would not disagree. Did she want to have her mother Janet in there with her? But could she rely on the fact that she lived far away and may not be able to get to NY in time? Imani was the closest to Precious, but she knew the strength and fire Mercedes carried inside her might be a great strength when Precious needed it. She decided that she would let Imani come with her into the delivery room. It was the right thing to do. On top of that, Precious knew that Imani would not take it well if she picked Mercedes.

That same day, Jasmine was feeling very excited. She went to the jewelry shop and ordered a necklace for the baby. She didn't care if Precious chose her to go into the delivery room, but she wanted to make sure that she knew that her Aunty had gotten her first piece of jewelry.

The next morning, she decided she would go out and let them both know in person. They had waited patiently for her to make her decision and she felt that she owed it to them to not tell them over the phone. Precious knew that they were all going to get their hair done that morning so she decided she would meet them over there.

Precious went downstairs and got into the car. She was feeling very positive with her decision. She checked her mirrors and pulled out of her parking spot. Precious looked down and noticed that she didn't have much gas in the tank. She decided to stop and get gas before she went to the beauty parlor. Ever since Precious found out she was pregnant; she always went to self-serve. She pulled up and told the attendant to fill it up. While she sat and waited, she turned from radio station to radio station to see what was on. Nothing as usual. She popped her CD in and the attendant came to the window. Precious handed him a $20 bill and a $10 and pulled off. She was in such a good mood she didn't realize that she gave him an $8 tip. Precious continued on her journey to the hairdresser grooving to the music. She wasn't even paying attention to the road. As Precious was crossing the intersection, through the corner of her eye she could see a car coming straight at her. She tried to swerve and stomp on her brakes but it was too late. The impact was so strong she felt as though a bullet was surging through her body. The airbags deployed immediately. Precious gasped for air. The jolt to her car pushed her thirty feet to the side, crushing it like a can of sardines.

Precious was shaken up bad but the only thing she could think of was her baby. She tried to move over to grab her pocketbook, but it flew too far over and she could not reach it. She could hear the sirens coming and all she could do was pray that they would hurry up and get there. Precious wasn't sure if she was bleeding, because she could barely move, but she could feel wetness between her legs. She just closed her eyes and started praying out loud. She thanked the Lord for the opportunities he had afforded her. She thanked him for blessing her with the chance to carry her baby. She knew at first she was very upset, but she reassured the Lord that she wanted nothing more than to have this baby.

She told the Lord if he had to take anyone, make sure it was her and not her little baby. She just kept assuring the Lord that she wanted her baby to have a wonderful life. She made all the right sacrifices and she would continue to do the same. Precious then thought to herself that the sirens were fading away. Why were they going somewhere else? She was cold and wasn't sure what was going on. Precious told herself to stay awake and hold tight. Help was on the way.

The fire department arrived at the scene first. They realized that they were going to need a helicopter. The fireman called on the radio for help. He banged on the window and realized that the female in the vehicle wasn't responding. The officer didn't realize that she was pregnant until he pried the door open. He quickly got back on the radio, letting the proper parties know that the female was pregnant and as he was moving the airbag out of the way he realized that she was bleeding and her pulse was very faint. Traffic around the accident scene had been stopped in all directions.

Meanwhile, Mercedes was stuck in the traffic. She was trying to figure out what was going on. She heard the helicopter flying above, realizing that the accident was bad and she would be there for a while. She cut off the key to her ignition and started dialing her phone. She wasn't sure why, but she just felt a chill in her body. She hung up the phone and got out of her vehicle, walking towards the scene. There were so many people gathered around. Everyone was asking each other what happened. One man who was standing there said that there was a big car accident. Apparently, one of the parties involved in the accident was hurt very badly. Mercedes yelled out to the crowd and asked if anyone knew what kind of cars were involved. No one seemed to have been able to get that close. Mercedes decided to see how close she could get. She wasn't sure why she was so curious, but she just felt that she had to know. The closer she got the more she started feeling a big pain in her belly. The pain got worse as she got closer to the accident, but she didn't realize what was going on. She just knew that whatever happened wasn't a good thing. She kept asking herself why this was affecting her to this degree. She kept trying to get the negativity out of her head. Mercedes knew that this year was crazy and that she didn't think she could take another tragedy. She tried very hard to shake the feeling off. As she approached the corner, an officer informed her that she could not go any further. Mercedes could barely see the vehicles. In the middle of the street, she could see the helicopter in the middle of the street. She was pretty amazed that it was able to land on the street. She looked at the officer and asked what happened. He just stated it was a bad accident and one of the parties involved was pregnant and she had to be transported by helicopter to the hospital. He wasn't sure the condition of either party but when there is a pregnant woman or baby involved and they are being teleported, it is serious.

"Can you tell me what kind of cars that were involved?" Mercedes asked. The officer looked at her with a very serious face and advised her that he had already told her too much info. Just then Mercedes saw the news van coming through the traffic. She quickly ran back to her car and got on the jack. She tried to call Precious, but the phone went straight to voicemail. This didn't even seem strange to her because she knew that she was going to get her hair done, so she just assumed she was most likely sitting under the dryer and didn't hear her phone. She then dialed Jasmine.

Jasmine picked up the phone and before she could say hello Mercedes was telling her to cut on the local news. "What happened?" Jasmine asked.

"Just hurry up and turn it on. I am sitting in traffic and there was a big accident. There is a helicopter taking a pregnant lady to the hospital and I have a really bad feeling in the pit of my stomach."

"I think you are just overreacting Mercedes, as usual. Hold on for a minute. They are showing the weather. You can't see the vehicles involved?" Jasmine asked.

"If I could, do you think I would be calling your stupid ass to turn on the news? But if you really need me to answer, NO!" The phone was quiet for a few minutes while Jasmine stared at the TV.

Then finally Jasmine spoke. "How bad is the traffic where you are stuck? Will you be able to back out of the block."

"Does it matter?" Mercedes asked.

"Yes," Jasmine replied. There was a deep silence between the phones and then Jasmine said, "Do you need me to pick you up and leave your car there, or do you want to meet me at the hospital?" Mercedes advised Jasmine to call Imani and Janet and met her at the hospital. She will figure out how to get her car moved off the block and meet her there.

Jasmine hung up the phone and called Imani. Imani was her usual happy self. Jasmine didn't want to tell her over the phone, but Imani could sense something was wrong from the start. Jasmine told Imani to get ready and she was coming to pick her up. She would not even get into details. She just told Imani she would be there in less than five. Imani knew when she hung the phone up that something was wrong. She began putting on her shoes and tried to dial Mercedes at the same time. No answer on the phone by Mercedes so she just put her jacket on, went outside, and waited for Jasmine to pull up. When Imani opened the door, she could see that Jasmine had been crying. Jasmine thought that it would be better to tell Imani before they started driving, because it would only get Jasmine more upset and the last thing she wanted to do was to get into a car accident herself. She explained what she believed had happened to Imani. No surprise that Imani took it the hardest because she and Precious had always been the closest. She was unsure if she should call Janet before she knew exactly what was going on. Imani didn't want to alarm her if there was no reason to do so, but Jasmine advised her that the crash was very very bad and that it was most likely best so she had time to get to New York. Imani agreed that she would call Janet and let her know while they were on their way to the hospital.

When they arrived at the hospital, Jasmine tried to call Mercedes. She didn't pick up the phone at first. They both tried a few times thinking maybe she was inside the hospital and she could not answer the phone, but just as they began to get out of the car Imani's phone rang. It was Mercedes. She asked where they were. Imani let her know they had just gotten to the hospital but had not gone inside. Mercedes begged them to wait for her; she was about five minutes from them. Imani let her know where they were parked and they would wait for her. Jasmine and Imani held hands and prayed for their friend. They asked God to take hold of her and her unborn baby. Watch and guide them through this time and do what is right whatever he knows would be right. They told him that they may not understand but they have all the faith. They know he will guide them thru.

Mercedes pulled up at the end, jumped out of her ride, grabbed their hands and prayed ending the prayer with Amen. All three of them knew they had to wipe the tears out of their eyes because they didn't want Precious to see them so upset. They were supposed to be there to cheer her up. Imani asked if everyone was ready to go in. The other two shook their heads and they began to walk over to the emergency room entrance.

Mercedes walked in first and went right over to the counter. The woman at the counter looked like she was busy doing nothing. Mercedes banged on the table making her presence known. "Hello!" she shouted. The woman behind the desk made sure she knew that they were in a hospital. Mercedes gave her a look that said bitch I will hurt you. "I am trying to get an update on Precious Gray. Can I go inside and see her?" The lady at the desk looked back at Mercedes and asked her who she was. Finally, Mercedes realized that being nice was the only way to get her in the back. She apologized to the lady and introduced herself as Precious' cousin. The lady behind the desk informed her that she had to go in the back and check and see if Precious could have any visitors at all, and if she could, was it okay for it to be her cousin.

They stood pacing back and forth. Imani's phone rang and the guard told her to take it outside. She quickly walked outside and answered the phone. It was Janet and she wanted to know if they had found anything out. She let her know that they were at the hospital but had not been able to see Precious yet. They didn't know her condition or the condition of the baby. Janet let her know that she is trying to make arrangements to get up there. As soon as she knew exactly when she would be on her way, she would call and let Imani know. Imani let her know that as soon as she heard something she would call her and let her know. They hung up the phone.

Imani went back inside and as soon as she got to the door, she saw Mercedes and Jasmine standing by the front desk. Jasmine was holding Mercedes' hand. Imani rushed up there and just caught the tail end of the conversation. Precious was in surgery and that they should go to the chapel and pray. The lady advised them to contact Precious' immediate family and the father of the baby if they could.

Imani rushed back outside and immediately dialed Janet's home. She told Janet she wasn't really clear on the facts, but told her to get her ass up here like yesterday. Janet hung up the phone before Imani could say another word. "Come on," Jasmine told them. "Let's go to the chapel like she said."

As they began walking out to go to the chapel, Mercedes again got another pit in the bottom of her stomach and the code blue was called out over the loudspeaker. Mercedes stopped as she felt it was for Precious. "NO!" Jasmine screamed out. "You can't be right. This cannot be happening!" They all turned around and went back to the front desk. The lady behind the desk just looked at them with sadden eyes. She didn't have to say one word. Her eyes spoke loud and clear.

They all rushed to the chapel as fast as possible. They fell to their knees in silence. Not one word was spoken. They all listened to their hearts and God's word. They were trying to take in the strength that he was providing for them. It was funny the effect it was having on Mercedes because she was the one who argued with Precious the most, but she was the one who had all these gut feelings. She realized that maybe it wasn't dislike she felt for Precious sometimes, but maybe a little jealousy. Maybe in her heart she wanted to experience growing up being super close to her siblings, being able to share her secrets with one another, not having to grow up too fast and enjoying her childhood like Precious did. She asked God to make it go away. She asked him to give her the strength to do what was right whatever that is. She asked the Lord not to take her friend away from her and to please don't take that little baby away.

Jasmine sat and kept holding her hands together, clasping them tighter and tighter. The tears would not stop running down her face. She looked up into the heavens and told God that she knows she does not pray often, but he knows what is in her heart. He knows that he would do whatever to keep their friendships together. She is not asking much and it is not really for her, but for everyone who loves Precious and that little baby that is growing inside her. She told God that Precious was brave to make a decision like she did about having this baby and having anyone rally around her to assist. "Please Lord," she started. "I know you are a great

God and please, just please no matter what you decide give me the power to get through this. And if I need to change, please guide me with this also."

Imani bowed down at the altar. She was constantly wiping the tears from her eyes. She just kept shaking her head up and down as she was in a two-way conversation and that person was standing in front of her. Precious's influence on Imani was profound. There was no bond between friends stronger than theirs. Everyone knew that Imani would be the most affected by this if it turned out to be catastrophic. Imani told God that she was giving it to him. She was putting all her faith into him and she knew he would not lead her down the wrong road. She just started saying out loud that he would not give her more than she could handle. Both Jasmine and Mercedes heard her, went over to her, put her arms around her and started saying the same thing over and over again. The bond between these girls appeared to become stronger this day. They decided to go back to get an update on what was going on with the surgery. They all hoped that everything turned out okay.

Meanwhile, Janet was on her way to New York. She had called one of her friends and asked if she could give her a ride. Janet was so anxious to get there. All she could think about was all the years that they had together and praying they would have a lot more, now to be shared with her grandchild. She kept thinking if she said I love you the last time they spoke before she hung up the phone. Did Precious know how much her mother truly loved her? Would she get a chance to tell her one more time? She kept telling herself that everything was going to be okay. It seemed to be the longest three-hour ride in the word. While she was in the car, she continued making phone calls to contact everyone and anyone she could that was important and needed to be at the hospital when she arrived. Janet had a sick feeling that she would need support herself. She didn't believe that if this turned out to be tragic she would be able to deal. Her girlfriend tried to keep her mind off of everything that was going on. She played the radio and talked and talked but it didn't seem to help. She understood that Janet had too many things on her mind. Janet told her friend that she wasn't always the best mother in the world by far, but when she found out that her daughter was pregnant she was ecstatic. She talked to her friend about some of the mistakes she felt like she made early on like exposing her children, especially Precious, to the bar scene. She was way too young to experience things that went on inside of those places. She would smoke her cigarettes and sometimes let Precious light them. At that time, she didn't think there was anything wrong with those things. She didn't take control of the men that came in and out of the house, which could not have been any guidance, and worst of all she never told her children that she loved them on a regular basis. This could not begin to describe the feelings that she felt. Now all she could think about was what kind of misfortune could come to her family. Janet knew that she had to keep positive thoughts, but she knew nothing and always assumed the worst. If it was that horrific she would not be shocked. Janet felt some comfort that she was able to talk for most of the ride. As she noticed they were halfway through New Jersey, she asked her girlfriend if she wanted to stop at the rest stop and she would drive the rest of the way. Her girlfriend thought about it and told her if she needed to stop she would, but it might be better if she jumped in the back seat and took a nap. Janet had a long day ahead of her and would need all her strength. She decided to take her girlfriend's advice. Janet let her know that she didn't have to pull over to the rest stop. She just jumped into the back seat and lay down and quickly dozed off.

When Janet woke up, they were getting off the highway and they could see the hospital. Janet wasn't sure if she was nervous or anxious. Maybe it was a little bit or a lot of both.

As they got closer and closer to the entrance she felt overly anxious. Her girlfriend parked the car and she asked if she wanted her to come inside or if she just wanted her to wait outside. Janet let her know how grateful she was for giving her the ride and that if she would accompany her inside, she could not express to her how important that would also be.

Janet went straight to the emergency room entrance but before she walked inside, she took out her phone and called Imani to let her know that she was here. Imani picked up the phone and her voice sounded distraught. Janet didn't ask what was going on because she knew that she would know soon enough. "I just wanted to let you know I am here. I am getting ready to go inside the emergency room entrance. Meet me there," Janet explained. Imani hung the phone up and let everyone else know.

When Janet walked in she could see Imani, Mercedes, and Jasmine. They all looked like they had been crying for such a long time. Imani's eyes were so swollen they were barely opened. That is when Janet realized it was worse than she could have imagined. They all hugged each other and Janet proceeded to the front desk.

The same lady was still sitting there. She asked Janet if she could help her. Janet asked about Precious. The front desk lady asked her to have a seat and let her know that the doctor would be coming out shortly. She picked up the phone and spoke with the person on the other end for a brief amount of time. Janet didn't wait for long when a female and a male doctor came from the back and advised her to come inside. Everyone stood up, but they were advised that they only wanted to speak with Janet. They took her to the back and sat her down. The female doctor spoke first with a very soft voice. She told her that she was a grandmother. She has a healthy beautiful granddaughter. Janet was very happy to hear this. A smile lit up her face but the smile was short lived. The male doctor then let her know that she no longer has a daughter. He explained that she lost too much blood.

The impact from the accident and the airbag made it a necessity to save the baby. In doing such, they had to perform a c-section. Precious wasn't strong enough and her blood stopped clotting. They tried to save her, but she bled out. Janet screamed so loud that everyone in the waiting room could hear her, that included Imani, Jasmine and Mercedes. Janet's body went numb and her knees began to buckle. The doctor had to stop her from falling. Janet couldn't get it out of her head that she wasn't going to be able to say I love you to her daughter one more time and get a response. She felt like she failed her somehow, and everything she feared had come to fruition. The agony she was now experiencing had never been felt before. How was she going to go into the waiting room and face Precious' friends? How was she going to keep it together for the family? She knew she had to pull herself together and put her sorrow and misery to the side for at least a little while. Back in the waiting room, they all came together and hugged. They weren't 100% sure about what happened, but they knew it was bad. It was just a matter of figuring out if it was Precious or the baby or both of them.

Janet took a moment in the back with the doctors before she came back out front. The doctors said that she could view the body before they took her downstairs. Janet wasn't ready for that. She didn't want to go and view the body by herself. She knew it wasn't possible to say goodbye to her daughter multiple times, and thought it would be better to see if she could possibly do it with everyone. If not, she would choose not to do it at this time. She knew that she would need to go out front and talk to the girls. She asked the female doctor to get her some tissues so she could wipe her face. The doctor showed her where the bathroom was so that she could go inside there to pull herself together. Not that the doctor thought that was even possible. She then let Janet know where the chapel was so that if she wanted to go there it was opened.

Imani asked the front desk lady if it was okay for her to go in the back. The lady told her no. She let her know that Janet would be out shortly. Just as she finished speaking, Janet walked out from the back. The pain on her face was evident. Her eyes were swollen, and her makeup had run down her cheek so much she didn't even attempt to fix it. They all knew that someone had died. Janet didn't say a word, she just hugged them all so tight. They stood in the middle of the floor and weep together. They held hands and said a prayer together, and in the prayer they all found out who they lost. Janet let them know by asking to take care of her daughter, and she would watch over her granddaughter. Janet felt that by saying this she didn't have to say the words that Precious was dead. She could not get her mouth to say it out loud. She knew eventually she would but not right now. It wasn't possible to embrace that truth.

Janet went back inside and asked the doctor if they could all go upstairs and see the baby. The doctor let them know they could. Janet came back out and told them where they were going. They all went and rode to the third floor. Not one person said a word. They were saddened and a little excited to see their little baby. They walked into the maternity ward and went right to the newborn babies. They were not sure how they were going to know which baby was Precious', but they would surely find out. They walked up to the window with all the little babies. Jasmine knew right away when she saw this little sweet girl laying in the incubator. They told them all to come over to her. "That is her," Jasmine exclaimed. Janet went over to the nurse to confirm and Jasmine was right. They all wanted to go inside to hold her, but they would only allow one person inside and they knew it had to be Janet. Mercedes said that the baby was beautiful and they all shook their head in agreement. They felt a little sunshine in their hearts. They knew that a piece of Precious was still alive. They stayed at the hospital for about another hour, then they all decided to go back to

Imani's house to try to put the pieces of the puzzle together. They knew that they would have to divide all the responsibilities up. There was no way that Janet could handle everything. On their way to Imani's house, they all took some time to reflect on everything. Imani started thinking about old times when they were kids and how they would say they would be friends forever. She never knew that forever would be so short. Tears rolled down her cheeks the entire ride, but every now and then she would put a grin on her face and chuckle because of something she remembered. Mercedes didn't have the same emotion. She felt bad, but she was angry. She kept thinking, *you wanted to have the spotlight, and now you finally do. You will always be talked about and remember for this moment in time.* She knew it wasn't right to have these feelings but she did. I didn't take away the love she had for Precious. Jasmine could only concentrate on what needed to be done. She didn't feel like she had time to grieve at this moment. She wanted to be the rock. Jasmine knew that everyone was going to need a shoulder to lean on and she wanted to be that person    She would concern herself about leaning on someone else at a later time.

They knew it was going to be a long night at Imani's house. They decided they needed to write a list of things that they needed to get done. Imani took out a pad and gave it to Jasmine, putting her in charge as she was good at keeping things in order. Imani advised them they had to call the claim into the insurance company. Jasmine said, "We need to find out where Precious' car was towed and someone also needs to pick up the police report to see what exactly happened." Nobody rushed to say they would do it, which kind of annoyed her. Jasmine decided that she should take care of that duty. She went on saying, "Someone needs to go to Precious' house and look through her stuff to figure out what kind of insurance policy she has."

Mercedes quickly responded, "I think I can take care of that."

Imani let Janet know that one of them could assist her with making the funeral arrangements. Jasmine asked Janet, "Maybe she may want to go to Precious' house to pick out an outfit for her to wear, or maybe go to the store and pick her something new out."

Janet wasn't sure about that. She replied, "I know this seems strange but picking out an outfit for my daughter to wear at her funeral seems so final. I'm not ready for that yet." She paused before continuing. "I will make a separate list of people that needed to be contacted starting tomorrow." She thought it should be tonight, but it was late and she didn't want to disrupt the family. Janet just broke down crying. Everyone knew that was going to happen over and over again. They just gathered around Janet and held her. They could not even muster the strength to tell her that everything was going to be alright, because they were not sure themselves. They just knew that it would take all their strength to help each other hold up at this bad time. Mercedes had gone to the store to pick up some munchies and alcohol for them to sip on. When she got back, the mood was still the same. It was very somber and stagnant. It didn't even feel like there was any fresh air moving around the house even though the windows were open. Everyone was in disbelief about what had just happened. She went into the kitchen and put the chips and dip into a bowl. She took out the beer and put in on the counter, telling everyone to just help themselves. Imani went over and grabbed a couple of beers, giving one to Janet. They sat down and made sure they had covered everything. They knew that this was going to be a long week. They all decided to sleep at Imani's tonight and start fresh in the morning. The funny thing though that Jasmine thought to herself, was that no one ever brought up the new addition to the family. Jasmine thought it may be too soon. She picked out a spot on the couch and started dozing off.

The next morning everyone got up pretty early. Jasmine asked Janet if she was able to get any sleep, and she shook her head yes. They all decided to go to their respective houses to get themselves prepared for the long day ahead. It was decided the night before that Janet was going to stay at Imani's house and so was her girlfriend, as Janet's girlfriend was going back home tomorrow. She told Janet she would come back for the service and if she needed a lift back she would take her. Janet knew that she had a lot to do, but first she needed to go to the hospital, view her daughter's body, and see the baby. Janet still had no clue how bad her baby girl looked and what kind of service she was going to prepare for her. She asked Jasmine if she could come and pick her up here after she went home and got dressed. Jasmine agreed without hesitation. Jasmine felt that she would do anything that she could do for Janet.

Mercedes went home and took a long hot shower. She didn't even check her messages. As she was in the shower, her phone rang but she wasn't about to get out and get it. She figured that now she would have to check her messages when she got out. It may be someone important. Mercedes in a lot of ways didn't want to be bothered today. She felt drained and knew that there was no rejuvenation in sight. At least she was home by herself and felt like she was in a safe place. She had hid her feelings the entire time, trying not to break down in front of anyone. Her anger had finally turned to grief. She cried and cried knowing that she needed to get it out. She didn't try to stop herself. Mercedes knew that once the explosion was over, it had to be over. When she finally got out of the shower, she went into the bedroom and dried off. After she got dressed, she went to her phone and hit the play button to hear her messages, which had eight. She only wanted to hear the last one which was the one when the phone rang when she was in the shower. That message was from Imani who let her know that she was going over to Precious' house and if she needed her to hit her on the hip. Mercedes' job today was to start calling the people on the list that Janet had made. She was really not too comfortable with this, but she knew she had to do it. Her calling people, some that she knew and some that she didn't, made her feel like she had no real direction. How was she supposed to approach this mission? She thought about it and wasn't sure what approach to take. She decided that she was going to run out to take care of some personal things for herself, and then she would come back home and get settled in and start making the calls.

Meanwhile, Imani was at the home of Precious. She was just walking around taking it all in. She knew that her best friend would never be returning home. Because of this, Imani's life would never be the same. She felt like part of her heart was ripped out. No matter what they had been through, they always had a chance to work it out. They no longer had that chance anymore and Imani had to come to terms with it. She just knew that she still had a part of Precious around, and she was going to make the best of this. What was to come of all the things that she had accumulated over the years? Imani could not even begin to think of where to start looking to find the important papers she would need. She went into the bedroom and began looking through the nightstand draws. As she looked through the top draw she saw a pack of photos. Imani started looking through them one by one. As she looked through them, some of the photos brought a smile to her face. Then, she looked at one photo and it immediately brought tears to her eyes. It was a photo of the four friends out at the club. They all looked like they were having a great time as they were. The photos brought back immediate memories to Imani's mind, and tears started to roll down her face. Even though she was crying, she was also smiling. The photos she looked at made her think about all the occasions when they were taken. She started feeling overjoyed as the great memories flooded her mind. Imani knew she was there for a reason, so she decided to put the photos down and look through the papers. She completed looking through the top drawer not finding anything she was looking for, then opened up the bottom drawer. She found a book that was wrapped in rubber bands. Imani thought this was a little odd, so she took off the rubber bands and opened the book. Inside the book was an envelope that was sealed. Imani was hesitant to open it up, but she knew that she had to open it as it might be the information she is looking for. Before she opened the envelope, she called the house to speak with Janet. The phone rang and the answering machine picked up. Imani hung up and called Janet on the cell. She got the voicemail. She left a message for Janet to call back but she wasn't going to wait for a return call. She opened up the envelope and she didn't find any legal documents, but she found a letter with money wrapped up inside. Imani opened the letter and began to read it.

*I wish that we could have spent more time together before I had to leave you. The most I can ask of you now is just to try to be patient and wait for me. I am going to deposit more money in your account once I get home to make sure this pregnancy runs smoothly for you. You are the best thing that could have ever happened to me. I think that you have a lot of things to sort out for a while but I will be here for you when you make your decision. Don't try to send the money back to me as I will not accept it. I will call you when I get settled in.*

*Love,*
*Your one and only.*

Imani was dumbfounded. She had no clue what this letter meant. Was Precious seeing a married man? Was the father of her baby this man and did Precious lie to everyone about what happened at the club? Imani's head was spinning, but after she counted the money up it was spinning even more. The total amount was $10,000.

Imani's first reaction was to contact Jasmine, but she wasn't sure if that was the right thing to do either. Imani sat on the couch quietly. What was she to do with this new information? She thought, *maybe I should give the money to Janet for the baby. What else could happen and what other questions would go unanswered due to Precious' death?* After contemplating for over two hours, Imani decided she would put the money into a trust account for the new baby. She wrapped the letter and the money back up and put them into her pocketbook. Imani continued to look around the house to try to find any important paperwork. She went into the kitchen and looked through the drawers. Precious was very neat and everything looked to be in order. Imani got to the last drawer and was quickly losing hope that she was going to find any insurance papers. She began to think that maybe Precious didn't have any insurance. Maybe she should take the money she found and tell Janet so this money could pay for the service. All Imani could think was she could use a cold one. She closed the cabinet draw and opened the refrigerator. Imani had a smirk on her face because she knew that Precious would have beer inside. She opened the beer and took a sip, just pressed her back against the frig and began to cry. It was finally starting to seep in that her best friend in the whole world was dead and wasn't coming back. *How could this have happened? It wasn't fair! Why would God do something so sick to my friend? How could God do this when she was doing everything to make everything right for her and her baby? God spared the baby's life to keep putting us through hell by making us make the decision of what would happen next.* Imani finished her beer and decided to give up on the search for the insurance papers. She picked up the phone and called Janet back. This time she actually picked up. She told her that she didn't have luck.  Janet thought they might have been beating a dead horse, so she told Imani not to worry about it.

Meanwhile, Mercedes had finished running her errands and went back to the house, staring at the list of names that she needed to call and let know what happened.   All Mercedes was thinking was the list was long.  She never realized how big Precious' family was.  She picked up the phone and thought she should start with the most important people first because once she hung up the phone with them they would be picking up their phones and calling the rest of the family, cutting Mercedes' job in half.  It was kind of selfish, but Mercedes didn't want to be the bearer of this bad news.  The first person she dialed was one of Precious' brothers.  She wasn't sure if she remembered if Janet called him or not.  The phone just rang and rang. Mercedes looked on the list and just began dialing numbers. The first person she got was the Uncle. She let him know what happened, and said she was sorry that she had to call him to tell him this. She told him that once all the funeral arrangements were set up she or someone else would give him a call back. Just as Mercedes had hoped for, he told her that he would call a bunch of people to let them know. Most of Precious' family had moved down south and they were going to have to make traveling arrangements as soon as possible. He wanted to make sure there wasn't anyone forgotten.  Mercedes sat on the couch for at least two and half hours making calls and explaining the same thing over and over again.  Finally, she just laid back and closed her eyes in exhaustion.  She knew this was going to be very difficult to do but she knew it had to be done. She felt dehydrated and worn out. Her body felt like it had just run a marathon and her mind had just solved an entire crossword puzzle and could not comprehend anymore.

At the police precinct, Jasmine was waiting to speak with one of the officers that were at the scene. She sat and waited patiently as she could not talk on her cell phone. The officer finally came out and introduced himself. He gave his condolences and walked her into a private room. Jasmine explained why she was there and what she needed. The officer was very helpful and stated that the report wasn't ready. He advised a few things that she was going to need. Jasmine took out a pen and paper and took all the info down. Jasmine wanted to know how the other driver was. She wanted to know if she was hurt or not. The officer advised that she did get hurt but he didn't think it was life threatening, pointing out the other driver was a male. Jasmine thought that was ironic since he wasn't the one carrying the baby, he wasn't the one who died. She asked the officer if he could at least get the other owner's information so she could report the claim to the insurance companies. The officer admitted that he could not give her that info but would let her know the minute that the reports were ready. He also advised her that they could still report the claim to Precious' insurance company to get things moving along. Jasmine asked the officer if he could at least give her the location where they towed the car and he agreed. He left the room for a few minutes and gave her the paper with the tow yard where the car was towed too. Jasmine thanked him and began walking out. Just as she got to the door, the officer touched her on the shoulder and gave her his information, telling her if she needed anything to contact him day or night. She wasn't sure if he was trying to hit on her or if he was just being concerned, but either way Jasmine appreciated it. Jasmine knew that she had a lot more work to do. She quickly got into her car and cut her phone back on, immediately calling Mercedes. The phone rang for a long time and then Mercedes picked up the phone. "Hey," she said. Mercedes sounded like the call woke her up, her voice drained.

Jasmine looked at the phone thinking *I know this bitch wasn't sleeping.* "Are you sleeping"? Jasmine asked.

"Yeah, I dozed off for a few minutes."

"I need you to get your ass up and meet me at the tow yard. We need to find out what we need to do to get Precious' car out of there and I might need your feminine wiles," Jasmine stated.

"Alright, what is the address?" Jasmine told her where it was. Mercedes let her know that she could get there in about 20 minutes at the most. Jasmine decided that she would first see what kind of condition the vehicle was in, and they would then decide what they were going to do next. They knew the insurance company had to look at the car. After they looked at the car, Jasmine would report the claim to the insurance company. She didn't have the policy information yet anyway.

Both Mercedes and Jasmine arrive at the tow yard at the same time. They both parked the cars and got out. Jasmine told Mercedes that she would do all the talking. They walked inside and Jasmine went to the front desk. She asked the female behind the counter if she could help her. The female continued to talk on the phone like she didn't even hear her. Jasmine waited for about three minutes and saw Mercedes getting impatient. Jasmine looked down at the girl sitting on the phone and politely said "Excuse me. I am sorry to interrupt your conversation, but I have been standing here waiting to get some help and you're acting like you don't even see me." The girl behind the counter sucked her teeth, saying something very low to the person she was talking to on the phone and hung it up. She then got up and walked into the back. About two minutes later she came back out. She put a phony smile on her face and asked how she could assist them. Mercedes began walking over to the desk but Jasmine grabbed her arm. Jasmine told Mercedes to be cool. "My girlfriend's vehicle was towed here because she was taken to the hospital from the scene of the accident. I wanted to know what I needed to do to pick up her vehicle." The lady behind the counter asked what kind of vehicle it was. Jasmine gave her all the information. The girl looked in the book for the vehicles they picked up on the date. She located the lot and the vehicle was towed too. Unfortunately, the lady stated that Precious' vehicle was taken to the other lot and it was locked. They would have to wait to speak with the officer manager who was gone for the day. She took down both Mercedes and Jasmine's info and explained they would give them a call tomorrow. Jasmine asked what kind of condition the vehicle was in. The lady advised that most of the time when a car is taken to the other lot it was totaled. They are keeping it there so it does not block the vehicle that can be driven out of here. Even though Jasmine didn't like what happened in the beginning of the conversation, she thanked the lady for her help and they walked out. Mercedes uttered, "Jasmine why the hell she is so fuckin' nice."

Jasmine casually replied, "What would going off accomplish.? By the way have you spoken to Imani?"

"No…. What are you going to do now? I'm starving and wanted to know if you would like to get a bite to eat before we get back on track with what we needed to accomplish."

"Bet, let's go get something to eat. How about the old faithful dinner? I will meet you there," Jasmine said enthusiastically.

They both arrived at the diner about ten minutes apart. Jasmine arrived there first and had a little attitude because Mercedes was late. She just kept thinking that she had a lot to get done and the day was going by so fast. When Mercedes got out of her car, she immediately apologized for being a little late and she stressed that word little. Jasmine didn't want to argue because she was starving and she knew it would be pointless. They went inside and ordered immediately. They didn't even really talk too much as they knew the urgency of the day. At the end of the meal,

Mercedes looked saddened, as if the whole traumatic experience had resurfaced like earlier. She was annoyed because she didn't want to express these feelings in front of Jasmine. She tried extremely hard to keep the dolefulness off her face as Mercedes was unable to achieve it. Jasmine went and sat next to her in the booth and just gave her a big gigantic hug. There was no need to say a word. Jasmine let Mercedes know that she understood the pain that she was feeling, as she was feeling it to. She wanted Mercedes to know that she didn't always have to be the rock. It was okay to display the emotions that she was feeling. As Jasmine was talking, Mercedes shook her head as though she was agreeing with what Jasmine was saying. In her head she was wishing that she just shut up, but she didn't want to seem inconsiderate. Jasmine knew in the back of her mind that if Mercedes didn't do it now that when they got into a public setting it would come out and it would not be for the best. Mercedes had a flare for the dramatic, and it was usually and all out spectacle.

As the next few days passed, everyone chipped in and did their part. The funeral arrangements were with not many issues. The group chipped in to get rooms put on hold where relatives and friends could stay. Because of her job, Mercedes basically worked with cash, so Jasmine just put everything on her credit card to hold them. None of them were concerned because it was understood that everyone would pay for their rooms at checkout. They were able to find the car insurance information and set up the claim. They also located Precious' life insurance policy which she had taken out a little over a year ago. Janet had continued to be short on words and tears while all the preparations were being finished up. Imani and Mercedes knew it was just a matter of time before she blew, but all they knew is that they just had to be there for her when it occurred.

As the night rolled around, everyone wondered what would be the next step to be taken. As Imani, Jasmine, and

Mercedes waited for the service to begin, no one said a word. The silence was too much and Mercedes could not take it anymore. Mercedes said, "How long will it be before someone asks the question, who will take the baby?" She would be getting out of the NICU very soon and there had been no discussion.

Janet decided on the adored baby's name. She would name her Karisma. She figured her daughter was charismatic and it would only be right to name her something close to that. She didn't consult with anyone, not that she had too. Mercedes assumed that everyone believed that Janet would take her granddaughter home when she left.

Everyone's eyes opened wide. It was like Mercedes said something she had no business saying on this day. It was about Precious and the friend they had lost.

About ten minutes passed and Jasmine replied, "Good question. Who is going to take the baby?"

Imani jumped in. "Why the fuck are you all discussing this? My best friend is being buried today. I know there is a baby involved and an issue that has to be addressed, but today is not the day for it. Today is the day when we are to mourn and pray for our friend. Let that be the last thing I should have to say about the matter today." Everyone looked stunned after Imani's reaction; it wasn't like her to articulate her opinion with such strength.

Jasmine was the only person who replied, "You are so right Imani, today is not the day. It is a day about Precious."

It was time, and the three remaining friends walked into the church right before the service was to start. The church was packed. There were four rows of just family members. Up in the front, Precious' mother had saved a space for Imani only. Mercedes and Jasmine sat with each other towards the back. The service lasted for about an hour and half. When it was time, Jasmine got up to read the Eulogy. It was supposed to be Imani to read it, but she was just too weak. Her eyes were bloodshot red and her hands could not stop shaking.

Jasmine stood up at the podium and began to read. "Precious was so loved and how her honesty pierced the souls of others. If she came into your life she left a footprint." The tears and cries were great. As Jasmine continued, Mercedes joined her at the podium and began to take over the Eulogy, "Words can't describe Precious," Mercedes said. "She was a skinny girl who thought highly of herself and everyone else could be underneath her." The whole church looked as if they were dumbfounded. Why Mercedes would be doing this. At one point, she and Precious had become good friends. The past few months Mercedes was assisting Precious when she had things to do. Mercedes would take days off from work to help her. Imani was sometimes jealous of the friendship they developed in such a short time.

Imani ran up to the podium and began to pull Mercedes off. Mercedes would not budge. Jasmine started to continue with the eulogy as though none of this had just happened. "Precious was given a gift. The gift to touch a person's head and make it alright. Yes, she was a little scissor happy, but it all worked out in the end. Precious is survived by her mother, Janet, her brothers Paul and Ricky and her daughter Karisma." The tears again began to drop. Jasmine had just made everything okay. She took over knowing in her head that the end was nowhere near. If there was a light at the end of this tunnel, it would not be shining tonight. There were a lot of broken hearts that needed to be mended and she would not even know where to begin.

After the service, everyone went to the burial and said their prayers, nobody spoke one word. After, the hugs were plentiful for the family. Jasmine whispered in Janet's ear "Everything is going to be alright." Jasmine went over to Imani and then Mercedes and said she was leaving. Jasmine was too disgusted to even address what Mercedes had done on this night. The truth was, she wasn't even sure how to address it. The fact that nobody even brought it up made her discomfort even more uncomfortable. It showed the Mercedes ruthlessness shined bright on a day it should have not and everyone was too scared to revoke it.

It was late when Jasmine got home. She ran a hot bath with some aromatherapy candles and put on her favorite slow jam CD. She just sat in the tub and cried. Only Jasmine understood what really lied ahead. She knew the foundation that was built over the years had just crumbled. She knew that this one death would be the death of all of them. A pierce of the fabric had ripped. The only thing she could do was leave it in God's hands.

The next day came fast. The telephone rang at Mercedes' home and she picked it up so fast as if she was waiting for this call. "Hello?" she said. It was a man on the other end, Mr. Oliver, and calling to confirm our appointment today at 1PM. "Yes, I will be there," she replied.

Mercedes got dressed and did something different. This particular morning, she put on hardly any makeup. She looked very respectful. She put on a pants suit and her shirt didn't show any cleavage. This was very unusual for her. She knew that it was important to be taken seriously this day. It was 12:15pm and she grabbed her pocketbook, looked for their keys, picked them up and went out the door. Mercedes was going to look to see if she had any chance to be a permanent fixture in Karisma's life.

Back at Imani's house, where Precious out of town family was staying since they had checked out of the hotel. Imani had prepared a big breakfast. She made bacon, eggs, pancakes, grits and French toast. The sound in the house was so lively you would have not known that just yesterday they buried their best friend, daughter, and sister. Everyone handles death in their own way. At least they had comfort and support with each other.

Jasmine, who didn't ever bother to get out of the bed this morning, just laid with the TV remote control in her hand, gazing out into space as if she was unaware of the surroundings. She finally looked over at the telephone and saw the answering machine was blinking. She rolled over and hit it. There were two messages. The first one played, *"Jasmine, hey just calling to check in on you baby. You needed some time alone and I'm waiting for your call."* The second message made her jump out of the bed. It was from Mercedes. *"Look bitch, I am taking things into my own hands. It is a new day and the girl is mine."* Jasmine wasn't pleased with this, because she knew exactly what Mercedes meant. Jasmine picked up the phone and dialed Mercedes' cell. It went straight into voicemail. She hung up without leaving a message. She then called Imani. That answering machine came on also. This time she started leaving a message but someone picked up. The voice sounded familiar; it was Janet.

Jasmine said what most people would. "How are you holding up today?"

Janet replied, "I just want to say thanks for everything you did yesterday. I still feel like it has not sunk in that my daughter is gone. She will not have a chance to kiss her little baby, hold her when she is crying for her. She will never see her take her first stop. I feel like it's not fair."

Jasmine was hesitant for a moment. "Janet, if we could talk seriously for a moment. I know that this might not be the best time, but it may be the only time because once you leave, all hell is going to break loss. It has already started."

Janet paused for a moment. "This is about Karisma right?"

"Yes."

"Go on."

"Okay, what is going to happen with her? Do you want custody of your granddaughter?"

It was silent over the phone. Almost like Janet didn't want to answer that question and then the line went dead. Jasmine waited a few minutes before she called back, hoping that Janet would dial her first. The phone never rang. Fifteen minutes later, Jasmine was pacing the floor wondering what happened. She then picked up the phone and dialed back. The answering machine came on and Jasmine began to leave a message but this time no one picked up the phone.

Jasmine looked in her closet to see what she could put on that didn't have to be ironed. She pulled out some blue jeans and a red top. She jumped in and out of the shower in five minutes. She threw on her clothes and was ready to walk out the door when she realized that she didn't even brush her teeth. She ran into the bathroom in haste and brushed her teeth and as she was heading out the door the phone began to ring. She waited for a minute and left out without seeing who it was. The machine came on and it was Mercedes saying, "I'm making it happen and nothing or no-one is going to stop me."

Jasmine pulled up in front of Imani's house. There were no cars in the driveway she recognized. She went to the door and didn't hear anything. She pushed the bell, but nobody came to the door. She pushed it again, but to no avail. Now she didn't know where to go. She wondered to herself, *did Janet leave and take Karisma or did they just go out?* She could not believe that Janet would take the baby and leave without at least letting everyone say bye. Jasmine looked in her purse for a pen and piece of paper. She jotted down a note saying, "I am not sure what happened or where you went, but please call me when you get in." She slid the note under the door and left.

About four hours had passed, Jasmine had not heard from anyone. Her phone just wasn't ringing with anyone who could tell her what was going on. She had not returned back to work since the funeral.  The phone company had been very understanding due to the situation.  Her boss assured her that her job would be there when she returned, and for that she was very grateful.  She had left numerous messages for Imani and Mercedes.  Neither had replied.  She was starting to think that maybe they were working together.

Three days had passed and Jasmine decided to go to see a private detective and find out what he could do to find everyone.  Jasmine did her research to find out the best one.  She would not spare any expense.  She knew she had to find out what was going on and she felt this was the best way to get there.  She located a very reputable person.  She did some quick research to see if any complaints were made against this firm.  Nothing.

She went to the office and spoke with the detectives.  He explained that it would be costly to try to locate four different people. Jasmine didn't care, she called the bank to see how much was available.  She asked the detective if $2000 would be enough to retain him.  He agreed.

When Jasmine returned home her answering machine was blinking.  She ran over to the machine to play the message and tripped, fell, and hit her head on the coffee table.  She reached over and was still able to play the message. She listened as the blood started running down her face.  The message was a female that sounded like Imani, but Jasmine's head was starting to feel light.  She tried to focus on the words…..  "Jasmine if you're there pick up, pick up. It's an emergency. I need you to come and get us…." Before the message finished Jasmine was passed out on the floor lying in a pool of blood around her head.

Hours passed while Jasmine lay knocked out.  Then her phone rang and like the miracle it was, she woke up and grabbed the phone. All she was able to say was call 911. About 15 minutes later there was knocking on the door, then banging.  Then the door was broken down.  It was the police.

One officer got on his radio, tell them to get an ambulance to this address right away.

It was moments before the ambulance was there. They came right in and took Jasmine out. They worked on her all the way to the hospital. By the time the ambulance arrived at the hospital, Jasmine was stable, but still not conscious.

Hours passed and Jasmine didn't have one visitor. No one knew where she was.

Finally, that evening, the detective came to the hospital to see her. He had found out what had happened from one of Jasmine's neighbors. The doctor asked her if he was a relative and he lied and told her yes. He knew if he didn't he could not see her since she was in ICU. He went to Jasmine's bedside. She still wasn't awake. He whispered in her ear and said "You can't die on me; I have good news. I have located two of the four people you asked me to find and it requires a trip for the both of us in an airplane." He didn't get a response from Jasmine. He had a book with him and he began to read it. He sat for hours until the doctor finally told him he had to go. He whispered again in her ear, telling her that he would be back tomorrow and she needed to wake up before it was too late.

The next morning rolled around and still Jasmine wasn't awake. The doctor needed to do a cat scan to see why she had not yet woken up. He had just gotten the orderly to roll her into the elevator and suddenly her eyes opened. She didn't utter a word. She just stared up, looking around as if she was trying to figure out exactly where she was. Finally, she spoke. "What am I doing here and how did I get here?" The orderly replied by saying, "I will go and notify the doctor that you are awake and asking for him." She just nodded her head. The doctor decided to do the cat scan anyway. He needed to see how much if any damage there was to her head. He would examine and answer any questions after that.

When Jasmine returned back to the room, the doctor wasn't there but the detective was. All she saw was his beautiful white teeth, teeth you only see on television. She smiled back at him but it hurt her to do so. "Good morning," he stated. "Hope you're up for a lot of info, got good news and bad news." She tried to continue to smile at him. Thinking he was fine, was this her husband or boyfriend and then it dawned on her, she didn't know who this man was. The look of a smile turned into puzzlement.

She spoke to him in a soft tone. "Don't take this personally, but who are you?" He smiled more in a 'you are joking' manner. She then repeated herself, "Who are you?" This time he knew she was serious. She didn't know who he was.

"It's me darling, Richard. The man you hired. You paid me dearly to find some of your friends. You have just recently been through a lot and I can understand why you would like to forget, but I have a great lead on two of the four people but I can't do anything without you."

Jasmine just stared at him still looking at his face thinking *damn he's fine. Did I ever date him?* She finally got herself together and asked, "Who are these people that I have you looking for?' Maybe if you tell me these things it might trigger something."

"What do you remember Jasmine?" Richard asked. "You tell me what and who you remember and maybe I can help you fill in the blanks. Just to make sure you understand, I am a PI that you hired to assist you. I haven't known you for very long and I don't know any of your friends. Just what you have previously told me."

Jasmine began to go over what she remembered. It was mostly the basics. Her mother and her cat. She talked about growing up the youngest of three girls and the family being dysfunctional. Jasmine then started talking about her three friends, Mercedes, Imani and Precious. She explained how

Imani was a great friend to her growing up and then Mercedes took over. Their friendship grew and grew. They had a personal respect for each other and then she began to speak about Precious. When she spoke about her, it was from the heart. She didn't realize or remember that she was dead.

She began by saying Precious was a name that she lived up to. Precious was a girl who thought that she was the shit and grew up to be a woman who was the shit. She was a pretty girl with a body that wasn't very sexy, but she had a sculptured ass for a skinny girl. She was thin and wore big clothes to appear that she was bigger. She always kept her hair fabulous and figured that since she was so into herself that she would express it by doing other people's hair, but she did it well which gave her something else to brag about. The thing that touched her was behind all that she was an insecure girl. She talked a good game and could give killer advice, but never looked into her own backyard. Sometimes she thought that is why she and Imani became so close. They both lived in the same world. Jasmine accounted for everything she could remember.

Richard was very enthused that Jasmine remembered the girls. He let her know that is who he was looking for and he had found two of them. He didn't want to go any further until the doctor came back with her cat scan results. He let her know he had to leave her for a while but would be back later on.

Richard left and went back to his office to follow up on a few leads. He started to feel very vested. As he sat and listened to Jasmine speak about her friends, he felt a genuine connection. He could tell that she had a good heart and he needed to help her out. He logged onto his PC and noticed that he received an email. It read, *"This is my last contact with you. If you want to find the baby, act fast. She is about to be on the move again and I am not sure she is going to be found again."* Richard hit the print button, still wondering in his mind who is sending him these messages. The person would never give him their real name and had many good facts so he knew it was someone on the inside. Richard had tried to get the information by the email address but was never able to get anything. This person really knew how to cover their ass.

He rushed back to the hospital to talk to Jasmine and her doctor. When he walked into the room, the doctor was just going over the cat scan results. "Everything appears to be fine. It will take some time and rest but everything should come back to you."

Richard quickly jumped in and asked, "Can she go home today?"

The doctor glared at him. "I don't recommend it but I will not stop her."

"What about flying?"

"Wait, wait, wait," Jasmine stepped in. "You guys are acting like I am not here. What is this shit about flying?" She felt a little embarrassed after blurting that out with the doctor still in the room. She quickly apologized.

Richard began handing Jasmine her clothes and let her know, "I will explain on the plane. Our flight leaves in an hour and a half." They rode in the car and both were very quiet. Jasmine had not really got her mind right. It was sort of bothering her. But Richard had been so sweet and nice to her. He acted very concerned and willing to help her anyway possible. The only thing that Jasmine didn't understand is why and what was in it for him..

Jasmine and Richard arrived at the airport about 45 minutes before the plane was to take off. Jasmine was starving. Jasmine let Richard know that she needed to pick up some food and he politely agreed. She ran and picked up a chicken sandwich from Burger King with small fries. Jasmine still wasn't sure where they were headed and why. When they got to the gate she realized they were headed to

Las Vegas. They immediately boarded the plane. She sat in first class. She had never sat there before.

Richard said to Jasmine, "Have you ever been to Vegas before?"

She took a minute to reply, "Yes, I believe I used to live there."

"Do you remember your exact address?"

"No," Jasmine quickly replied, and continued by saying, "I have not remembered everything yet. I do get a feeling that I enjoyed living here. Not even sure why I left. By the way, why are we going there? Are you trying to help me get all my memories back?"

"No, we are going to find the baby," Richard replied.

There was a moment of silence and the tears swelled in Jasmine's eyes. Everything suddenly flooded into her head. She remembered who Richard was and why he was so important. First she had flashes of Karisma, and then Precious. Everything that she had forgotten was in the forefront. Jasmine felt overwhelmed with guilt. How could she have forgotten something so important, especially that darling little baby girl? She kept telling herself that it would not make any sense to blame herself. What was important was that she now had her memory back. She felt an astounding sense of relief. Jasmine leaned on Richard's shoulder to reflect. They flew the entire plane ride in silence. Richard had realized just what had taken place. Jasmine was remembering everything. The fasten your seatbelt sign flashed on. They knew it would not be long before the plane was to land. Jasmine looked out the window and observed Las Vegas lights. They were closer to landing than she had thought. She clinched onto Richard's hand as flying wasn't her favorite.

They got off the plane and were still in silence. Jasmine was still not sure where they were headed exactly. Richard hailed a cab and asked the driver to take them to Rio. The

Rio she thought. *Hmm that is a casino hotel. Is he taking me gambling, maybe?* He didn't know that she loved to do that, how could he know?

In the cab ride Jasmine finally spoke, "Do you know more about me than I think?" He smiled with those beautiful white teeth and laughed. He put his hand over her lips and never even answered the question. She thought that was odd, but she was trying to be patient because he was being so helpful. Jasmine took in the entire ride. She looked around at all the traffic and the people walking around outside looking like they were having the best time in the world. She took a deep breath and smiled. With everything that was going to wrong she felt like being home was right.

They arrived at the front desk and already had reservations. They had a suite with two queen size beds. The view wasn't that great but Jasmine didn't really care. She knew they were there for a reason and she wanted to get to the bottom of everything. At this point, she was consumed by everything. She had just remembered what had recently gone on with her life. The funeral and the pain that all her friends and Precious family had just experienced. Where was Karisma and who took her? Then it dawned on Jasmine, if they were in Vegas it must have been Mercedes.

They sat in the room for hours. They didn't really talk about why they were in Vegas. Jasmine decided that she would go down to the casino and take some of the pressure off. Richard was looking at his laptop and was very distracted. Jasmine asked him if he minded if she went downstairs for a while. He just shook his head up and down. He didn't even look up at her.

Jasmine walked around the casino for a while before she started to play. She found a slot machine that was right up her alley. She sat down and began to play. About ½ hour later, she was down $150. She had just dumped a lot of money in one machine. She got up and started looking around again. Jasmine noticed a bunch of one-dollar Wheel of Fortune Machines. The area was crowded. She just sat and waited. Finally, someone got up. Jasmine dropped a $50 bill in the machine and it dawned on her. Where was this money coming from? She didn't remember putting it in her bag. Jasmine just smiled and kept gambling.

It didn't take long for Jasmine to triple her money. She was on a winning streak and loving it. She was also in the process of getting hammered, being on drink number five. Her luck was going great. She then felt a hand on her shoulder. Jasmine turned around and it was her buddy the investigator. "Are you ready to get going?" he asked. She really wasn't but she hit the cash out button and picked up her ticket. She proceeded to the cashier and cashed in. She was very excited because she had one all the money she lost and won some too. Jasmine looked over at Richard, grabbed his hand, and put something in it. She told him don't even count it just put it in your pocket. Richard knew that he could not win this so he obliged. They got back into the elevator and went to a different floor. Richard told her they were going to meet up with someone. He was going to do all the talking. He let her know that he needed her to pretend that she still does not have her memory back yet. Jasmine asked him what was going on. She had been very cooperative since they got on this journey but she needed to get some answers. He advised her that once they finished the meeting he would clue her in on what was going on. Hopefully, this lead would turn out to be all of the information they needed to find the baby. "Just try to be a little more patient. I know it has been hard but I promise I will give you full disclosure once the meeting is over," Richard.

They got to the room and Richard didn't even knock on the door, he just opened it up. He looked back at Jasmine with a stern face and put his finger up to her lips. She got it. Inside the room were two men and a beautiful woman. The first thought in Jasmine's mind was she was a hooker. She had way too much makeup on and her heels were at least four inches high. Her dress was provocative and didn't leave much to the imagination. The two black men were dressed in fancy business suits. One man told them to take a seat. Jasmine sat down but Richard stood. One of the men pulled out a little box, but Jasmine could not really see what was inside. The guy spoke very softly to Richard. Based on their body language, it looked like the conversation was very intense. One of the men kept pointing at the box. They all shook their heads in agreement. Richard walked over to Jasmine and whispered in her ear, "Remember what I said." He grabbed her hand and walked her over to where the box was. The man looked at her and told her to look inside the box. Jasmine opened up the cover and saw a locket inside. Memories of the locket came fluttering down. She remembered the day she purchased it. She was so. excited to buy this for Karisma, her first piece of jewelry. She took a second to compose herself and shook her head no. She believed that this was the answer that Richard wanted her to say. The man looked at his friend and then looked back at Jasmine and asked her if she was sure. She shook her head no again. Richard said to the man that he thinks that he made a mistake. He didn't have the valuable information that they were looking for. Both men looked puzzled as they knew that this locket was the one that was brought by Jasmine for Karisma. The beautiful lady walked over to Jasmine and asked her if she needed a drink. In Jasmine's mind she was thinking hell yeah, but she knew that wasn't the right thing right now. She said "no." "Would you like to go on the balcony and get some air?" the lady asked. Jasmine looked at Richard and he shook his head letting her know that was fine. Jasmine told the lady to lead the way. The lady opened up the balcony door and they walked through, then closed it behind them. Jasmine could tell that they wanted her out of the room. Jasmine looked over the balcony at all the pretty lights. She wondered to herself what was going on inside, but just kept silent. The lady stood beside Jasmine and put her hand on her shoulder, startling Jasmine a bit.

"Are you enjoying your time in Las Vegas?" the lady asked.

Jasmine thought for a minute and responded by saying "Yeah, it has been pretty fun. I love coming to this city." Jasmine thought about it and wondered if she should have made reference that she had been her before. She decided she would do a little probing since the lady wanted to talk. "How long have you been living here?" Jasmine asked.

The lady replied to her, "I don't think we have formally been introduced. My name is Talia. I have been living out here for quite some time. I am thinking about moving and trying something new."

"If you don't mind me asking, what do you do out here?"

Talia gave her a shady stare and laughed. "Do you really not know what I do here? Look how I am dressed. I mean I know that people wear sexy dresses in Vegas all the time, but I am surrounded by men with stacks of money all night long. Do you think they keep me around for my look? Need I say more?" Jasmine shook her head up and down in understanding.

Jasmine turned her head and continued to stare off the balcony admiring the view again. Talia looked back into the room and noticed that the conversation looked to be getting heated. There were a lot of fingers pointing at each other and the box. At one point, it appeared that Richard was going to leave the room, but one of the men grabbed his arm and he apparently changed his mind. She wondered to herself if she should continue to talk to Jasmine to try to distract her, but looked over at her and realized that she wasn't even focused on what was happening in the room; she was more concerned about just getting through the evening. No more words were exchanged as they waited on the balcony. At least a half an hour went by before a man came over to the balcony door and tapped on it. Both Talia and Jasmine looked at the door at the same time. The man waved his hand as to signal us to come inside. Jasmine let Talia go first and followed behind checking around the room to see if she could spot Richard. At first, she got a little nervous because she didn't see him, but he shortly came walking into the room. Richard put his arm around Jasmines' waist and asked her if she was ready to go. She smiled and said her goodbyes. Talia waived at Jasmine almost like she was sad to see her go. They walk out of the door into the hallway and Jasmine could not wait to open her mouth. "How could you let me sit out there so long? Don't get me wrong, I did enjoy being outside that stuffy room but I was getting such a weird vibe from Talia. Did you know that was her name?" Jasmine didn't even give him Richard a chance to answer as she continued firing question after question at him. As they got into the elevator, Richard had finally had enough of her questions. He put his finger over her mouth to let her know to be quiet for a minute. He finally spoke. "Just be patient my friend. We have a lot to discuss and you firing all these questions are not giving me a chance to even get my thoughts together and absorb the information I just obtained."

When they walked outside, it was hot. It wasn't the same kind of hot as New York. The humidity wasn't even an issue. Jasmine asked, "Where are we headed?"

"Home," Richard replied.

"Home as in back to New York?"

"Yes."

"I thought we were coming here to do something special, to find that beautiful baby girl. I thought we had a purpose for this trip. Please explain why you dragged me on a plane, brought me to a casino, put money in my pockets to just turn back and go home?" He could sense how upset or maybe confused Jasmine had become. First, Richard just showed those pretty white teeth and then he began to laugh.

This infuriated Jasmine even more. "What type of games are you playing Richard? What is the deal?"

Finally, Richard had an answer. "While you were having fun gambling, I was out following some leads, one of which panned out. Do you think I was in that room just hanging out with those guys for no reason? This possibility has led us back to New York. Home. Now can we go?" Again, Richard showed those pearly white teeth and put his arm around her and told her that everything was going to be alright.

"First tell me the one thing that you may have found," Jasmine stated.

"We can discuss this on the plane ride home. We are losing precious moments just standing here bantering while valuable time is being lost. It will be late when we arrive in New York and we will both be tired. Let's get a move on it okay?"

They arrived at the airport just making their flight. They were unable to sit together on the ride back home. Jasmine thought to herself, *maybe this was intentional.* Maybe Richard didn't want her to get her hopes up for what he had found out or maybe he didn't find anything out and he didn't want to let her down. She could spend her whole plane ride guessing or she could try to get some sleep. That is what she decided to do.

# Chapter Six

Imani found herself stranded. She never heard from Jasmine, and she started to wonder what happened. As she sat on the stool of the little diner in the middle of nowhere, Janet sat beside her. They had made numerous attempts to contact Jasmine and Mercedes. To Imani, this was a nightmare that just would not end. Janet was very calm through the entire ordeal. She just wanted to get out of this god forsaken place. They had run out of money and there wasn't anyone who was willing to help them. All they knew was they were somewhere in the Catskills, Upstate New York. Who brought them there was anyone's guess to Imani. Janet's only concern was what happened to Karisma? Where was she? Was she okay? Who had taken her?

Imani now believed that Jasmine and Mercedes had to have done this. Neither had responded to their phone calls. It was like a knife in Imani's back. Why couldn't her friends, her lifelong friends, come to her? They could have all talked this out. This was an innocent little girl who belonged with her family. She didn't need to be on the run, with Lord knows who. Imani was angry and hurt. She couldn't figure out why they would betray her. How could they deceive her? This feeling of abandonment was real. Imani felt like she was experiencing the death of a friend all over again. Her mind could not even comprehend anything because she was exhausted, not only because of this but everything she has not had a chance to get over.

The owner of the diner came over. He was a large white man with teeth the color of stained wood. His belly laid over his striped pants and his shirt was no longer white, but grey. He said to Imani, "Are you ladies going to be having anything to eat here or are you all just taking up space?" Imani had to catch herself before making things worse.

She took a deep breath and began to explain. "It has been days since we have been out here, walking down roads trying to find a warm place. We were dropped off in the middle of nowhere. We didn't ask to be here but we are kind of stuck. We have no money left and really need to get back to Westchester County. If there is any way you can assist us, I will give you my guarantee that we will repay you. If you could even call the police that would be a great help." The tears began to swell up in Imani's eyes. She was at the end of the line. She stared up at the stranger and he stared back.

He waited a moment and finally replied. "What is your name?"

"Imani," she replied. She began to go into her pocket to pull out identification and he moved back. "Wait, just getting some ID out."

"That's not necessary," he replied. "Here is the deal. I will help you on two conditions: your friend over there sucks my dick and you, beautiful one, you fuck me lovely." Imani quickly stood up, ready to call the police. He quickly pulled out his badge. He wasn't only the police; he was the sheriff of this small town.

Janet pulled Imani to the side and said, "Let's do this. We can get the hell out of here."

"Are you crazy?' I am not sleeping with this guy and you are not sucking his dick."

Janet replied after looking around. "It doesn't appear that we are going to be able to just walk out of here. There are way too many of them and only two of us."

Imani replied with an attitude. "We can do better all by ourselves. What if we get them to throw us in jail? At least we know we could most likely get a phone call. Then again in this hick town who knows what they may do to us."

Janet thought about it for a little while and appeared to think that maybe Imani was right. She thought for a few moments and remembered something that might help them. "There is a pay phone outside. If you could get to the door, I would distract them. Go outside and dial 911. Make an excuse, do whatever you have to do to get the State Troopers here. Keep the phone off the hook so they know where to come. Do it now. Now!"

Imani got up very slowly, eyeing the door to see if someone would try to stop her. Could she get around them? Janet called the fat sheriff over to distract him. "Where should I suck your cock at? Show me the way." He looked at Janet as if she was lying. She smiled at him. "Hurry up before I change my mind. You don't look that appetizing to me right now. Matter of fact, you got some liquor in this joint? Bring me a shot, no make it two." As the man began to go behind the counter, Imani made her move. She headed towards the door. As she got her first foot out, someone grabbed her arm. She tried to jerk it so they could not get a hold of it, but to no avail. She turned around and it was Janet.

Imani said, "What are you doing?"

"I had to do this," she replied. "I need to make it like I do not want you to walk out. Once I go into the backroom, then you make your move but go fast. Not slow like this because if I am able to catch you, someone in here will too." Imani went back and sat down. Janet sat across from her and told her she needs to loosen up to not call attention to herself. "Talk to me until the guy comes back. Don't just sit there. If we are going to get this right, you have to get your mind right, girl. I need you to pull all your strength from somewhere. I don't give a fuck where but get yourself together." Imani put a smirk on her face to try to ease Janet's mind. It wasn't that impressive.

"I think I will be okay," Imani informed Janet. "I have the easy job I think. You have to go and violate your own body by choice. I don't think I can do that no matter what the circumstances."

"Don't worry about me," Janet replied. "I got this one."

The sheriff came back to the seat and gave Janet two shots. Imani asked her if she should drink that.

"Do you even know what it is? Tequila," he replied. Janet drank the first and then the second.

"Wow," she yelled. "I'm ready now, I can take on anything." She grabbed the sheriff by his belt loops and said show me the way.

As they approached the door to the back-room Imani made her move. She got up and headed towards the door. She opened it with ease and walked out. This appeared to be too easy, but she kept it moving. She looked around and located the pay phone. She began walking towards it taking her time, but in the back of her mind was the idea that Janet was in that back room doing who knows what. Imani tried to reason with herself that Janet was only doing this because she thought it was our only way out, but she wished that she had not decided to do it. Janet had already been through a lot herself and the shit just kept coming. It seemed like forever before she reached the pay phone. She picked it up and could not believe there was a dial tone. She began pressing 911. A woman answered 911, "What is your emergency?" Imani was about to talk but the phone was snatched out of her hand. It was another white guy she remembered seeing in the diner. He covered her mouth so she didn't scream.

"Wait," he said. "Let me explain, don't call the police because they are all linked together. I will try to help you."

Imani began to cry. "Why are you doing this?" she screamed. He covered her mouth so hard this time she could barely breathe.

"Shut up," he said again. "I can help just don't scream anymore." The man took his hand away from Imani's mouth. She started coughing trying to catch her breath. The man told her to come with him, and she reluctantly followed. They went towards the parking lot. Imani stopped, telling the man that she would not leave the lady that she came with. He smiled and told her they needed to get to his car so they could talk and nobody would notice them sitting there. He would need to pull off, but he promised her that he would bring her back if after what he told her she wanted to still return. Imani was curious to hear what this man had to say so she agreed. She was uncomfortable with the idea of leaving Janet, but if there was any way she could contribute to getting them back home she was willing to give it a try.  At this time, Imani was desperate.

Back at the diner Janet and the sheriff were in the back room. They were both sitting down having a drink. It appeared as if Janet was enjoying herself. She didn't even look like she was nervous or scared.

Janet began to take her clothes off seductively, almost dancing around the chair like music was playing. She started with her shoes and then she unbuckled her belt. She pulled it off and swung it around striking the man. He didn't seem to mind, just looked on smiling. Janet unbuckled her pants slowly pulling them down around her knees and then pulling them back up as if she was teasing him. He moved closer to Janet and she pushed him back. "Be patient," she said. She continued her seductive dance removing her shirt and then her bra. Her tits were now exposed. Her breasts were not large, and for an older lady they still sat high. Her nipples were large and erect. The sheriff was completely turned on. It was like Janet could get away with just about anything if she wanted to. This was her chance, but she continued with her dance. She pulled her pants back down and began to remove one leg at a time. Slowly and with precision, Janet looked as though she had a purpose behind every move.

Janet was down to only her panties. She moved up close to the sheriff and rubbed her ass across his hands. He gently caressed her ass, like he had done this before.  Janet's panties remained on, but she knew it wasn't going to be for long. She could see how this was turning the sheriff on and how much it was turning her on. Her pussy was becoming extremely wet.

Janet moved away from the sheriff and began to remove her panties. She pulled them down with her ass facing the sheriff as she got low to the ground. She put her hands on her ass and pulled it wide open. A moan escaped the sheriff's mouth. He was ready. She took off her panties and rubbed them between her legs making sure her juices got on the panties. Janet then turned around butt naked and rubbed her panties across the sheriff's face, making sure he felt the wetness and smelled the scent of her. She loved licking her lips, making him even hornier but how did she know this?

He pushed everything off the desk and began to remove his pants. She quickly stopped him and advised him that was her job. She pulled down his pants and noticed that he didn't even have on underwear. She didn't seem to care. As she began to lick his nuts, he grabbed her head. To him, she didn't appear to mind. She continued sucking and licking his nuts, moving her tongue in a furious manner.

The sheriff was a somewhat well-endowed man. He was about seven inches hard and the width was enormous. He wasn't circumcised. Janet put her hand on his dick and pulled the foreskin back. She licked the head of the penis. There was more moaning by the sheriff. All at once, Janet opened up her mouth swallowing the sheriff's dick. She pulled it out and spit on it. She moved the spit around with her tongue keeping the foreskin back. She put his dick back in her mouth enjoying it. Janet proceeded to continue this same procedure over and over again for at least 10 minutes.

Finally, the sheriff jerked his dick out of her mouth and ejaculated all over her face, mostly her lips. Janet stuck her tongue out and licked the cum off. She then stuck his dick back into her mouth, proceeding to start the ritual all over again.

She looked up at him and said, "Are we done or would you like more?" He stuck her head back down on his dick and said get to it. It didn't take a long time for the sheriff's dick to become fully erect again. He pulled her head back and turned her around. He put one of her legs on top of the desk. He spit on his dick to make sure it was moist and stuck his dick inside her soaking wet pussy. Janet's pussy swallowed his dick. She didn't even seem shocked that he didn't put on a condom and she didn't request one either. He stroked the pussy in and out, sometimes with force and sometimes so gently as if he knew what she liked. They shared a very strange connection. She was enjoying every second of this trade off as if she didn't have a worry in the world.

Janet asked him to turn her over so he did. They continued to fuck for over 45 minutes until finally Janet reached her peak. She came all over the sheriff's dick holding his ass so tight. He yelled out to her that he was about to cum but she didn't let his ass go. Instead she wrapped her legs tighter around him as he dropped his load inside her vast pussy. When it was all over, they kissed each other like it was natural.

# Chapter Seven

In New York, Jasmine and Richard arrived at Jasmine's home. She walked in feeling great, for the simple fact that she now remembered everything. Through it all, she still managed to enjoy some down time despite what was going on. Richard came inside and sat down. She went into the kitchen and poured both of them some water. He quickly sucked the water down as if he were in a rush. She was thinking to herself how she could get him to stay awhile so she could get more info from him. Jasmine knew that he knew more than he was willing to give up. Jasmine asked if he was hungry, but he told her he wasn't. She continued to make small talk trying to figure out how she could get to all the questions she wanted to ask. Richard got up and went into the bathroom. Jasmine wondered how her bathroom looked. Was it even clean? When he came out, he didn't seem to complain. Richard let Jasmine know that he was going home and would get with her in the AM. She tried to stop him to find out what he knew, but before she could say something Richard was out the door.

Jasmine went into her bathroom and cut on the water in the bathtub. She made sure the temperature was just right and put the stopper in the tub, closing the bathroom door as she walked out. Jasmine went into the bedroom and saw her answering machine blinking. She had over 15 messages. First she thought maybe she would listen to them after she took her bath. Then she thought about it again, it might be something very important regarding Karisma or something else upsetting. Jasmine decided to just relax and take her bath and deal with everything afterwards. She didn't even bother to take the phone in the bathroom with her.

As she laid her head back she began to think about all the things she needed to do.

She knew that she was running low on funds, and she hadn't been going back to work on a regular basis due to all the things going on. She needed to figure out if she could make time to get a second job, if only for a little while, just to get back to where she was before everything had changed.

She began to doze off and she was startled by her phone ringing. She listened to her answering machine. She could not hear it that clearly so she cut the hot water off. She only caught the end of the message. It was a female voice telling her to call her as soon as she got this message. Jasmine wasn't too sure who it was. She cut the hot water back on just to get the water warm again and continued to relax. About a half an hour later Jasmine realized her body was shriveling up like a bad grape. She stood up and began to soap up her washcloth. The water was now a little cold so she pulled out the stopper and turned the shower on. As she was washing she heard her phone ringing again. Jasmine listened closely and heard the same voice as she did before, but this time she knew who it was. It was Mercedes and she sounded like it was important.

Jasmine quickly finished washing her body and hopped out the shower. She grabbed her towel and went immediately into the bedroom. Jasmine pressed her answering machine and began to listen to all the messages. She picked up a pen and paper that was sitting on her nightstand and as the messages played, she realized that mostly all of them were Imani and Mercedes. Mercedes' messages were all over the place. She was saying that she had some information on what happened to Janet, and she was sorry she had not returned any of her calls. Then she would call back saying she made a mistake. Imani's messages were more like distress calls. Every message sounded like someone was in her face and she could not say what she meant. The only thing she knew was that Imani was up in the Catskills and had no way to get back home. Each one was more distressing than the last, and one so distressing that she stopped the messages, picked up the phone, and called Richard. Jasmine felt the need to make him aware of this.

Richard sounded like he was asleep when he picked up, "Hello."

"Hey," Jasmine said. "Sorry for waking you up but there is something that could not wait until the morning."

"What is it?"

"Listen," she said as she pressed the play button on her answering machine. The message played and when it was over, Richard asked Jasmine when that message left was. Jasmine let him know that she had no clue as her machine date and time wasn't set.

"Damn," Richard cursed. "If we knew that it could have helped a lot." Richard asked Jasmine if she would be up for a while. She stated yes because she could not sleep due to that message. "Is it okay for me to come over?" he asked.

"Yeah, that would be okay. "She let him know that she was going to leave the front door open so that she would not have to get up to open it. Richard informed her he was on his way and they hung up the phone.

It took about twenty minutes and Jasmine had begun to doze back off. Her body was in a very relaxed state. She didn't even hear her door open and close. Richard walked into the bedroom and smiled as he saw her lying down. She still only had her towel on and half of her body was exposed. He walked very quietly towards the telephone and picked it up. He spoke in a very soft voice as he didn't want to disturb Jasmine. All he said was "I'm here and will probably be here all night, will catch up with you tomorrow" and gently hung up the phone. Surprisingly to Richard, woke Jasmine up.

She looked up at Richard wiping her eyes. "Who were you talking to?

"Nobody important," he replied. He smiled and asked her if she was planning to get up or should he go into the living room and watch some TV so she could rest. Then he laughed and said, "Maybe you want to put some clothes on too." Not really thinking, Jasmine grabbed her towel and threw it at him. She quickly realized what she did and threw the covers on top of her naked body.

Jasmine sat up and slowly got up from the bed. "Are you hungry?"

"Not for food," he replied and quickly noted that he was just joking. "Yes. It's kind of late though so we can't order anything in."

Jasmine went to the kitchen and looked into the fridge, which didn't have anything appealing in it to make. "The diner," she remembered. "It's open all night; I can have a nice cup of coffee and you could get something to eat. We can have some peace and quiet and talk about everything that we both just learned."

"Do we have a date? I mean a deal." Richard grinned.

He rubbed his hands all in her hair and said, "do something with that too." Richard flashed his pearly white teeth and walked out of the room.

# Chapter Eight

Imani and the stranger continued to drive off getting farther and farther away from the diner. Imani felt some sense of relief, but also was worried that she had left Janet behind. She sat silently wondering what this man was going to say to her. Was he actually there trying to help her, or was he part of this little town's corruption? She knew that she had to see it through.

They drove for about twenty minutes and pulled into a driveway of a house that was so large and beautiful, Imani just stared in amazement. The house stood four stories high and was as wide as an amusement park. The grass was so green she knew it was tended to daily. The house had a beautiful large fence around it and she turned and watched out the back window as the gates closed.

*Did this man own this house?* she thought to herself. She could not imagine that as this man didn't appear to be a man of substantial wealth. He appeared as a common man, a man who didn't own much more than a pickup truck and a tiny plot of land.

The man got out of the car and asked Imani to come with him. She was very hesitant and sat in the car questioning herself why she even got into the car with this man in the first place, but it was too late. She was here now. He opened the door and let her know that they didn't have much time. This was a do or die mission and if she wasn't willing to trust him, he would take her back to the diner and she would be on her own. "You will not get any answers at that diner at least any that would get you any closer to the truth. I know the fucking truth now get out of the car so you can know it too." He put his hand out and Imani grabbed it, took a deep breath, and got out of the vehicle.

As she took the long journey to the front door she wondered again to herself what she was walking into. The man opened the front door and they stepped inside. The inside of the house was breathtaking. The first room they stepped in was painted a pale blue color. There were flowers all over the room. In the middle of the room was a clear elevator that went up to the top floor. Imani was mesmerized by the décor of this room. The scent smelled as if they were in an enchanted garden filled with every exotic flower that existed. The curtains on the window were the same pale blue as the walls. They were tied back with satin string. The window glass was so clean it was as if glass. Who was this man? And if this wasn't his house, whose was it? The stranger watched as Imani was taken in by the beauty of this house. He remembered how it felt the first time he walked inside the home.

The man led Imani to the elevator and told her to step inside. He told her to press the third-floor button and he would meet her upstairs in a few moments. Imani walked to the elevator and did exactly what he requested. The ride was quick. So fast that her stomach dropped after arriving on the third floor. The elevator door opened and Imani walked off. She wasn't sure where to go from there. The hallway was long and wide with many doors to choose from. None of the doors were opened. She stood in front of the elevator trying to decide what she should do next. Should she wait for the man, or choose a door to start at? Imani realized as she was standing there that her body was trembling. Her palms were sweaty; she was totally anxious and unsure. She was curious about what was behind the door but also hesitant to find out. Imani knew she was taken there for a reason. It was to show her something important. She didn't like the feeling. Her anxiety level was higher than she had ever felt it since

Precious passed away and she wasn't sure how that was possible.

Imani decided that she would take her chances and take a look around. As she began to walk down the hallway, she heard the elevator going back down. She decided that she would wait for the elevator to come back up to see if the stranger was in it. She stood for a while and waited but the elevator didn't move. She began her journey back down the hallway. It seemed to Imani like she was walking forever. She arrived at the end of the hallway and tried to open the door. She didn't even bother to knock because she figured she had not heard a peep since she arrived on the third floor so she would take her chances. The door was locked. She then continued to try to open each door. As she arrived almost at the other end of the hallway there was one door she had not tried, she grabbed the doorknob and began to turn the handle and heard the elevator doors open. Imani turned around and saw the man get off the elevator. She turned back around getting ready to open the door and he yelled "Wait, wait for me!" Imani paused but opened the door anyway. The room was pitch black. She whispered as if she knew someone else was in the room. "Hello? Hello, is anyone in here?" She didn't receive a reply. Imani could smell the scent of perfume, a scent she has smelled many times, but this scent was faint as if the person wearing it had long gone. She took her hands and rubbed them across the wall searching for a light switch. Just at that second the room was bright.

The man stood in the doorway and said, "I told you to wait for me." Imani looked around the room but her and the man were the only two people in there. Imani was now getting angry. "What kind of games are you playing with me? You brought me here for what? I thought it would help me. My friend is back at that diner and I don't have a clue what kind of trouble I left her in. I know that a friend left me before and our friendship paid the price and many people suffered." The man began to laugh. He laughed so hard he started choking. Imani was totally offended by this. "Fuck you, take me back now," she belted with authority.

He immediately stopped laughing and got serious. He informed Imani to sit down for a second and after he said what he needed to, she could make up her own mind and if she wanted him to take her back, he would do so, ASAP. Imani had her reservations but figured she came this far so she might as well hear him out. "Proceed," she stated.

He replied by saying "Now, let me speak and do not interrupt me until I am finished and if it is okay with you I will take a seat." He began by clearing his voice and then starting to speak with a clear, distinct almost morbid tone. "Imani," he continued, "your friend Janet is not the person you think she is. Do you think it was strange how you wound up all the way up here in an area where you would never find yourself going? A place where there is not one black face that you have seen? A place where not one person is friendly, even the police? But a place, so foreign to you, that your supposed friend would be willing to go into a back room with some strange white man not even thinking twice about leaving you with a bunch of strangers?"

Imani tried to interrupt but he quickly stopped her. "I am not yet finished. I haven't even really begun. I have met Janet many times. She has made several or should I say numerous trips to this destination. She has been fucking Buddy, the sheriff, for months. OH, by the way the sheriff his name is Buddy. They have been dating each other for quite some time. I am still not sure why she would have brought you up here with her, but I knew that eventually two plus two would equal four. She needed you to believe that she was innocent in this game she had orchestrated. Janet had talked about her elaborate plan that she put together and she knew that she needed one of her daughter Precious' friends as an accomplice. One who would not even realize it."

Imani quickly interjected by saying, "What do you know about Precious?"

"I will answer you this, Janet let us know about her beautiful, boney, hardheaded daughter she had. She bragged about how her daughter had made a life for herself leaving mommy behind. Janet would say that Precious wasn't really good for much unless it was going to benefit herself, but for the first time she did something that would benefit Janet. She was raped, got pregnant, decided to keep the baby, and died."

Imani now had tears running down her face. She was in disbelief of what this man was saying. Was he lying? He couldn't be, because how did he know all this information? *There was only one person he could have learned this information from but why?* Imani wondered to herself. Janet didn't have to go through all these theatrics to get Karisma. She was her granddaughter. *I mean it might have been a struggle but judges like to give custody to blood relatives.*

He continued his story as if he really didn't want to hurt her feelings anymore. "I believe you also have a friend named Jasmine and Mercedes. Janet felt as though Mercedes was too unruly and she would never go for this, and Jasmine was way too smart and she would figure everything out. Now I can imagine what you are thinking. What is the point of all of this? What could Janet want to gain? She had all rights to Karisma so what would be the point of going through all this? Well, once Janet realized that everyone was so interested in what would happen to Karisma, she came to the conclusion that she would profit from this.

She talked to Buddy who helped her come up with this elaborate plan. What helped her execute it even better, was that Jasmine had her little accident and lost her memory and Mercedes was off chasing leads that Janet fed her. This made you think that one of them had taken Karisma. Am I right?" Imani just nodded her head agreeing with him.

He continued by saying that he never agreed with this whole ploy. He felt a baby should not be used as a pawn but he really didn't have a choice until now to speak up. The man took two deep breaths and continued with his story. "Buddy told Janet that if they pulled it off right they could collect the money and disappear without a trace. But Janet felt like someone needed to take the fall for this and it looks like, lucky lady, you are the chosen one. I know you are wondering why I think that you are going to be the fall girl. That would be because she brought you up here and I believe she may try to kill you and say that she did it to protect the baby, which I am sure you have figured out that she is here too. Now I am not sure where they are keeping her, but she must be close because she would have not dragged you up here for nothing. By now Buddy has placed some calls for ransom demands to as many people that they could think of, and as soon as that comes through they will turn the tables on you and it will be a wrap.?

Imani raised her hand as if she was in class and was interrupting the teacher during his lesson. "Go head", he replied.

Imani proceeded to clear the tears from her eyes and spoke with a quivering voice. "Do you have any idea how I am supposed to believe one word you are saying? If you are telling the truth, what am I supposed to do? I cannot even begin to fathom the idea that Janet would think or even say those things about her daughter, Precious. Precious was my best friend. She made a huge decision to keep that baby and I believe that if she knew that this was going on she would be turning over in her grave. I cannot believe that Janet would let me take the fall for this. I have been a fixture in her life for most of my life. She always treated me like I was one of her kids. She has shown me nothing but respect and love. My heart is breaking into a million pieces just thinking about this. Who the fuck are you and what is your part in this? What do you have to gain by telling me these things?"

"I never formally introduced myself, did I? My name is Jr. My real name is Buddy Graves and yes before you say anything, big Buddy is my father. I wanted to wait until you knew almost everything before I let you know who I was. I believe that this knowledge of who I am is going to make you even more suspicious. Trust me though, everything that I have told you is the truth. I am putting my ass on the line by even just bringing you to this house."

"So, what is the purpose of bringing me here?" Imani asked. "Whose house is this because I cannot believe it is yours."

"Take a walk with me please." He put out his hand to lead her to another room. Again, Imani was very hesitant to go, but also something inside of her knew that she had to find out everything. They stopped at the elevator and Jr. pushed the button. The elevator doors opened and they stepped inside. This time, he went into his pocket and pulled out a set of keys. He stuck the key into a panel on the wall, the elevator doors closed, and they began their journey down. This ride seemed much longer to Imani than her ride up to the third floor. Once the elevator stopped, the door didn't open right away. Jr had to stick the key back in. Imani thought to herself *who would take these kinds of precautions? What would they be trying to hide?*

The elevator doors opened and they both walked out. The hallway was identical to the third floor, same amount of doors, same faint smell that she had recognized upstairs. Jr. turned to Imani and put his finger over her mouth advising her she should be quiet. They walked all the way to the end of the corridor to the same exact door that they were in on the third floor. Imani remained silent through the whole walk. Jr. again went in his pant pocket and pulled out the same set of keys. This time though he handed Imani the keys but the one that opened the door was sticking up. Jr. stepped away from the door and waved his hand signaling her to open it. Imani's heart was beating so fast she could barely catch her breath. Her palms were sweating so bad she wand up dropping the keys. The sound of them hitting the ground echoed through the hallway. Jr. quickly ran over and picked them up. He located the correct key again and this time he took it off the ring. He slowly handed her the single key, looking at Imani so intensely as if he was saying without saying it, don't drop it this time.

She put the key into the door and turned the lock. She opened the door with all kinds of thoughts going through her mind. She was reserved and anxious of what she would find. Once the door was fully opened, she again realized that this room too was pitch black. She remembered that the light switch was on the outside of the door. Imani put her hand on the switch and clicked it and the room was lit up, an overwhelming feeling consumed her as she fell to her knees.

Back at the diner, Janet and Buddy were still in the afterglow of their tryst. They weren't even thinking about the time that had passed since they first left Imani sitting at the counter. Janet got up and began putting her clothes back on. She threw Buddy his pants and told him to get dressed. She could tell that he really wanted to stay where he was, but could sense the urgency on Janet's face. He slowly rose off the desk, his limp dick soiled from her cum. He went over to the sink, stuck it over the counter, and began to rinse it off. He looked over at Janet. "You want to put some water on your face and pussy before you go back out there." She smiled and replied, "Why? She knows why we were back here. Let her smell the scent of a real fuckin lady."

Janet continued to get dressed and then there was a knock on the door. Buddy told Janet to move to the corner so she would not be seen when he opened the door, and she obliged. Buddy opened the door and there was a large woman standing there. By his reaction you could tell they knew each other very well. Jane was very curious about what she was about to say. Unfortunately, Buddy stepped out the door, closing it behind him. Imani could not make out the conversation at all.

Buddy quickly came back into the room and continued getting himself together. He didn't even say a word about what had just happened. After he was completely dressed, he said to Janet, "You ready?" She shook her head advising yes. He told her to go out first and he would follow behind in a few minutes. Before Janet walked out she turned to him and asked how much money he was going to be giving them so they could get back home. He informed her that everything has been arranged and as soon as he comes out they could be on their way. Janet took him for his word and walked out the door with the door slamming shut behind her.

As Janet walked into the dining area, she only thought about what she would do as soon as she got home. Maybe take a long bath and relax for a moment or two. When she arrived at the counter, she looked a little puzzled as she didn't see Imani there. For a second she thought to herself, *did Imani make it to the pay phone? Was she able to contact the police or someone else?* She knew that Imani had no money to call anyone she knew or maybe she phoned collect but who? They were unable to contact anyone since they had been out there. Janet got on the stool at the counter and ordered a cup of java. She sat shaking her leg wondering where Imani was. She continued to look around the room. Janet took a sip of her coffee and heard the diner door open. Imani walked through the door looking very disheveled. Janet ran over to her and gave her a huge hug, kissing her, and thanking God that she was okay. She had to make sure that she showed her concern so that Imani wouldn't get suspicious. Janet needed everything to run smoothly because she had more plans to execute.

"Where have you been?" She asked.

"Outside, exercising my legs. I got tired of sitting waiting for you to come out. I wasn't really worried about you because the waitress had assured me that you were okay. I didn't hear any loud noises coming from the back so I stepped out for a minute or two." Imani stood staring at Janet with a weird smirk on her face, her look puzzling to Janet.

Janet questioned Imani on if she was able to make it to the pay phone and whether she was able to reach anyone who could help them? Imani came up with an outrageously believable answer. She said she made it out of the door and took the journey to the phone as she tried not to look back, she could feel that someone was following behind her. She started running towards the phone in hopes that she could just make it there. Imani continued her farce of a story now with tears running down her eyes, building up to the biggest bullshit of it all. "As I put my hand on the phone," she continued, "a man came up behind me breathing heavily on my neck. I felt a sharp object in my back." She added some flavor by adding that she almost peed on herself. "He put the knife under my shirt and slowly rubbed the blade across it. I tried to jerk away but he pulled me back and when he did…" she took a moment to wipe her tears and pulled up her shirt in the back, revealing a cut that Janet was well aware was fresh. Janet immediately put her arms around Imani and wept. What shocked Imani most was the fact that it felt and sounded genuine. She could only think of the last thing that Jr. had informed her. Janet was the best actress in the world. He told Imani that Janet would put on an Oscar performance but to remember it was a performance. Nothing more nothing less.

Buddy came from the back and handed an envelope to Janet. He informed her that it was enough to get them back to safety. He let her know that he would contact a car service to pick them up and take them to the bus stop. Janet looked so excited and relieved. Imani again was a little confused by this. Again, Janet appeared genuine. They both walked outside not saying a word. Imani watched Janet like a hawk, seeing if she would turn around and make any kind of gestures toward Buddy. She didn't.

They waited in front of the diner for the car service. Imani finally spoke, asking Janet what happened in that back room. Janet remained silent. The car pulled up and they both got inside. Imani was a little annoyed because Janet didn't answer the question right away. She was wondering what was going on. Imani knew that something was off, but she wasn't sold on Janet being part of it yet.

"We are going to the bus station. The one that will take us back to Westchester County," Janet said. The driver just shook his head. Janet got comfortable in the seat like it was going to be a long ride. Imani just stared at her wondering when she was going to answer her question, feeling that she deserved an answer. She then started to think that maybe Janet did this for them to get back home. Maybe she should not be pressing the issue. She sat quiet for about two minutes and again asked, "What happened?"

Janet looked at Imani with a look of disgust. "The fucking shit went down like he wanted. I sucked his dick well and he fucked me well. Are you happy now? Now you know. Do you think we would have gotten this money if I didn't do something?" As Janet was spurring her reply, she was also opening the envelope. When they looked inside, they both were shocked as there was only green colored paper stuffed inside.

# Chapter Nine

Jasmine and Richard sat quietly at first, both trying to figure out where they would start. Richard was staring at the menu trying to figure out what he was going to order. Jasmine never even picked up the menu. The waitress came over and asked if they were ready to order. Jasmine ordered coffee only. Richard on the other hand ordered a steak and egg breakfast with hot chocolate. The waitress picked up both menus and walked away. Jasmine smiled at Richard and of course had to say a smart remark.

"Hungry huh?" Richard smiled. "Let's get busy. I have heard that there have been some ransom requests for Karisma. Have you received one?"

"Yes," Jasmine quickly replied. "I had a message on my voicemail. At first I could not figure out if it was a female or a male. The person was definitely making sure I was unsure. I played the message over and over again."

"Tell me exactly what the message said word for word if you can remember," Richard commanded. Jasmine took a minute to think about it. She was about to speak when the waitress came back and brought over the hot chocolate and the coffee. Jasmine thanked her and then requested an order of French toast and informed the waitress that she didn't want it soggy in the middle and if it was, she would send it back. The waitress sort of rolled her eyes and walked away. Jasmine asked if she was too direct.

Richard replied by saying, "You know what you want, nothing is wrong with that. Back to the matter at hand, he continued, what did the message say?"

Jasmine thought for another minute to make sure she got it right. "Okay, it went like this, she began. "Hello Jasmine, I have a deal for you. If you want Karisma back safe in your arms do exactly what I say. Gather all your money together because you will pay dearly. You can stop this message now if you don't intend to do what I say, but again, it will cost you dearly. I will call back soon with my details.' That was the first message." "I was so confused." Jasmine stated. "Why would someone ask me to pay for Karisma." She was trying to figure out if it was possible that everyone was getting the same calls, and if so why wasn't everyone reaching out? Or could it be that someone was playing a horrible joke? The thought made her stomach curdle.

Richard looked puzzled at this point, "First message? There was more than one?"

"Yes, three."

"Do you remember any of the other two?" he asked, still having that puzzled look on his face.

"Of course," she quickly responded. The second message was the same jumbled voice. Still could not make out if it was a female or male. There was something eerie about this message though. There was a baby crying in the background.

This time they said, *"Hello Jasmine, hope you put all our money together because here is my price. $10,000. No more and definitely no less. Borrow, steal it or fuck for it, but get it. You have two days because this fuckin kid is getting on my last nerve."*

"This is not good," Richard stated. "This second message wasn't a joke. This person may be serious. We have to figure out what is their next step and beat them to it."

Jasmine interjected. "If I had the money I would take it anywhere, anytime. I don't have that money; I already depleted my bank account."

Richard let her know that he had no intentions of paying a coward one copper penny. "What about the third message?"

"Well it gets even more bizarre. The last message was even stranger and more intense than the other two. *'Hello Jasmine,'* the voice always started. *'I have a surprise waiting for you when you come and meet me with my money. I think you will be pleased when you arrive. You must arrive alone and if you try any tricks you will be mourning more than your dear brat Karisma so skip, skip, skip to my lue and bag the money because I'm coming for you.'*

"That message scared me because on one hand the voice said I would be coming to them, but then it made that silly nursery rhyme making it seem like they were coming to get the money themselves. What is your take on all of this?"

"Not sure," Richard replied, "but we can go back to your place and listen to the messages and see if I can pick up on something maybe you missed. I guess that is a good time to go over what I learned in Vegas," Richard stated.

"The men that I met with were old acquaintances of Mercedes. They advised me that she was out there before we were working hard to make some money. They didn't know or didn't tell me what the urgency for the money was about, but they did her a solid and fronted her a large sum of money. She was one of their favorite dancers out there. They could always send some of their partners to her club and she would take care of them and never call them back complaining. They let me know they would contact me if she went back to Vegas or if she called one of them to hit them up for more doe. They let me know that no matter what they would not tell her no. They just couldn't."

"You could have told me that on the way to the airport or when we first got back," Jasmine said with disgust.

"I needed to follow up on some leads first to make sure they were on the up and up. I don't know if you knew this but they contacted me for us to come out there. They made the reservations and they were the one who put the extra doe in your pocket. I would love to take credit for that but I am keeping it real." Jasmine respected the fact that he was honest with her.

The waitress came over with the food. She stood and waited for Jasmine to check her French toast. Jasmine took her knife and cut the middle of all four slices. To her surprise they were not soggy.

Jasmine was delighted. "I'm good," she said, and thanked the waitress as if she cooked it herself.

"Everything good with your food sir?" she asked Richard.

"Yes, fine," he replied.

Both of them sat silently while they ate. Jasmine was so excited about the French toast she devoured it. After they were finished they both lay back in their seats and looked at each other and began laughing. It was refreshing that at a time like this, they could share a smile on their face. Then reality dawned on Jasmine and she blurted out "Mercedes called me!"

Richard didn't look the least bit shocked. "She called me too," he said. "I put out a lot of feelers to make sure that once she was located she had my number to reach me."

"So, you've spoken to her?" Jasmine asked.

"No," he answered, "but she has called me. She left me messages while we were in Vegas."

Jasmine was still unsettled with the information that Richard had given her about their Vegas trip. She asked again if he had told her everything.

The waitress came over again and asked if they needed anything else. Of course, Jasmine requested another cup of coffee. She was trying to stall to get Richard to clue her in on the entire story about what went down in Vegas. Richard also ordered another cup of hot chocolate. "Okay, here it goes. We went to Vegas for two reasons. The first was for you to relax because you really needed it. The second reason was I got a lead that Mercedes had gone back to Vegas, which I already told you about. I found out that she requested several different loan extensions. I could tell that she was trying to acquire a large sum of money and the money trail led to Vegas. I believe that she went back to the strip club and met with a few of her past favorite clients. I don't believe she was successful though. I am thinking that she also received a ransom demand and she was trying to put her hands on the cash as quickly as possible. By the time we got to Vegas as you know, we met with the people that the informant gave me. They had already helped Mercedes out. I did leave out that they also booked her a flight back to NY and paid for it."

"Are you sure about this?" Jasmine asked. "Because if this is true, why did she not call me first, why would she try to go through this all by herself? Mercedes knew she could count on me."

"I am sure," Richard replied. "But this is the weirdest part of all, after her plane landed she rented a car. She left her car in the airport long term parking lot. I have made several attempts to contact her but she has not returned any of my calls until last night. But I didn't hear my phone ringing and she left me a message. When did she leave you her last message Jasmine?"

"Tonight, or should I say last night since it is now past 2 am." She answered.

"But like you, I missed her call as I was in the shower."

They returned back to Jasmine's house a little after 3 AM. Both felt exhausted but they knew their work wasn't done and they needed to go through the messages again to see if Jasmine missed anything. They went into the bedroom and Richard hit the machine, luckily Jasmine had already erased all the unrelated messages. Jasmine sat next to Richard as he kept hitting play over and over again. Richard looked at Jasmine and noticed that she had fallen asleep. He took the blanket off the edge of the bed and gently laid it over her. He didn't want to wake her. Richard cut the answering machine down low to continue to play it. He checked the caller ID to see if he saw any numbers that he recognized. He noticed that all were out of the area. One of the numbers was private which was strange to Richard. This meant they were most likely calling from a pay phone. Richard had a friend who worked for the phone company and maybe able to at least find the area where the calls were coming from, but he knew he had to wait for later this morning to contact him. Richard knew he was getting a little delirious because he was dead tired. He gently slid over Jasmine and lay down next to her. It didn't even take a full minute before he was asleep.

Later that afternoon, Richard woke up with the aroma of food and coffee brewing. He laughed to himself because he knew there was hardly any food in the fridge last night. Jasmine must have gone to the supermarket. At that very moment, Jasmine walked into the room. She smiled at Richard, stating, "I see we finally woke up. Plan on getting out of my bed? I put a new toothbrush, a washcloth and towel on the sink for you. Clothes, I am sorry I can't provide," she smirked at Richard and walked out of the room.

It was about an hour before Jasmine saw Richard again. He walked into the kitchen and flashed those pearly whites at Jasmine, "What's to eat?"

"First," Jasmine said, "I made you your favorite, hot chocolate. I wasn't really sure what you like to eat so I made a couple of things, scrambled eggs, waffles and potatoes. Does anything sound appealing?"

"Yeah, I will make my own plate if that's okay because I think you've done enough." They both sat down and consumed their meals. Richard informed Jasmine of what he discovered while listening to the messages and checking the Caller ID. He let her know that he needed to go home and change his clothes and contact his connection at the phone company. Jasmine wanted to go home with him and waited while he got dressed so she could hear what the phone company connection told him. But, he told her that she needed to stay home in case Mercedes or the mystery caller tried to contact her again. After thinking about it, Jasmine agreed. Richard grabbed his coat and his keys and walked out the door. Two seconds later he knocked back on the door and Jasmine opened it. He put his head through the door and kissed Jasmine on the check and thanked her for the meal. Jasmine closed the door back smiling.

Jasmine sat around, flipping through her TV channels not finding anything to watch. She grabbed her phone and called Imani. The phone rang and went right into voicemail. She received a message that it was full. Jasmine found this strange because Imani never liked people to leave messages and she would always listen and delete. She would yell at her whenever she left her a message because it annoyed her to have to take the time out to listen. She then dialed Mercedes and got the voicemail. She opted to not leave a message. Jasmine sat still trying to find something to occupy her time. She lay back on her bed and started thinking about Richard. She remembered his pearly whites as he smiled at her. She pictured in her mind what she imagined what they possibly could have. She figured this wasn't the right time for this as there were so many other things that were more important.

Suddenly there was a knock on the door. "Who is it?" she asked.

"Me," that same familiar voice answered.

Jasmine was almost paralyzed as she heard the voice, unclear if she was buggin. "Who?" she said again.

"Me bitch, open up the door." The voice behind the door blurted out.

Jasmine quickly opened the door. A flood of emotion came over her. She hugged Mercedes before she could totally get through the door. Jasmine pushed Mercedes and asked what was that call about. Mercedes closed the door and said for them to go into the kitchen. Jasmine was very firm that she wanted an explanation about where she has been right that moment. Changing the room, they talked in didn't make a difference.

Mercedes reiterated, "Let's go into the kitchen and talk, please."

"I'm hungry, you got anything in your fridge." Mercedes went into the kitchen with Jasmine following behind.

"Are you going to let me know what that's been going on?" Jasmine asked.

Mercedes continued to rummage through the fridge looking for something to munch on. Before Jasmine could say another word, Mercedes put her finger up as to say wait one minute. Mercedes stuffed some cheese in her mouth and chewed like she hadn't eaten in months. Jasmine just stared quietly.

After Mercedes finished eating all Jasmine's cheese, she tipped the water bottle to her mouth and guzzled the last of the water. Wiping her mouth, she finally spoke, "Let's go."

Mercedes grabbed Jasmine's hand and pulled her back into the living room. She told her to grab her bag as she might need it. Mercedes grabbed her pocketbook and pulled out her car keys and let her know they needed to go converse.

"Go where?" Jasmine asked confused.

"I will explain to you on the way there. I will give you the entire 411 of where I have been, what I've been up to, and what the plan is now. We need to leave now though because we are working on a time schedule that is crucial. Are you in or are you out?"

Jasmine was hesitant to go. She has some feelings of apprehension but something in her gut made her feel like if she didn't go the outcome could be much worse than going. Jasmine decided to follow behind Mercedes and into her car. Right before Mercedes began to pull off Jasmine realized she forgot her purse. Jasmine ran back into the house and grabbed her purse and saw her cell on the bed and stuck it inside her bag. She was about to run back out the door when her phone rang. She thought about picking it up, but she didn't have time. She knew that Mercedes was serious about time being crucial. She locked the door and ran back to the car.

If only Jasmine had waited a few more minutes to hear the message or had picked up the phone. It was Richard and he told her to stay put. *"Do not go anywhere too far and contact me immediately once you get back into the house."* But it was too late, Jasmine was gone.

On the drive to wherever, Jasmine continued trying to get Mercedes to explain where they were on their way too. Mercedes remained tight-lipped to Jasmine's surprise. Mercedes had promised to explain what mission they were on. Jasmine told Mercedes to pull over and let her out if she wasn't going to let her in one what was going on. Jasmine was also a little upset on how Mercedes was driving. She was flying up the highway like she was invincible, like the police would not stop them for speeding. Jasmine noticed the tank was under a quarter and Mercedes would need to find somewhere to pull over to get gas. They were approaching the split on 87 where the Harriman exit was, with a rest stop not even a mile away. Jasmine quickly reminded Mercedes about the gas. Mercedes looked down as if she was totally concentrating on something else that she didn't even realize it.

They pulled off at the rest stop and Jasmine asked, "Do you need money for gas?" Mercedes shrugged her shoulders no and rolled down the window. "Fill it up," she said to the attendant and the window rolled back up. Mercedes opened her Gucci bag and pulled out a stack of money, not even trying to hide it. Jasmine eyes were open wide $100, $50 and $20. Jasmine could not stop herself from asking, "What's up with all the cash, where did you get that from?" Mercedes gave Jasmine a look that almost said out loud, mind your business bitch. That look wasn't going to silence Jasmine. "You better start talking," Jasmine demanded. "Because if you want me to continue this journey I need answers. I need the truth and I mean the entire truth. So, what I would like you to do Mercedes is think about that while I go inside to find the bathroom. When I come out, have answers. Just don't split and leave me here by myself."

Jasmine opened the door and made sure she grabbed her bag just in case Mercedes did try to split without her. Jasmine knew she had cash and a cell phone in her bag. When she went inside the rest stop she saw a Starbucks. Jasmine was excited; going to the bathroom became a second thought. She went over and there were only three people in line. She stood for about five minutes and thought maybe she should call Richard and give him a heads up in case something goes wrong, but hell she didn't even know where they were going, so what kind of heads up would that be? She knew all she would do was make him worry and probably about nothing. Jasmine thought for the life of her could not figure out where all that money came from. Mercedes always had men in Vegas giving her dough, but did she get it when she was down there or did they send it to her. Jasmine had to know. Jasmine got her Starbucks and realized she still needed to go to the bathroom. She didn't want to take her Frappuccino with her so she went back out to the car. Thank goodness Mercedes was there waiting. She put her drink into the cup holder and informed her she would be right back, not thinking about if she dropped her bag in the seat. Jasmine ran into the bathroom almost pissing in her pants. She felt relieved when she was done. As she got to the exit she could see Mercedes pulling off. Jasmine ran out the door screaming at the top of her lungs. Mercedes didn't even turn her head. She continued proceeding forward like Jasmine wasn't there.

Jasmine reached into her pocket looking for her phone, no phone. She patted her other pockets and nothing. Then Jasmine finally realized she put her phone in her bag after she decided not to call Richard, and her bag was on the front seat of Mercedes car, her Frappuccino was in the cup holder too! What was Jasmine going to do now and why did she not call Richard? But the biggest question of all was why Mercedes would leave her out here with any money or any identification. Jasmine wondered if this was a plan to strand her friend.

Back in her vehicle Mercedes was jamming to her CD. She was singing without a care in the world. There would have never been a guess that she had just left her best friend stranded at a rest stop with no money and no phone. As Mercedes continued jamming, her phone rang. She checked out the Caller ID and picked it up.

"Hey," she said with a soft voice.

"What's up?"

"I completed the first part of the plan. Jasmine is out of the way. She has no idea what is going on. She just knows that I have a shit load of money and headed upstate somewhere. I have her bag with all her cash, cards, and her cell. I feel pretty uneasy because I stranded her, but hey we gotta do what needs to be done to get what we want. So, what's next?" The voice on the other end was husky, definitely male. He explained the rest of the plan to her as Mercedes just kept replying. "Okay, okay, sounds good. See you in about an hour," and she hung up the phone, pumping her music back up and continued on her journey.

# Chapter Ten

Back at the rest stop, Jasmine was talking to anyone who would listen. She would ask to use their cell phone or for money to make a phone call. She wasn't having much luck. She realized that people upstate are really not that friendly. By this point, she was distraught. Tears were constantly flowing from her eyes. Jasmine was perplexed about how this could happen. Mercedes was her good friend. She was like a sister to her, like the same blood ran through them both. Jasmine felt the most betrayal ever. Her spirit was fractured by this incident. She had nothing, not even a cigarette which she felt would calm her nerves and she would have a chance to put everything into perspective. Jasmine went to the curve and sat down. She wiped her eyes with some napkins that she took from inside. Jasmine took about five deep breaths and thought about what is next. *What can I do to get myself out of this?* Just as she was at her wits end, a guy came up to her and asked what's wrong? Jasmine was very hesitant to look up. Her eyes were bloodshot red from crying and extremely puffy, but she knew this could be her only chance. She looked up with a half-smile and slowly began to speak. She never made eye contact at first.

"I got stranded out here, my so-called best friend left me, and inside her vehicle I left my bag and cell phone. I have been unable to get someone to let me use their phone and worst of all, I really, really need a Newport." Jasmine finally at that point made eye contact and much to her surprise, pleasant at best was a fine, brown skin small framed muscled man smoking a Newport. He opened up his box, took two out, and handed her the pack. She smiled, took one out, and handed the pack back to him. For the first time, she felt like things could be looking up. Maybe there are some good people up here, but she still was very hesitant to trust anyone.

"For you mommy," he said' as he gave her a light. Jasmine inhaled the smoke like it was her last puff. "Where you headed?"

"I guess back home so I can figure out what went wrong."

"Where's home?"

Jasmine was very vague in her reply. "Westchester County. I know you're not headed that way because this rest stop is headed North up 87."

"You're right," the man admitted. "I am going to Woodbury Commons, but missed the exit. I got off here to get a bit to eat because the food at Woodbury is ridiculous. But after Woodbury I am heading south to the Bronx, if you want to hang. You can get a ride back to Westchester County with me."

Jasmine thought about it, thinking this may be her only chance to get back home. She would have him drop her off at Richard's house since her keys were in her bag. Jasmine also wondered if she can trust this guy to actually take her home. At this point, Jasmine was having a very hard time trusting anybody. Jasmine decided that she would ride with him to Woodbury and feel him out, and then decide what her next plan of action would be. In the back of her mind, she thought that there was a slight chance she would run into someone she knew.

"Let's do it,"      Jasmine out loud. He put his hand out to grab hers to help her up and said.

"I'm Anthony".

She smiled and replied, I'm Jasmine. "Let me just run in and get a bit to eat and we can get on the road.

He started walking away and turned and asked Jasmine, "you hungry?" You must be sitting out here. She nodded her head no even though she was starving.

He put a grin on his face and walked back to Jasmine and grabbed her hand and said, "This isn't any date, you can eat." He paid for the food at Nathan's counter and began to walk out the door. Jasmine quickly jumped offline and started running to the door yelling out for him to wait. Anthony turned around and smiled. When Jasmine caught up to him she was sweating and out of breath as if she'd just had run a marathon.

"Listen Jasmine, I am not going to leave you. I was just going outside to smoke. I repeat, I am not going to leave you. Go back in line and get whatever you want from Starbucks under five bucks and come outside. I promise I will be here." Anthony thought to himself, *Damn, what the hell is going on with this girl because she is fucked up?*

It took about five minutes before Jasmine walked back out the doors. She thanked Anthony for the money and waiting for her, and told him she only had one more request for now. She asked for another cigarette. He pulled out the pack and he took two out. Anthony put the cigarette in Jasmine's mouth and did a little trick with a book of matches by folding the match back and lighting it without the rest of the book catching on fire. He put it up to Jasmine's cigarette and then to his, put his lips together and blew the match out. They both smiled and enjoyed their smoke.

After they finished Anthony asked, "What if I take you back home now? Forget Woodbury, it is obvious to me that something is heavy on your mind and, at this point, I think getting you home to solve whatever it is going on is a matter of priority. I don't think the boots I wanted are on the top of my list right now. Are you okay with that?" She didn't even have to think about the thought that she had before vanished. "Yes, let's go."

Jasmine practically ran to the parking lot and then realized that she had no clue what Anthony's ride looked like. Anthony caught up to her and was laughing. Jasmine thought he must really think I'm crazy. "This way to my ride," he said. "I see you enjoy running around." Jasmine smiled and followed him. They walked past a bunch of cars and she wondered what kind of car does he look like he would drive. There were two SUV's and two little cars, A Mazda Protégé and Golf GTI. She walked over to the black GTI, guessing it was his car, and laughed. He confirmed it was his and walked over to the drivers' side door, telling her to stand back. She took two steps back and he pushed a button which automatically opened the doors. Jasmine was a little impressed. She sat in the car and Anthony pushed another button closing the doors. He started the car and they were on their way. He asked her what type of music she wanted to hear. She smiled, and said she loves old school R&B. He put in a cd and it was just what she was thinking about. She found herself not even really listening to the music that was playing, but more how she found herself in another situation that could potentially end badly. She prayed to herself that it would please work out fine. Everything she has done was in good intention. Anthony had been a gentleman the entire time trying to put her worries at ease. When Anthony was on the Hutchinson Parkway, she informed him that she would show him where to go. He said to her in a very low voice if he could have her phone number. Jasmine was flabbergasted by this man. She took a pen that she saw sitting in his ashtray, took his hand that wasn't on the steering wheel, and wrote down her phone number. She advised him that her cell phone was in her pocketbook in her girlfriend's car and she wasn't sure if she would ever see it again. This was her home number. Then she let him know he could drop me off at the corner. Jasmine thanked him as she got out of the vehicle. Jasmine walked until she reached the front of Richard's crib. Jasmine was more frustrated than anything else. She had a ton of questions and not one answer. All she could think about is what the fuck was wrong with her girl Mercedes. Why would she do what she did? Jasmine knew that it was pointless to drive herself crazy because she knew she would be unable to get immediate gratification. Jasmine went and rang the bell. It seemed like forever and she was getting impatient. In reality, it had been less than two minutes before Richard came to the door. As soon as he opened the door, the tears immediately began to fall from Jasmine's eyes. She put her arms around Richard and squeezed him so tight he almost couldn't breathe. He quickly asked her what happened. She could barely get the words out of her mouth without spitting all over his shirt. She tried to explain as best as she could but Richard wasn't sure what she was saying.

He finally was able to get her arms from around him so he was able to close the door. He walked her into the living room and sat her down. He told her to take a deep breath and calm down. Richard went into the kitchen and poured her a glass of water. He thought about getting her a drink, but knew that would not be wise. He brought the water back to her and sat down. Jasmine had somewhat calmed down. She began to explain all over again about what she had just gone through.

Richard sat in amazement and disbelief. In his head, he was putting all of the pieces to the puzzle together. He asked Jasmine if she had any clue of where Mercedes could have been going. She knew that it was somewhere upstate, but she wasn't entirely sure. Richard advised her that he needed to narrow the area so they could start a search. He picked up the telephone and began dialing. Jasmine wasn't sure who he was calling, but she could hear what he was saying. Jasmine had just learned how great of a private eye Richard was. He told the person on the telephone to start tracking Mercedes' vehicle. After Richard hung the phone up, he looked over at Jasmine and gave her a play by play on what he had done.

He told her that when they went to Vegas and found out the Mercedes had rented a car. He had another one of his PI friends locate her vehicle in the airport and put a tracking device underneath. It would be in a location where she would never see it and she would have no reason to suspect anything. Richard noted that he had tracked some of her movements since she picked her vehicle back up from the airport. Mercedes wasn't doing anything out of the ordinary to him, but maybe if he went over it with Jasmine maybe they could figure some stuff out.

Richard went into the bedroom and got some paperwork. Richard spread the paperwork over the couch, and to Jasmine everything was foreign. She didn't have a clue at what she was looking at. Richard explained to her what the lines meant and the locations they represented. Only one thing struck out to Jasmine. *Why was Mercedes making so many trips back and forth to the bank and also a few trips to Precious' home? Why would she be going there? But maybe she was going there to try to stay connected to Precious and Karisma.* She pointed out to Richard those two things as being strange. Richard felt the same way. He thought that maybe if Jasmine still had the key to Precious' apartment, they could go over there and check the place out. See if anything was out of place that would give them a clue. Jasmine told Richard there was no way to get inside of Precious' place because she had the key at her home and she didn't have her house keys. She smirked and stated "Remember, Mercedes took my bag." This made Richard think that was done intentionally. They didn't want Jasmine to have any access to her crib, because if she did she would have the keys to get inside of Precious' home. But why would they even think that she would think to go there? Richard asked Jasmine if there was anyone that had a spare key to her apartment as they really needed to get inside. Jasmine let him know that the super wasn't even an option. She never trusted anyone and refused to give them a spare key to get inside. Richard looked up and stated, "We are going to have to break in. It is not technically breaking in though. If we get caught, the super knows that it is your place. Or, you could call a locksmith and they could open the door for you."

"And what kind identification could I show proving that it was my place? I think the best chance we have is for you and me to go to my house and try to pick the lock," Jasmine responded. They both agreed on the plan and left.

As they pulled up to Jasmine's building, she felt anxious. She wasn't sure why. Richard parked the car and immediately got out. Jasmine just sat in the car. Richard came over to her side and told her to come on. He opened up the passenger side door and grabbed her hand.

"I know this is a lot but we are clearly running out of time. If we do not check every possible lead, that one that we don't check could be the one that causes us to miss what we need to find out all the answers. Please Jasmine please, work with me. Help me out baby, please."

She got out of the vehicle and swiftly walked into the building. Richard was a little behind. Jasmine rang every bell in the building until someone answered. A male came and she informed him that she misplaced her key to get inside the building. The male rang the buzzer to let her in. She held the door until Richard caught up, then they got into the elevator and rode up to Jasmine's floor. Richard stood in front of the door and Jasmine stood behind him to shield other people if they walked into the hallway. It took about ten minutes before Richard was able to open the bottom lock. He knew that the top lock would be a little trickier since Jasmine was so paranoid. She put a special lock up top and it was supposed to be tamper proof. This took a little longer than even Richard thought it was going to take. Finally, about a half an hour later the deed was done. Jasmine jumped on Richard. "You're a genius!" she blurted out.

Jasmine was so excited that she was inside her house. She ran into the bedroom and looked around. Nothing appeared to be out of place. Richard walked into the bedroom. "Is everything like you left it?" "It appears so," Jasmine answered. Richard looked around like he knew what he was looking for and Jasmine guessed he did because he was the private eye. He saw that her answering machine was blinking. He sat down at the edge of the bed and told Jasmine to get a pen and paper so they could listen to the messages. There might be something that they may need to write down. Jasmine immediately went into the kitchen to get the items out of the drawer. When she walked into the kitchen, she noticed that something didn't seem right. She wasn't sure exactly what it was, but something was out of place. Jasmine went into the drawer and pulled out her notebook and a pen, and went back into the bedroom. She figured she would not mention anything to Richard at this point until she could figure out what was wrong.

Richard hit the play button and they began listening. The first couple of messages were unimportant for what they were listening for, but Jasmine still wrote them down. The next few messages were from Mercedes. They actually were taunting messages. The first one stated that she was wrong in what she was thinking. Things are not always what they seem. She promised to take care of her possessions and would return them when the time was right. Naturally, Jasmine thought that she was talking about her pocketbook and the items inside. Richard paused the messages and asked Jasmine what time they left to go on their excursion. Jasmine told him that it was in the morning.

Richard began thinking out loud. "Give me a minute. Why is this message strange to me? This message was left while y'all were still together. I think that message is not about the pocketbook. This is about something else. Maybe she didn't plan on taking your cell phone, or maybe she was hoping you listened to your messages before you got home.

Something is off." That made Jasmine realize what was off in the kitchen. Her prize possession was the keys. Jasmine ran into the kitchen and looked up on the wall. All her keys that were usually hanging up were gone. That included the spare key to Precious's home. That was the prize that Mercedes was talking about. Richard looked puzzled as he was clueless to what was going on. Jasmine was just pointing to the wall. "It's over. It's over." She kept repeating.

"Tell me what you see or don't see" Richard commanded.

"My spare keys are all gone. I keep them right there." She pointed to the wall almost breaking her finger as she pressed it up against the spot. "What are we going to do now? We can't go and break into Precious' house. If we get caught doing that, we'll go to jail."

For the first time, Richard had a look of anguish. He could not hide the worried look on his face. His facial expression looked like someone punched him in the gut. He tried not to show the hopelessness affected him. Richard advised Jasmine they should go back into the bedroom and take the remainder of the messages of her voicemail. Maybe they could get a clue to Mercedes whereabouts when his private eye friend calls him back. Jasmine asked could he put a rush on that. Richard went back into the kitchen to make a phone call. Jasmine didn't even bother to try to figure out why he left the room. He never had done that before. The truth was that Richard didn't want Jasmine to know how ominous the situation really was.

When Richard returned to the bedroom, he stated that his man told him they were close to pinpointing a location and once they had a destination, he would hit him back. Richard sat back on the bed and told Jasmine to pick up the pen and paper again just in case there was something to write. Richard hit the play button and the next message played. To no surprise, it was Mercedes again. This time she was a little more cryptic.

*"Guess what I've got. I bet you'll never figure it out. By now, if you are home, you have figured out that you have no spare keys to your buddy's house. Well, that is not the only thing you are missing. I could let you know all my secrets but that would take all the fun out of this. You are usually so smart but this time, I don't think you have a clue. Or maybe you do. I guess we'll never find out because you are just too damn slow. Well, darling, the best advice I have for you is catch me if you can. By the way, remember, things are not always as they seem. Look deep inside and you will find the answers. Look inside."*

At the end of the message, you could hear her laughing. It was like a dagger in Jasmine's heart. The friend that she loved just doesn't seem true. Richard was sitting on the edge of the bed with a puzzled look. That was the last message on the machine. This would weigh heavy on both of their minds for a while. Richard looked over at Jasmine and asked her to take a minute to get her thoughts together. "Do you have a clue on what she meant by saying look deep inside? That means something significant because she made a point to challenge you to figure it out." Jasmine could not even think at this point. She was exhausted. She knew it wasn't right but she knew that she needed some rest. Jasmine asked Richard if he thought it okay for her to take a little nap. Richard looked at Jasmine's face and could tell that she was worn out. "Go ahead and get some rest. I will continue to try to put the pieces of the puzzle together. If I get a call from my buddy, I will wake you up immediately and we can get back on the grind."

Jasmine was so happy that he didn't give her a hard time. She smiled and laid her body down on the bed, and within a few minutes she was knocked out. For a little while, Richard just stared at Jasmine. He knew that through all of the ups and downs he had developed feelings for her. He knew that there was no way he could act on them at this point. Unfortunately, Richard realized that he was just as tired as Jasmine was. He tried to fight it for a while, but was unable to fight his heavy eyes and he lay next to Jasmine and dozed off. Richard slept for about fifteen minutes before his phone woke him up. He barely could get to it quick enough. He didn't even bother to look to see if who was calling.

"Hello," he said with a deeper than normal voice."

The voice on the other end was a male. "I got it," the voice said."

Richard quickly woke up. The man continued by telling Richard that Mercedes' vehicle had stopped moving. The vehicle was stopped in the Catskills, and he had pinpointed the exact address. Richard looked on the bed trying not to wake up Jasmine too soon. He found the pen and paper and began writing some information down. He thanked his buddy for his hard work and hung up the phone. Richard still didn't wake Jasmine up. He got up and went into the bathroom.

Surprisingly to Richard, when he flushed the toilet he heard Jasmine moving around in the bed. He wasn't sure if she was up but he knew she was moving. Richard went back into the bedroom and saw that Jasmine was still knocked out. He didn't want to wake her up but knew that he had to. Richard rubbed her back until she woke up. Jasmine took a minute to get herself together and then asked Richard if everything was okay.

"I got some new info that I thought you might be interested in. It hurt me to my heart to have to wake you up though. You looked so peaceful."

Jasmine quickly sat up and to hear the news. It was like someone shot her with a jolt of energy. "Come on give me that 411." Jasmine was amped up. "I just hope it is good news. I almost think that if it is something that bad that you should let me go back to sleep." Richard put his fingers over her mouth so she would stop freaking out.

"Take a deep breath." He stated. "I have the location where Mercedes is at right now. The problem is, it's a long drive to her location and there is a good chance that if we do get up there, she may be gone."

Jasmine quickly replied by letting him know that is no reward without risk. "Let's do this. But first let me go and freshen up. If this is a long journey like you said, I don't want my breath to be kickin' for the ride. You won't want me to talk to you. If you need to freshen up, I have something for you too."

For the first time in a little while, Jasmine smiled. She jumped out the bed and ran into the bathroom. She didn't even take a shower; she was in and out of the bathroom. When she walked out of the bathroom, she just pointed her finger at it showing Richard it was all his. Richard was even faster than Jasmine. They were out of the apartment in less than a half an hour. Just as they were walking out of the door, something important dawned on her. She stopped right in her tracks, almost stumbling into Richard while trying to stop.

"What's up?" Richard asked.

"I think we need to go back into the apartment. I think I figured out what Mercedes was speaking about when she told me to dig deep. At first, I thought she was trying to tell me to look inside myself. But now, I think she was trying to tell me to look deep inside a place. Let's just go back inside for a few minutes. If I don't find what I think I will, we can get on the road immediately." Richard quickly opened the door back, knowing that he should trust Jasmine's instinct. She swiftly walked into the kitchen and looked up at where she kept the spare keys. She then looked down and kept repeating to herself look deep, look deep. She stopped moving for a minute and closed her eyes. "Trust yourself," she said out loud. Something made her open the bottom cabinet. Inside this cabinet Jasmine kept some keepsakes that she didn't want anyone to touch. There was one keepsake in particular that was near and dear to her. It was a jewelry box that was given to her from an ex-boyfriend. She still kept the jewelry inside that she never wore. She picked up the box and opened it. She turned to Richard and shook her head. Richard looked inside and saw the items inside, including a bunch of keys.

He looked puzzled at Jasmine before speaking. "Are these..."

He could not finish before Jasmine started screaming. "I don't get it. I don't get it. Why would she move the keys and then give me clues on how to find them? Isn't that a bitch. She is really confusing the fuck out of me. Now I don't even think we have the time to get over to Precious' house before we get on the road." Richard shook his head no. She knew he was right. Jasmine put the spare keys in her bag so that she would have them with her in case nothing panned out on their search upstate.

They stopped at the gas station before they got on the road. Richard advised Jasmine to pee if she needed to before they got on the road. She knew he was right but she had a big problem with going to the bathroom in public places. She decided it was best to go ahead and try to be on the safe side. Finally, it appeared to Richard that they were on their way. The ride was smooth because there wasn't a lot of traffic. He guessed they picked the perfect part of the day. There wasn't really too much talking during the trip. About thirty minutes into the ride, Jasmine was asleep. Richard decided to crank up the beats and just enjoy the ride. As it began getting dark outside, Richard realized they had been traveling for a minute. He decided to call his man to see if Mercedes' location had changed. His man's phone just rang and rang until the voicemail came on. Richard didn't want to leave a message because he needed to confirm. He hung up the phone and dialed again. This time the man answered. He let Richard know that nothing had changed. He also let Richard know he was fucking up his time with a lady friend he was entertaining. Richard apologized but made it clear that if that car moved he needed to let him know right away. Even if that meant he needed to take the dick out of the chicks pussy. He laughed to himself.

# Chapter Eleven

Imani was perplexed. Why would Buddy do this to Janet if they were cohorts? *Maybe this was one way I couldn't get back home and continue my search with the rest of my friends*, she thought. "Fuck!" Janet screamed out. "I did all this sucking and fuckin for nothing! I just let some mother fucker violate my body for absolutely nothing! What in the hell are we going to do now, because I am fresh out of ideas." Again, Imani thought to herself *could Jr. be telling me the truth about everything? If so, how is Janet able to pretend so well? She genuinely looked and acted distraught. She could not be faking.*

Janet yelled to the driver to take us back to the diner, but the man turned around and told them in a very stern voice. "I have my orders so sit back and enjoy the ride."

"We have no money," Imani replied. He rolled the window up that separated the driver from the passengers and turned the music up so he didn't have to hear them. "I have a really bad feeling about this Janet." Janet took Imani's hand and suggested they pray, and they did. Imani thought to herself as they prayed, Janet could not be playing around. She would never use god in her plan. She knew how wrong that would be.

When they finished, Imani stared out of the window and started thinking about what she saw when she opened that last door in the house. In that room was a crib and bassinet. There were photos of Karisma all around. It was a shrine of Precious' little girl. There was no sign of Karisma, but Imani knew in her heart that she had been there.

"Janet," Imani said. "Do you have any clue about what is going on here?"

"Yeah right, why would you ask me a stupid question like that? I know exactly what you know, nothing." Imani thought about telling Janet what she had found out because she thought that maybe Jr. had set Imani up to turn against Janet, but if he didn't she would be tipping her hand. The one little edge that she may have had would just be thrown out the window. Imani also thought to herself if somehow she could just drop hints she could get some kind of read from Janet. But how could she do this and not get her suspicious?

As they continued to ride around, Imani could not help but feel like she had seen this area already. Could they be going back to that house? Could this all be a set-up from Janet after all? In that instance, it all came flooding into Imani's mind, panic, panic, damnit, panic. She quickly started banging on the glass that separated the back and front seat. "Please, please, please," she screamed, "Tell me where you're taking us. Let me know what the hell is going on!" Imani managed to bring herself to tears unintentionally.

Finally, the window comes rolling down. "Please lady," the man replied. "Stop banging on the window and shut your fuckin mouth. I do not want to have to hurt anyone."

"Fuck you!" Imani screamed. She was about to spit at him when Janet covered her mouth.

"Okay, enough already! Are you trying to get us killed? I still value my life enough to be patient and see what is next." Janet stopped talking to Imani and spoke to the driver. "I apologize for my friend's behavior. Can you just roll the glass back up so we can talk privately?" The driver didn't even acknowledge her words with words or a gesture, the window just went back up.

Janet turned her body towards Imani and grabbed her hand. She placed Imani's hand on her chest so she could feel her heart beating. Imani could feel Janet's heart and wanted

Janet to know that she was just as scared. So, Imani grabbed Janet's hand and put it on her heart. "Everything will be okay," Janet softly spoke. "I feel that if we keep cool we will make it through this." It took a minute for Imani to get her head straight. The ride was over a half an hour. Finally, they pulled up to this big house that Imani knew she had seen before. She had an unsettling feeling in her stomach that she might have something to worry about. Imani believed that this house had all the answers to everything that was going on. After they stopped, no one got out of the car except the driver. Imani tried to listen because he was talking to someone, but she could only hear one voice. She wasn't sure if he was talking on the phone or to someone else who was too far away for her to hear or see. Imani finally looked at Janet and asked, "What is going on?"

Janet just told Imani to be patient and she would see what she had been working on for so long to make sure everything was right. Imani didn't know how to take this new information. She thought to herself, *what she would need to work on for so long? Why were they out at this house and why were they still sitting in the car?* Imani went to open the door but Janet stopped her. "That is not the smartest thing to do, girl. Just be patient for a little while longer and all darkness will come to light. I think you will be very pleased with what you see. This journey will have been well worth it. I believe that we have found out much about each other on this trip. Things that I always knew were in you and you just needed some help letting it out." Imani felt a little taken back by what Janet had just said. What did she mean by that? Was she thinking that Imani was a lesbian all this time? Did she know things about Imani that Imani wasn't even sure about? Imani just sat in the back seat with her mouth shut, unsure why. Maybe because she didn't know what to say, or maybe she was a little embarrassed about what Janet said. In Imani's mind, she was about to learn everything that she needed to. The whole mystery of why they were out there was about to come to an end.

Finally, the door opened and Janet got out first. Imani watched her hug the female figure. Imani recognized this person, but didn't want to believe that this was her. Imani didn't rush to get out of the car. She just sat there in disbelief for a minute and Janet yelled to her to get her ass out of the car. Imani put one foot out and then that familiar hand grabbed her and pulled her out of the car. "What's up? You are not talking to me?" Imani still didn't reply. She kind of looked like she was in some kind of haze. She didn't understand what was going on. Why was she here and what was her dear friend doing here? How was this possible? Imani looked at Janet as she wanted an explanation from her. Janet looked at Imani. "I know this is a lot to take in. We will explain when we get inside the house. If you don't want to speak to me anymore I will understand but at this point I cannot let you leave until you understand what is going on." Imani still didn't speak and neither did Mercedes.

They all walked into the house and it was decorated like there was going to be a party. There were balloons hanging up with streamers, bottles of champagne and beer on ice. Imani still didn't know what to make of all this. Imani still didn't crack a smile because she didn't feel right. She felt betrayed.

Janet told Imani to go upstairs into the first bedroom on the left. There was something in a box for her to put on. There was a towel and washcloth on the bed for her to take a shower. "Take your time because there is not a rush. We have about another hour before the rest of the guests arrive." Now Imani was even more confused. "Be patient," her friend said. "I will explain everything to you once you get refreshed. I heard you had a very eventful ride here. Think about that as you are showering."

Imani walked up the stairs to the first bedroom on the left. She opened the door slowly, because at this point she wasn't sure what she could expect. As Janet had stated, there was a big box and a towel and clothes next to it. But instead of walking inside the room, Imani decided to walk around to see what else was in the other rooms. She took her time observing the area, went to the door on the right, and turned the knob slowly. Unfortunately, the door didn't open; it was locked from the inside. She continued down the right side of the corridor and tried every door, but they too all were locked. This made Imani more curious of what was going on, but instead of going to the doors on the left she went down the hallway and got into the elevator. She hit the button for the top floor but the elevator didn't move. She kept hitting the button and the close door button but it still didn't move. Finally, she got tired of just standing there so she just started hitting all the buttons. The elevator doors eventually closed and started to move, but instead of going up it went back to where she came from.

The doors opened and Imani saw Janet and her dear friend standing there talking to some guy that Imani had never seen. They saw Imani standing there and Janet walked over, staring directly into her eyes. "What's the matter, honey?"

"I was feeling a little weird up there by myself. I am not sure why I am here. I need some questions answered before I go and take a hot shower. I can't think of anything except my friend over there acting like nothing is wrong and you doing the same. I need some questions answered like yesterday." Imani had never talked with this kind of force before but Janet didn't even take her seriously.

"I told you that everything would be explained in the next hour. Why can't you be a little more patient? We are not asking you for much more. Just go back upstairs and take a shower. Get yourself together to party and all will be understood," Janet offered.

"Party," Imani said. "What is there to party about? I am not in the partying mood. I think that it is best for you to clue me in on what the hell is going on. If not, I will just walk out this door and find a way to get home and let everyone know what I have been through and what I have seen. I am sure that is not what you want because you have not put up with all this bullshit to get me here and let me just walk out this door."

"You are right," Janet said. "But there is no way we can let you just walk out this door. I promise you this. When it is all said and done and you come back downstairs in the next hour, all your questions will be answered."

Imani just gave up and walked back toward the elevator. Janet stopped her and told her to take the stairs. Imani just shook her head and walked to the staircase and didn't look back.

This time Imani entered the room. She looked at the box on the bed, sat right next to it and began to cry. She sobbed hard and long. Imani just didn't have a clue. She was so confused that it hurt. She didn't remember feeling like this since she was at Precious's funeral. Imani got up, went inside the bathroom, and looked in the mirror with disgust. Her eyes were now red and swollen. She could only think that Janet knew that she would break down and Imani would look horrible when she came back downstairs. All she could wonder is why they would do this to her. She had a heart of gold. She never treated her friends badly. Imani thought she was one of the most giving people in the world. Imani cut on the shower and took her clothes off. She went back into the bedroom and opened up the box. Inside the box was a beautiful full-length ballroom gown, the perfect fit for her size. Imani could only think to herself that on the perfect day it would be the perfect dress. But today could not have been it. Imani went back into the bathroom and got in the shower. The water was nice and warm and felt like a blanket of comfort to her, the first good feeling she felt since she walked into the house. Imani let the water run over her face over and over again. Imani enjoyed her shower for over twenty minutes and realized that she was shriveling up. She took one step out of the shower felt a draft like the door was open. She looked around the room and with a low voice asked if there was someone out there. There wasn't a peep. Imani continued to get out of the shower and walked over to the bed to dry off. Just as she was almost completely dry, Imani again started crying. She quickly pulled herself together and stopped herself. Imani made a conscious decision to get her mind right, get dressed, go downstairs and tackle any and everything that they throw at her. Imani pulled the dress out of the box and began to admire it. It was a beautiful dress and she was going to rock it the way it should be. She walked into the bathroom and looked into the cabinets to see if there was any makeup inside. Funny to her, there was lipstick and eyeliner, the shades that she would prefer to wear and next to the makeup was her favorite perfume bottle. This kind of spooked Imani, but she just shrugged it off and said to herself "be strong baby."

She took off her shower cap and started playing around with her hair. She finally got it like she wanted and started feeling excited. *Funny*, she thought to herself, *where was these feelings coming from?* Imani went to the bed, put the dress next to her body and looked in the mirror. She felt some fluttering through her body. Imani thought that she had to make this the best that she could. She was going to walk down those stairs and shock everyone. Then after getting to the bottom of the stairs, feeling great, she'd get her answers.

Imani put the finishing touches on her outfit and felt as though she was a beauty queen. She thought that it was a fairytale nightmare. That description would appear to be a little odd to someone who was about to see her and didn't know what was going on, but Imani felt that everyone but her knew the deal. She took a few deep breaths and began to walk towards the door. As she began opening the door, she could hear the music banging. Imani was very hesitant to walk out the door, but she knew that she had to see this through. She needed answers. For once and for all, she needed some closure to what was going on. Imani walked out the door and put her head up high. The hallway appeared to be such a long journey. She walked to the elevator and pushed the button and waited for the doors to open. Just as the doors opened, a male got off and advised her that it wasn't time. He sent Imani back to her room, but this time she didn't want to comply. She did what everyone had asked. She put the enchanting dress like they wanted. Imani felt it was her time. Nothing was going to stop her. Even this guy.

# Chapter Twelve

Richard and Jasmine's journey to their destination was almost complete. Richard was constantly on the phone trying to make sure that Mercedes' vehicle had not left its location since they had last talked. Richard advised Jasmine that they were close. He warned her that he wasn't sure what they were getting themselves into. It could have just been a long journey that led them to nothing. Jasmine quickly assured Richard that it was well worth it. She knew that they needed answers and she was enjoying the time they had shared together.

Richard laughed and asked Jasmine, "Are you flirting with me, girl?"

Jasmine smirked and answered him that best she knew how. "Of course, but I hope that is not a bad thing at a time like this."

"I was waiting for you to come out of your shell girl. I know this whole ordeal has been very painful for you and I am glad I was just there to help you through it. Now, does that sound too mushy?" Jasmine could not contain herself from smiling. Richard had not seen Jasmine this jubilant at all. This made him feel he did the right thing by taking his time with her. Jasmine and Richard continued their kind of intense discussion regarding their possible relationship until Richard's phone rang. As usual, Jasmine could only hear one side of it but she could tell it was important. This call lasted for about fifteen minutes before he hung the phone up. The longer the conversation went on; Jasmine thought that something bad had happened. Maybe Mercedes' vehicle was on the move. Were they too late? Jasmine just sat in silence but her stomach was in such pain. She wasn't sure if it was from all the aggravation of everything, or was she just starving.

Richard turned to her after waiting a few minutes to speak. "Apparently, there are a lot of people hanging out at this location where Mercedes' vehicle is located. Some kind of big party. The problem is the house is gated, and if there is a big party more than likely it will be heavily guarded. This could pose big problems."

"Are we fucked?" Jasmine quickly interjected.

"I don't think so. The best thing now is to pull past the house to see what we can do to get inside. If there seems to be no way around the gate we are going to have to go straight through it."

"You can't be serious." Jasmine replied. "I think we could be in a world of hurt right now. We have been facing challenges in every move that we have made. Nothing has come easy for us. I just don't get it. What are we doing wrong?" Jasmine had turned from optimistic to pessimistic. Richard knew that he had to find a way to reel her back in. He really was going to need her focused for the rest of this journey. He wasn't willing to lose her now, especially since they had just put their feelings out there. Richard dialed the phone and started inquiring if they thought there was a way for them to get around the gate. By the look on Richard's face, Jasmine could tell it would not be easy. As much as he tried to act as though things were not grim, Jasmine knew it was.

Richard hung the phone up and let Jasmine know that once they turned this corner they were going to be passing the house. "My man let me know it's huge. First thing we are going to do is just drive past it. I need to see if there are any open bush areas that we could possibly walk through. Like I said before, if no sneak attack is possible, straight through the front entrance."

Jasmine joked around and said maybe she should have worn all black to camouflage herself. "Or since there is a possible party going on, maybe I should have worn my Sunday's best."

"Glad you still have a sense of humor," Richard said.

"Stop, stop!" Jasmine blurted out. "I think I see a possible opening."

Richard pulled the car over a little puzzled as he didn't see any opening. "What are you talking about?"

"Look over to your left about twenty feet down. There is a small slither of space that I think we could possibly get through. Hopefully undetected."

Richard walked down to the left to see if he saw what Jasmine seemed positive that she saw. Low and behold, he saw the small space between the bushes. He was kind of surprised because at first he thought she was buggin. Richard ran back to the car and signaled Jasmine to jump in. She quickly got back into the car with a little swagger as if to say I told you so, I told you so. Richard drove the car a little further down and parked it as close to the bushes as possible trying to make sure it would not be spotted. He opened the glove compartment and took out a flashlight, making sure it was working.

He looked at Jasmine. "The moment of truth. This is do or die for us. Either I am going to get you the answers you are looking for, or we are just going to be crashing someone's party, might get arrested and go to jail but again, at least we'll be together." Jasmine looked deep into Richard's eyes and felt this was the right time. She leaned in and kissed him passionately. He obliged and kissed her just as passionately. A calming came over them both. Richard grabbed Jasmine's hand and pulled her toward him to kiss her one more time. The moment between them was extremely intense but endearing at the same time. They knew that it was time to get back to business. The two of them walked toward the bushes where they could fit through. Richard let Jasmine know that he would go first and check to make sure that the path was clear. He told her to wait for him at the entrance. He would not go too far before coming back or signaling her that it was okay.

Jasmine was a little hesitant about agreeing to this idea, but she understood why he wanted to do this. She watched as he walked through the bushes. It was only a few minutes before his body was barely in her sight. The next thing she knew she could not even see the light from the flashlight. Jasmine tried not to get nervous, but the longer it took for Richard to come back the antsier she became. She thought maybe she should try to walk through the path and see if she could find him. Jasmine stood at the entrance for another three minutes and thought *fuck it, I can't stay here anymore*. She thought that something may be wrong. She began walking through the bushes and could not really see anything. The next thing Jasmine knew, someone had put their hand over her mouth. She didn't want to fight because she just assumed it was Richard and he didn't want her to scream. The male turned her around slowly not to hurt her. Jasmine looked at him and realized it wasn't Richard. Who was this guy? Was he about to hurt her? He didn't remove his hand from over her mouth. She knew that this wasn't good.

The male began to speak with a soft voice. "I do not want to hurt you. I am not sure why you are sneaking around in the bushes but I need to take you up to the house. I don't want you to try to run from me. Do you understand what I am saying to you young lady?" Jasmine shook her head up and down. The guy removed his hand from over her mouth. Jasmine was able to get a better look at the guy. He wasn't too tall, but what surprised her was that he was white. She wasn't sure why this would have surprised her because they were in the back roads of the Catskills. The guy guided Jasmine through the bushed without a problem. The only thing Jasmine could think about was what happened to Richard. Could he have met the same fate as her? The only way she would know this answer would be by just cooperating with the strange man and letting him take her to their destination. The further they walked the more Jasmine's feet started hurting, but she could not complain.

Finally, she could see the big house. It appeared to be close but as they continued to walk she knew it was still a little hike before they would reach the entrance. The man stopped and informed Jasmine that he was going to lead her into an entrance through the basement. He didn't want her to touch anything in the house or say a word. If she tried to scream, it could get very ugly. The man reached into his pocket and showed Jasmine his gun. She quickly tensed up. She knew that whatever her and Richard was walking into was big. Jasmine let the man know that he wasn't going to get a hard time from her. She did ask him that if it was at all possible he could take to the bathroom because she had to go bad. The man acted like he didn't hear a word she said. He just grabbed her arm and kept walking. They went down a few stairs and he opened up a door that led to another staircase that went further down. As they walked through the door, it looked like a wine cellar. The room was kind of dark and dank. The man didn't cut on any lights. He continued to walk with his flashlight on. They came to another door and he opened it. He pointed inside and handed her the flashlight. He told her that she had three minutes and if she wasn't out by then, he was coming inside. He patted the side of his pocket to remind her of the gun. Jasmine entered the room and shined the flashlight around to see everything that was inside. There were no windows in the room. Jasmine looked over at the toilet which was very clean. She pulled down her pants, squatted down, and took a piss. She hoped that the man didn't walk inside as she felt she could not stop peeing. She knew that she was inside the bathroom for longer than three minutes but the man didn't bother Jasmine. The sink had no soap on it so Jasmine just rinsed her hands, took the toilet paper, and dried them off. Just as she was doing that she heard a tap on the door. She

Joanne Monteiro

knew that her time was up. Jasmine opened the door and thanked the man for letting her go to the bathroom.

"Can I ask you a question?" she asked the man.

"You can ask but that does not mean I am going to answer," he replied.

Jasmine thought for a minute but decided she was going to try to get some info, anything that could shed some light on the situation. "What is going on in the house tonight?"

"I thought you may already know the answer to that question. If you don't, why are you here? Most people do not walk through dark woods to sneak up in a house clueless."

"If I told you that I didn't really know would you believe me?".

"No," the man replied. "I would think that you were most likely stupid or thought that maybe I was. Nonetheless, I guess that eventually all your questions would be answered one way or the other."

"I have heard that phrase enough that I would be rich if someone paid me a dollar every time it was spoken to me." Jasmine figured that she didn't get any information and that is exactly what he planned. The man needed to make a phone call and he needed her to be quiet for a little while. Again, he pointed to his pocked to remind her of his little friend that he was holding there. The man walked over to the corner where there was a wall phone. Jasmine thought to herself *for this to be such a fab house the phone was very outdated*. He spoke very quietly to make sure she really couldn't hear him. Jasmine was able to hear his name though. He called himself Junior. Whatever he was saying to the other person on the phone was intense. It looked like he was getting some kind of instructions. She kept hearing him say "got it" over and over again. The man hung the phone up and walked back over to Jasmine. He let her know that they were going to take a little trip inside the elevator. He pointed over to it like she had not already noticed it.

"Once we get inside I am going to take you upstairs and again I don't want you to say one word. I will put you inside a room and don't touch a thing. I will be locking the door from the outside, and you are to sit still until someone comes into the room and gives you further instructions. Got it?" She just shook her head at him acknowledging the information he had just given to her. He grabbed her hand and took her to the elevator. He took out a set of keys and put one inside the hole. She heard the elevator as it moved down the shaft. Jasmine was really uneasy about the entire thing but what could she do? The elevator opened up and it was empty. Jasmine was happy about that. She got onto the elevator and again Jr. put the same key inside of a hole and turned it. He then pressed the button to take them upstairs. The ride was swift. The door opened and all Jasmine saw was a long corridor with a bunch of doors on both sides. She wasn't even sure which floor she was on. Jr. walked three doors down and pulled out his set of keys again. He opened the door on the left side and cut the light on. He didn't put his hand inside the room, so she assumed that the light switch was in the hallway. Jr. gestured his hand to let her know to go inside. He didn't walk inside with her. He stood at the door and advised her "remember what I said." Jr. closed the door behind him and she heard it lock.

Jasmine quickly started walking around the room to see if there was anything she could use to try to pick up the lock to open the door. Jasmine thought about it and realized that the lock was on the outside of the door. She walked over to the window and noticed that there was no way to open them. The room was decorated immaculately. The bedding was extremely fancy. The duvet cover was made with a fabric she never felt before and the stitching was flawless. It looked like something out of a romantic movie. The drapes were exquisite, the type of accessories that Jasmine could only dream of owning. She sat on the edge of the bed making sure she didn't knock a ruffle out of place. The mattress was plush. She wished she could just lay down and take a nap, but the only thing she could really think about was what happened to Richard. *Was he out there walking around looking for me, or was he in the house too being held against his free will?* Jasmine knew that she wasn't going to find out just sitting around thinking about it. She jumped up and started looking around the room again. She noticed another door in the room. She went over to the door in hopes that it would at least open, and it did. This room was dark but she thought it might be a bathroom. She put her hand on the wall and tried to find a light switch. She didn't feel anything. Jasmine remembered that everything in the house was different so she walked back outside the room and looked for a switch outside of the door. Low and behold she found it. The light went on inside the room and Jasmine was right, it was the bathroom. She looked through the medicine cabinet to see what was inside. She noticed the makeup and nail polishes lined up, knowing this must be a women's room. She looked under the sink to see what was hiding under there, but didn't see anything unusual inside. There was one other wall cabinet. Jasmine opened up the cabinet and saw the towels and washcloths. As Jasmine closed the cabinet door she noticed on the wall was a telephone. She could not believe it. Could her luck have changed? Jasmine walked over to the phone and picked it up. She heard a dial tone and was surprised. Then reality set in. The face on the telephone didn't have a keypad. There was no way she could dial out. Jasmine could not fathom why someone would have this type of set up in their home. *Was the owner of this house a kidnapper? Was this the type of thing they used the house for?* Jasmine felt a sense of dismay coming over her. She was locked in a room. She had no way to reach out to her friend Richard and was clueless on what was going on outside of those doors. She went back into the bedroom and cut the light off in the bathroom. Jasmine took her shoes off as she felt like she was in a hopeless situation. She laid her head on the pillow and threw her legs up on the bed. It wasn't more than ten minutes until Jasmine was asleep.

# Chapter Thirteen

Richard was back in the bushes trying to locate Jasmine. It had been a long time and still no sign of her. He had his flashlight pointed to the ground by the entrance that he entered inside. He didn't see any signs of a struggle. Was he to believe that Jasmine left there on her own free will? Richard was clueless. He just kept walking around looking for clues. Richard knew that he could make it to the house undetected and knew that his flashlight didn't have much more life. He was faced with a tough decision. Should he just continue on without Jasmine? Richard thought of one other possibility. Could Jasmine have gone back to the vehicle because she got tired of standing there waiting for him? Richard made his way back to where he parked his vehicle. He walked up to the door and peeked inside. He didn't see Jasmine or any sign of her. Richard thought that this was a good sign since his vehicle was still parked there. He walked back to the opening in the bushes and made the decision to go ahead to the house. The house had all the answers and now his main focus wasn't what happened to the baby; it was what happened to Jasmine.

Richard moved through the bushes like he had a purpose. He knew exactly where he was headed. It took Richard about ten minutes to reach the house. He wasn't sure how he was going to get inside but he knew he had to. He kneeled down as he watched the activity around the place. There were multiple cars pulling into the long driveway. Richard noticed that everyone who got out of the car was dressed to impress. He also noticed that just about all the windows in the home had drapes. There was no way just to see inside. He sat down for a minute to get his thoughts together. He knew that he could not go inside blind. Richard knew he was taking a chance, and if he was to get caught what would be his plan of action. What would be his back story? As Richard sat there, he noticed a figure to his right a semi far distance away. This figure looked familiar to him though. He wanted to wipe his eyes to make sure he wasn't buggin. He got very focused to look at the person to verify he wasn't seeing things. Richard just kept staring at the figure and staring. He could not be 100% confident that was the same person, but the way things had been going he was sure it was Mercedes. He stood up and began walking slowly towards the side of the house. He figured there had to be somewhere he could get inside undetected.

Richard located a side door that was slightly opened and he thought this was his opportunity. Maybe things were about to go his way. Just as he started to slide inside the door, Richard's phone rang. He could not cut the ring off quick enough. He looked around to make sure it didn't attract any unwanted attention. Richard felt as though it was safe, so he proceeded through the doorway. Once inside, Richard didn't have a clue on which way to go. There were too many options. There was one door that he thought would lead him right into all the action; this wasn't the door he should be going through right now. Richard decided that he was going to pick door number two instead. He walked over and tried to pull it open, but the door was locked. He decided that he was just going to exit through any door that would allow him. Richard tried about three doors until he was successful. He peeked his head out of the door to see how much action was going on in the area. He noticed that everyone who was in the area had on waiter clothes. Richard figured this was perfect. Maybe he could get an outfit himself and try to blend in.

He waited until he saw a young guy about his size. Richard grabbed the boy up quickly, and pulled him inside the door he had just exited. He showed the boy his private eye badge and asked if it was possible if they could switch outfits. Richard told the young guy that he was on an undercover assignment and needed a disguise. The boy thought that it was pretty cool, but wanted to know what was in it for him. Richard pulled out his wallet and gave the boy two crisp Benjamin Franklin's. The boy looked at the money wondering if it was real. Richard laughed and shook his head yes. Before he knew it the boy was standing in front of him in his draws. Richard quickly took his clothes off and gave it to the boy. Richard put the waiter suit on and informed the boy to wait about ten minutes and get out of here. He also advised him that if anyone stops him, just let them know that he changed his mind about working tonight. Richard made it clear to the boy not by any means to inform anybody that he gave his waiter digs up. The boy smiled and answered okay.

Richard walked out the door and never looked back. He went through the swinging doors and there was a kitchen filled with workers and food. Richard thought to himself *this party must be huge*. One of the tables had caviar, escargot and shrimp cocktail. Another table had key lime pie, peach cobbler and chocolate mousse cake. Richard was already hungry and by looking at this food his hunger was upgraded to starving. He kept trying to remember to stay focused. A female came into the kitchen advising the staff that the party would be starting in about fifteen minutes. Richard kept his head down in hopes that she would not notice him and she didn't. The woman walked out the door and then a male came in. He walked over to another waiter and gave him some instructions. The male then walked over to another waiter and gave him something to do. Richard stood with his head down the entire time, praying that the male would not walk over into his directions. Just as the man started walking over to Richard the same lady came back into the room and called the man over. Richard knew that he had escaped for the time being.

He walked around the room trying to see if there was something that he could fake like he knew what he was doing. He saw a sifter sitting on the table with some powder inside. Richard picked it up and started sprinkling the powder over the cake. Another waiter walked by and smacked him on the back. "Good looking out," the guy said. Richard felt a little safer but he knew that could be short lived. Richard knew his next step would be to get out of the kitchen area somehow and find his way to the main part of the house. He knew that if Jasmine was inside the house, she must be in trouble and scared as hell. The problem was that Richard knew that his time was short. He had to make a decision and make it quickly. Richard continued to shift the powder on top of the cake. What was he to do? Finally, he decided that he could not wait any longer. He just had to walk out of the door and take his chances. Maybe he could take one of the platters out with him and if someone stopped him and said it was too early, he could just act dumb. Richard picked up the platter to make his move. Just as he was walking out the door the same male waiter who was happy that he was sifting the cake stopped him.

"Man, what are you doing? It is not time yet. Remember we got the speech earlier. This has got to be perfect. Anyone who fucks up is going to be fired and never work around here again."

"My fault," Richard replied. "I thought she said that we were supposed to be starting in fifteen minutes. Fifteen minutes have come and gone."

"You are probably right but no one has come back and told us to go out yet, so if I was you, I would stay put until we get the word."

The guy walked away. Richard felt as though he was fucked. He could not just walk out the room bare handed.

He put the tray back in its place and thought about another plan. This was his last hope to get out without causing any attention. He walked back over to that same guy and asked him if he could show him where the bathroom was. The guy told him to go out the door and make a left turn, and halfway down the hallway was the bathroom. He told him to hurry back because he was pretty sure that it was almost time for them to get ready to go out and serve. Richard thanked him for the info and kept it moving. He immediately walked out the door and took a peak to see if he saw anyone else in the hallway, which he didn't. He could hear all the noise coming from his right, but the other waiter informed him to go to the left if he wanted to go to the bathroom. Richard knew that wasn't the direction he wanted to go. He checked again and started walking down the hallway to the right. The further he walked the louder he could hear the voices. Richard knew that this was his only chance and had no clue how he was going to make it happen.

# Chapter Fourteen

Jasmine was still sleeping like a baby. She was exhausted and the bed was so comfortable. Jasmine was awakened by an alarm going off, but it took her a minute to realize where she was. She looked around the room to see where the alarm was coming from. She got out of the bed and walked over to the dresser and hit the clock. Jasmine was a little confused because she didn't even remember seeing the clock in the room. Jasmine looked around and noticed that other things had changed. Someone had come into the room while she was sleeping. She ran into the bathroom and pulled down her pants making sure one had touched her body. Jasmine checked herself over and over to confirm that she had not been violated. She went back into the bedroom and noticed a big box on the chair. She was so curious to see what was inside but didn't really want to touch it. What if it was some kind of trap? Jasmine curiosity got the best of her. She walked over to the box and opened it. She saw an envelope on the top of what appeared to be a gown. The envelope had writing on the top and said *"Jasmine, this is for your eyes only."* Jasmine wondered how this note had her name on it. Who told them who she was? How did they know her name?

She opened up the envelope and began reading the note out loud as if she was reading it to someone else. *"Surprise, I know you are wondering how I knew your name. That is the last thing that you need to think about. This is going to be a night for you to remember. I am glad that you made it here on time. Inside the box is a dress just your size. On the corner of the bed is a pair of shoes that goes with the dress perfectly. Under the cabinet in the bathroom is your favorite brand of panties still in the package, as I know if they were not you would not put them on. There is also some make up for you to utilize. I know you don't want to put it on, but for this occasion you will. Make yourself beautiful so I can be proud. You don't have much time to get yourself together so hurry up. There will be an escort to pick you about in thirty minutes. Don't make me angry and not be ready. You will not want to miss this night. See you later, Jasmine."*

Jasmine didn't know how to take this info. Was she to do as the letter said and get herself all dressed up, or should she just sit on the bed and wait for her escort to pick her up looking like she did at that moment? She thought that whoever wrote this letter wasn't playing but she didn't feel comfortable in this situation. Jasmine sat on the edge of the bed debating about what she was going to do. Could that be Jasmine's moment of opportunity? Could she somehow break something off in the bedroom and knock this person in the head and be able to escape? Maybe this person would have a cell phone and she would be able to contact Richard and let him know where she was and he could come rescue her. Jasmine knew that she wasn't in the right state of mind to handle what had been happening. She got on her knees and prayed for God to help her make the right decision. Jasmine's body was frozen in that same spot for at least ten minutes when it came to her; she had to go along with the program if she was going to get the answers she so needed.

She quickly got up and went into the bathroom. She cut on the shower and looked under the sink and took the items she needed to get herself together. Jasmine knew that she was running out of time. She looked in the mirror and noticed the bags under her eyes. Jasmine looked a mess and didn't think she would be able to get herself together in such little time. She threw her hands up in disgust, went and sat back on the bed feeling defeated. She sat for a least five more minutes and realized that the shower was running and the bathroom had steamed up. Jasmine jumped up with a sense of urgency. She snatched her clothes off and jumped in the shower She jumped back out of the shower and looked back under the cabinet for lotion, but didn't find any Jasmine kept checking the cabinets until she found some. To her surprise, it was a bottle of Eucerin Calming Cream.

This made Jasmine even more curious. Only her friends knew what she always used. This entire ordeal was getting stranger all the time. Why did it seem so familiar? Too many coincidences were occurring. How would this be possible? Jasmine went into the bedroom and opened up the box again. She picked up the dress and admired it. Jasmine knew that under the right circumstances wearing this dress would be a dream but this night, she knew that she was only headed for disaster. She put the dress back on the bed and went back into the bathroom. Jasmine cleared the steam off the mirror and looked at herself. She still looked a mess. Her hair was sticking up all over the place. She again looked under the sink to find the comb and brush. She remembered seeing a blow dryer so she pulled that out too. Jasmine plugged it in and started trying to blow her hair straight. She didn't see a curling iron under the sink so she decided to throw her hair into a ponytail. In order to make it somewhat stylish, she made the ponytail high. Jasmine decided not to really put any makeup on, just lipstick. Jasmine went back into the bedroom and started getting dressed. First she put on the sheer stockings. The color was perfect for her dark chocolate skin. She stepped into the dress and noticed that it fit her body like a glove. She was a little uncomfortable due to her little belly pooch, but despite that she felt like a beauty queen. She felt like she was going to a gala and she would be looked at and admired by everyone, something that she dreamed about as a child. She picked up the shoes that were sitting by the chair. The heel was about 3 inches high which made Jasmine very nervous. Maybe the person that picked out this get up wasn't anyone who knew Jasmine, because they would have known that she never really walked in heels. That wasn't her cup of tea. She stumbled in her shoes to the bathroom to take another looked at her face. She mumbled to herself "it is what it is." Just then it was a knock at the door. Suddenly, Jasmine's dark skin paled. Jasmine didn't move. She heard the door unlock and she was greatly disturbed. Her heart started beating so fast, she knew if she didn't get it under control she would start sweating and that would never be good. She knew the time had come.

Down in the main hall where the party was happening, people were trickling inside. The place had gotten packed. Janet had been making her rounds greeting all of the guests. She was radiant. She looked as if she was an older version of Cinderella. Her confidence was like she had just been named Miss American. No one could tell her different. Janet knew that tonight was going to be a smash hit. She had taken a lot of time to make all the right arrangements. She wanted the night to be perfect and go off without a hitch. So far, everything was running effortlessly. Janet thought maybe she would run upstairs and touch up her makeup and squirt a little more perfume to make sure she smelled divine. She went over and let one of the staff know where she was headed. She also advised him to go inside the kitchen and let them know that they will be starting shortly and make sure everything is ready. Janet walked to the middle of the main room where the beautiful clear elevator was, took her key out, and opened the door. As she went up in the elevator, she was admiring what she thought was her accomplishments.

Little did she know, Richard could see Janet in this elaborate dress riding up in the elevator. He had managed to get into the main room without causing any suspicion. Now he needed to figure out how he could get upstairs. He knew that Jasmine must have been up there somewhere, but the house was huge and how would he be able to find out.

Richard tried to count the floors that the elevator went up before it stopped. He thought it stopped on the third floor. Richard continued to walk around the room closest to the walls thinking that maybe somewhere there was a staircase, and if he found it he would go floor to floor trying to locate Jasmine.

As he was walking he heard someone tapping a glass trying to get everyone's attention. Richard looked around the room and saw another familiar face. The person that was tapping the champagne filled glass was Mercedes. Just like Janet, Mercedes had on a stunning dress. The dress was definitely Mercedes fashion. It was very revealing, black, and the split was in the front of the dress not the side. Mercedes had on three and a half inch heels, making her look like a statue. Richard looked on with amazement for a moment before he got his thoughts together. After seeing this, it just confirmed to him that Janet and Mercedes were in cahoots together. He knew that he had to act fast before Mercedes noticed him.

As everyone quieted down Mercedes started speaking, "I want to thank everyone for being patient due to our lateness. We had planned to have the party start earlier, but you know the best laid plans." Everyone started laughing. Mercedes continued joking around blaming Janet for the delay. "We are having a great coming out party tonight and you all have the privilege to be a huge part of it. I am very excited about tonight and I hope that when you leave here you will be excited too. I will be giving some instruction to our very capable staff to bring out all the great food we are providing tonight and make sure you drink up. If you have any questions during the night direct all of them to Janet. Now enjoy yourself, and God bless." Mercedes picked up her glass and told everyone in the room to do the same. "To a new beginning. Cheers."

Everyone tapped their glasses together and continued partying. As Mercedes began to mingle in the crowd, she thought that she noticed Richard and Richard thought she noticed him. He tried to quickly blend back into the crowd but he saw Mercedes quickly pick up her cell phone and started dialing. He knew this wasn't a good thing. He looked around the room to try to make his exit keeping an eye on where Mercedes was. Just as Richard thought he was caught, the same waiter who had told him where the bathroom was called him over. "What are you doing out here man? I told you the bathroom was to your left. I know you are anxious to get out here but if they catch you, I told you there will be hell to pay."

Richard decided to take a chance and come clean with this fella. He could no longer play it safe. "Look man, I am not a waiter. I am here looking for one of my friends. It is very important that I find her because there is a good chance that she is in danger."

The young man felt a sense of urgency in Richard's voice, believing what he was saying. The guy told Richard that he had done some parties at this home before and he knew his way around. "Where do you need to go?" the guy asked him.

"I need to find a way upstairs so that I can search and see if she is up there. But I have to stay under the radar."

"Not a problem," the waiter assured him. "I can lead you to the back staircase where you can go upstairs undetected. Those stairs are used for servants in the home only."

Richard quickly told the waiter, "Let's go now. I don't have a second to waste." The waiter told him to stay as close to him as possible. He pointed into the direction they were headed. Richard followed behind him as if they were one. He closely watched to make sure Mercedes wasn't following them. The waiter opened the staircase door and told Richard that he was on his own. "I will try to buy you some time in case someone comes snooping around." Richard shook the waiters hand in thanks and disappeared into the staircase.

In the meantime, Mercedes was looking around the room trying to see if she could spot Richard. She no longer could see him. A man came over to her and Mercedes barked some orders to him. The night had just become serious all of a sudden. She didn't want anything to ruin what she had planned for the night. Finally, Mercedes saw Janet coming down in the elevator. The crowd was cheering as if a prize fighter was coming into the ring. Mercedes immediately walked over to the elevator to meet Janet as she came off. She whispered in Janet's ear not to alert anyone who was standing around "I think we might have a little problem. I think I saw Richard lurking around here. This could be a problem as the night progresses if he shows up and ruins our surprise."

Janet looked a little confused. "Are you sure you saw Richard here? How do you think he could have gotten inside?"

"At this point, I do not think it matters. He is dressed like one of the waiters. Get all your men out looking for him now!" Janet knew that Mercedes was worried and should be. Mercedes advised Janet to have her men go upstairs and get Imani and Jasmine to the elevator so they could come downstairs.

Imani was sitting in the room sweating in her dress. She was getting very impatient at this point, wondering when this ordeal was going to end. She went into the bathroom and washed all the makeup off her face to wake herself up. She looked back under the cabinet and pulled out the makeup and put it back on. As soon as she finished, the door opened up and the same guy as before told her it was time. The man put his arm around Imani's and they began to walk to the elevator. At the same time, another man was opening the door to pick up Jasmine. The man let Jasmine know that he would be escorting her to the elevator where she will go downstairs. The man put his hand out but Jasmine didn't do the same. He told her this wasn't a game and there was a sense of urgency and he didn't have time to play games with her. He put his hand back out and this time Jasmine grabbed it as they walked out together.

As both Jasmine and Imani were walking down the hallway to the elevator they both noticed each other, both confused. Where were each one of them at? Could both of them been in the same locations all this time, and why were they meeting at the elevator now? Neither one of them said anything at first, they just looked at each other. One of the escorts put the key into the elevator to open it up. After the elevator opened, he advised them that they were now on their own. He would press the correct floor and then they should act accordingly when the elevator opened at their destination. As soon as the elevator closed, Imani and Jasmine hugged each other and began to cry. For the first time they both felt as though they could show their true emotions. They felt they were in the same boat and now they were in it together. Both of them had overwhelming feelings and neither knew how to express them or even if it was safe to do so. Imani felt like she had so many questions to ask Jasmine, but figured it would be better to just stay silent. Jasmine felt like a weight had been lifted off her shoulders, but still was very hesitant because she didn't know what they were about to embark in. They didn't speak one word in the elevator the entire ride. As the elevator went down, Jasmine could see all the people that were downstairs and the elaborate decorations. Imani looked at her but still stayed silent, an expression of amazement on her face. Jasmine made a motion to Imani to wipe her eyes as the tears had made her eyeliner smear. The elevator stopped but the doors didn't open immediately.

Finally, Jasmine spoke. "Where have you been? Do you know what is going on here?"

Imani quickly replied. "We don't have enough time right now to get into where I have been, and I am clueless to what is going on here. I have spent the majority of today in a locked room crying and trying to figure out why my so-called friends would do something so bad to me."

Jasmine almost cut Imani off with her reply by assuring Imani that she had nothing to do with what was going on. She let Imani know that she was also locked in a room for hours and is very upset by the entire situation. "Let's see if we can find a way to cooperate long enough to get the hell out of here. Not sure how we can make it happen but I know we both got..."

Just then the elevator doors began to open. Imani grabbed Jasmine's hand and squeezed it tight. Neither of them immediately walked out. Instead, the same two male escorts came inside the elevator and put their hands out and escorted them into the party. Both of them continued to look around the room in amazement. The escorts made sure they took them to the opposite sides of the room. Jasmine made sure she didn't lose sight of Imani. She was hoping Imani was doing the same. It wasn't long before the waiters and waitresses started coming out with trays of food. *And it isn't any cheesy food* Imani thought. She wanted to stuff her face immediately. She had to take into consideration the beautiful gown that she had on, not wanting to mess it up. As the waiters walked by, she took samples off the tray. What Imani was waiting for was the waitress carrying around the champagne. She needed a drink badly. Jasmine had just picked up two glasses of champagne as the waitress walked by. She took a sip and then gulped down the entire glass knowing that champagne was hardly her favorite. She put her empty glass on the tray of the passing waiter as she continued to look around the room in search of familiar faces. She really was looking to see if she could spot Richard. She was hoping he was inside the room doing the same thing. She wondered though; would he be able to spot her since she looked different from when they got estranged from each other?

Richard had made his way to the second-floor door.  He opened the door cautiously trying to see if anyone was in the hallway before he walked out.  He saw that the coast was clear and walked in the hallway.  He tried all the doors but they were all locked.  Richard called out for Jasmine with no reply.  Just dead silence.  He quickly walked back to the servant door and continued his journey up to the next floor.  Richard did the same exact thing.  He checked the hallway before going.  He quickly checked all the doors which again were locked, and continued his journey back into the stairwell.  He knew that the house was big but his journey was coming to an end.  When Richard got up the next flight of stairs, he felt himself getting a little winded, but he knew somehow he had to continue his mission.  He cracked the door to again make sure the floor was clear.  This time it was different.  Richard heard a voice in the hallway talking but Richard never heard another person replying.  He realized that the person in the hallway was talking on the telephone.  Richard needed to figure out if he could make a move on this guy just in case he gets caught.  He opened the door a little more to try to see how big the guy was.  Unfortunately to Richard, the door made a noise which startled the guy and made him walk over in his direction.  Richard tried not to panic and keep his cool.  He tried to close the door a little so the guy didn't see him in the hallway, and if he came into the hallway he could knock him over the head, hoping to knock him unconscious. The guy walked right over to the door and noticed it was cracked.  He knew something was out of place because that door should not be opened.  As soon as the guy walked through the door, Richard cocked him right in the side of the head with his fist.  The man fell to his feet immediately.  Richard took a good look at the guy. He looked very familiar, but he couldn't place where he had seen him before.

Richard knew he didn't have a lot of time to waste so he gave up the do you remember game and walked into the hallway. He checked all the doors and this time to Richard's amazement the first door he tried opened. He walked into the room and looked around. All he saw were women's clothes lying on the bed. He picked up the shirt and pants but they didn't look familiar. He walked into the bathroom but that was no help. He walked out of the room, went across the hallway, and opened another door. This room was different, decorated like a baby's room. There were bottles around and a changing bed. On the left side of the room was an elaborate crib. The bedding on the crib was gorgeous. It was made with silk and had pillows laid around the crib that looked like they were hand made. The curtains in the room matched the bedding. The setup was made for a princess.

Richard thought to himself *could this be where Karisma has been all this time? But how could Janet afford this house and the extravagant items inside of it?* He checked around the entire room for clues, but there were none and there was no sign of the baby in the room. He walked out of the room and this time he didn't check the hallway. He went to the next door which was locked. The next door across the hall was also locked. He got down to the end of the hallway and knew there were only two doors left he had to check. As he grabbed the door on the left side, the guy that was knocked out grabbed Richard. He warned Richard to not enter the room. Richard tried to punch the guy in the face, but this time the guy was ready. He blocked the first three shots that Richard threw at him. Fortunately for Richard, the fourth time was a charm, again knocking the guy out. He pulled the guy's body into the room and laid his limp body on the side of the bed. Richard immediately noticed one of Jasmine's shoes next to where he had just laid the body. He picked it up just to confirm. A dreadful feeling came over Richard, sensing that Jasmine was in trouble. He got up and continued to walk around the room, every step he took he located more and more of Jasmine's belongings. Her shirt, pants, the other shoe, and when he went into the bathroom he saw her earrings sitting on the side of the sink. Richard went into panic mode, but at least he knew that Jasmine was in the house. He could sense that his blood pressure was rising. He knew that time wasn't on his side and kept trying to figure out what he could do and whether it have a good outcome. He began to realize how much he really started to care about Jasmine but couldn't let that cloud his judgement. He had to believe that she was one of the guests downstairs.

Richard checked the passed-out man to make sure he wasn't going to wake up anytime soon. Richard decided that his best bet was to swipe clothes with the guy. This would at least give him a better shot of fitting in downstairs. He knew that Mercedes had already seen him in the waiter outfit, so he would definitely have a better chance to stay under the radar. It took Richard about five minutes to get himself together. He went back to the door and checked to see if anyone was in the hallway which was clear. Richard felt as though he could go downstairs and find Jasmine now and get her out of this place without a problem. He knew he still had to be careful but he felt confident. Richard walked out the door and looked at the last door that he didn't check. He knew he didn't have much time to waste, but he felt something pulling him towards the door. He had a gut feeling that the room had more answers to what was going on. Richard could not resist, so he went to the door and like he hoped it was unlocked. He slowly opened the door and to his surprise it turned out to be the biggest shocker of all. The answers to all Richard's questions were just answered. He almost fell to the ground in amazement. Richard thought to himself *this could not be true.* His body went limp. Richard didn't know what to do at this point. Was he to run downstairs and start yelling and screaming about what he had discovered? Or should he just hope that what he saw would still be there after he found Jasmine and bring her upstairs to show her? Richard could not even think straight. His whole entire reasoning had just disappeared. He kept telling himself over and over again to get it together. *Get your mind right.* He tried to be as quiet as possible so that he would not disturb his discovery. What he didn't understand is why she was in the room alone. He walked over to the bed and just watched her sleep. Karisma was sweet and beautiful, so pure. She had no clue what everyone that loved her had been through. Richard kissed her on her forehead and decided he should go. Just as he was walking out he noticed the little intercom sitting next to the bed. When he walked away, he turned back for one last glance and saw her with her eyes opened and an endearing smile on her face. He smiled back and left the room.

The party was in full swing. Everyone appeared to be having a great time, but Jasmine and Imani were not. They were trying to make their way across the room to get to each other. Mercedes and Janet were in the kitchen talking. Mercedes asked Janet if her people had caught up with Richard yet. Janet assured Mercedes that they were covering the entire house. They would make sure he was caught and taken care of.

Mercedes said to Janet, "Do you think it is time yet? I mean everyone is here and in place. I don't think we should give Richard a chance to take away our joy."

"I think you're right," Janet replied. "I will get everything in place. Do you think that we should reveal ourselves first before bringing in the real deal?"

"Well if you ask me, I think we should come out first so they can see us. All the commotion of us shocking them and having all our friends out there gathering around will give us a chance to sneak back out for the grand finale."

"That's a perfect idea. I could not have thought of it any better. But check this out bitch; you are not as smart as I am," Janet joked.

They gave each other the head nod and walked out of the kitchen. They both felt they were on the top of the world. They had pulled off the biggest cue, and they had raised some cash in the process. Of course, they knew that some people were hurt behind it and they were hoping that the party would make it all just a little better. They walked down the hallway and Janet stopped and made a phone call. She let the person know that it was time.

In the main room, where the party was going on the light went dim. Jasmine knew this was her chance to get to Imani. She quickly walked in her direction hoping that Imani would do the same. Luckily, Imani was as she walked in Jasmine's direction. They met exactly at the halfway point. Things appeared strange to Jasmine though because her escort had disappeared, almost like he wanted to let her walk away. When they caught up to each other, they gave themselves a big hug. They felt a sense of safety when they were around each other. It didn't take long before someone was speaking on a microphone. Both Jasmine and Imani recognized that voice. It was Janet. She was standing on the stage which was really not noticeable at first because of the guests. Everyone in the party started gathering around where she was standing. They were cheering like she was some kind of goddess. Jasmine looked over at Imani and shrugged her shoulder. When did Janet spend time up here? Janet asked everyone to settle down because she needed to introduce her co-host of the party and her dear friend.

"I would just like to take a few minutes before my co-host comes out and say a few words about what a real friendship consists of. A true friendship is when someone can go through the good times as well as the bad times. A true friendship can stand the test of time. When everything seems to be hitting rock bottom, that true friend will be right there holding you up when your legs feel like jello and you want to collapse. I learned a lot from this person. They showed me how to get a thick skin fast, how to become ruthless, and also how to have a great time while doing it. When I introduce this person, I want everyone to put their glasses of champagne in the air and toast to this person.

Appreciate her like I do. Waiters, please make sure everyone's glasses are full. I would also like to point out that two very dear friends of mine are special guests here today. Jasmine and Imani, can you come up to the podium? I see you two over there looking beautiful. I cannot believe how regal you both look. The dresses that were picked out were superb. I must bask in my own great taste." All the guests chuckled from Janet's remarks. "Come on girls, don't be shy. I want you standing right by my side. One of you on the left side and one of you on the right. Will my escorts go over and give them a hand. Friendship is the theme here tonight. It is something that could make or break a person. Make sure that when you have a great friend, you let them know all the time how important they are to you. Never take your friendships for granted. I am not going to keep going on and on. Trust me, what I feel for this person I could go on forever."

Jasmine and Imani made their way to the podium next to Janet's side like she requested. Janet turned and kissed both of them on the check. "Without further ado I would like to bring out my dear friend that I keep bragging about. She is a diamond in the ruff. Please give a warm welcome to my good friend Mercedes."

Jasmine's mouth fell open so wide you could have stuck a basketball inside. Jasmine knew that Mercedes was involved but not to this degree. Imani had just about the same reaction, but instead of having her mouth drop the tears fell. She could barely contain herself. Imani was flooded with emotions. How could her friend Mercedes have a hand in helping Janet? She finally had total conformation she had something to do with everything she had went through in this fucking hick town.

Mercedes walked through the crowd like she was a queen, her dress trailing behind her. Mercedes had on jewelry that sparkled. She had that same look on her face that she had when she disrupted Precious' funeral. Imani felt sick to her stomach. As Mercedes walked up the platform, Jasmine thought about pushing her off but she knew that would not solve anything. It would only get her in more trouble. Mercedes walked over to Janet first and gave her the biggest hug in the world. The crowd was cheering so loud Jasmine and Imani could not even hear themselves think in the room. After Mercedes finished hugging Janet she walked over to Jasmine and put her arms out. Jasmine reluctantly put her arms around Mercedes and they hugged. Mercedes whispered in Jasmine's ear. "I had to do what I needed to. I am sure when the night is over you will understand. If you don't I will spend the rest of my life trying to explain it to you." Mercedes let her embrace of Jasmine go and walked over to Imani. She went to hug Imani but things didn't go as planned. Imani could not be as nice and turned her back towards Mercedes. Janet was shocked. She could not believe Imani's defiance, especially because she was embarrassing her dear friend.

She got on the mic and asked for everyone to quiet down. "I know that everyone just saw this fat bitch disrespect my friend. Just because you put on a fancy dress, nice shoes and some makeup doesn't change who you are. I need you to apologize to all my guests. I think you may be feeling a little overwhelmed with all the attention. I am going to hand you this mic and I want you to make it right."

Imani grabbed the mike out of Janet's hand with force. "You want me to apologize to your guest, your so-called friends? I thought we were friends. Maybe I should let these people know how you treat your friends. But what would that accomplish? Here is my apology Janet, I am fucking sorry." Imani dropped the mic and began to walk off the podium.

Mercedes stopped Imani. She pulled her into an embrace and whispered that she was sorry. "Sorry for shocking you like this. I knew it was wrong but I had to do what was needed. Don't make this any worse by acting out of your character. You know this is not you."

Imani knew that she was treading in deep water and she would not be able to swim her way out. Imani walked back up on the podium and Imani picked the microphone back up and spoke. "I apologize for my behavior. I had a little bit too much champagne. I hope everyone can forgive me, especially you Janet and Mercedes."

Janet took the microphone back and replied, "Of course, I forgive you and I hope you can forgive me for acting a fool too." The two of them hugged.

Mercedes walked over to Janet and whispered in her ear. "Does this mean you have everything in place? Because it is definitely time." Janet got back on the mic and told everyone to enjoy themselves and have some more champagne because the best was yet to come.

Both Janet and Mercedes walked off the podium and went to the side to talk. Janet got on her phone and made a few calls. Imani and Jasmine stood to the side drinking glasses of champagne. They didn't want to feel any more pain. People around the room were enjoying themselves. The music was pumping and they were dancing. It was about fifteen minutes before Janet's phone rang back. The person told them that they have not been able to find Richard yet. It wasn't looking good as they had already searched over half of the house, and most of the rest of the house he had no way to get into. Janet didn't want to hear that. She told him to find him now. Janet made another phone call and when she hung the phone up she was even more annoyed. She walked over to Mercedes and told her they had a problem.

"We have got to sound the alarms. The place has to go into lock down."

"What is the matter?" Mercedes asked.

"The phone call I just got wasn't good. I am almost afraid to say it out loud because it will make it true. I have to let you know though."

"Just spit it out damnit!"

"The baby is gone. Karisma is gone. One of my men went into the bedroom and she was gone. All the bottles and diapers are missing too." Mercedes could not believe it. All of their hard work could now be for nothing. Both of them looked at each other and at the same time yelled out "Richard!"

Even though the music was loud and the crowd was all speaking, Jasmine and Imani looked up because the yell was so loud. They didn't know exactly what had happened but they knew it was bad. Imani looked at Jasmine and asked, "Who do you think this Richard guy did and what could he have done that made them so upset?" Jasmine didn't want to scream over all the voices so she asked Imani to walk with her and she could explain to her exactly what she knew. Jasmine didn't know how far they would get before someone would stop them but she knew they needed some quiet. She thought for a second and realized that the bathroom would be a perfect spot. As they walked through the crowd, Jasmine located a guard and asked him to point out the direction of the women's bathroom. He didn't even look at them sideways, he just gave them the directions. Jasmine grabbed Imani's hand to hurry her along. She didn't want anyone to realize they were missing until they had a moment to speak privately.

When they reached the bathroom there was a guard posted at the door. First he said they would have to go in separately but Imani was quick and said they needed to help each other with the zippers on their dresses. The guard looked at them both and said okay. They got into the bathroom and it only had four stalls. They looked underneath them all to make sure there was nobody inside. Imani made an observation that it was the cleanest bathroom she had ever seen and it smelled sweet. Jasmine just looked at her like this wasn't the time.

"So, we do not have too much time, Richard is the private eye I paid a lot of money to try to find you all when everyone disappeared. He has been wonderful to me. He helped me so much and made me realize that there are still good people out here because I was definitely losing my faith."

Imani had a big grin on her face. Jasmine asked her why she was smiling. Imani started to cry and said "I'm so happy that you would do that for me. I would have said all of us but under the circumstances, it appears that we both were hoodwinked by our so-called friend. I still have not gotten my head wrapped around the entire situation. I don't think that the night is over but I think it just took a left turn that wasn't expected. I'm not sure exactly what Richard has done, but it appears to be big."

Just then there was a knock on the door. Jasmine ran into the stall and flushed the toilet two times just to make sure that it was heard in the hallway. The guard outside the door cracked the door open to tell them to get a move on. "I have instructions to get you two back to the party. Apparently y'all are important guests. I'm glad I didn't do anything inappropriate to get myself fired." They walked out of the bathroom and he escorted them back to the party. He made sure they were in the eyesight of Mercedes. Mercedes didn't come over to where they were standing right away. This gave Jasmine time to tell Imani a few more details. She just hoped she could hear her.

Jasmine tried to whisper to Imani that Richard was the one who drove her to the house. He came to look around and someone found her and locked her into a room. She never got to see him again but she hoped that somehow he got into the house. She just prayed that he would not leave her and now she knows the answer. He never left her. He must have been looking for her and stumbled into something he shouldn't have. She just prays they don't find him. Just as Imani was about to reply, Janet was right next to her. She asked them if they had time to talk to take a walk with her, but it didn't really sound like a request. They walked over by the elevator and Janet signaled to one of the guards to come over and open the elevator door. They got in the elevator and went to the third floor. Both Jasmine and Imani both thought *not back here again*. The door opened and Janet said, "after you." She walked down the hallway and Jasmine's stomach started to feel like someone had just sucker punched her. Janet opened the second to last door and advised them to go inside. This time they will be able to stay together, but it was too risky to let them stay downstairs at the party. She needed to be able to be seen at all times. She let them know if they decided to take their dresses off to remember to not get them wrinkled because there will be a time that she will be sending for them to come back down. She walked out the door and turned the lock and left.

Janet went into a different room before heading back downstairs. She opened the door and just stood in the middle of the floor. Tears started rolling down her face. She wasn't even thinking about how her makeup was getting messed up. She went over to the dresser and opened up a drawer and grabbed a pen and paper. She sat down and started writing a letter, but it wasn't addressed to anyone in specific.

*To Whom it may Concern,*

*I am so sorry about the disappointment that I have become. I thought I was doing something right to secure a great life for my grandbaby, but it turns out I even failed at that. I am not really sure why I did all this and put my daughter's best friends through the grief and agony after they lost their friend. Maybe I was persuaded by others. Maybe I was just too greedy to see the truth. I am not sure if I will ever know the answers, but I believe that my time is just about up. I think it's time for me to go and join my daughter. Maybe by the time this letter is read, Karisma will be back and with Mercedes. If I had a choice, to be honest, I think that Karisma belongs with someone who could love her entirely. Will teach her to be a better person than all of us. Please make sure when she gets old enough she knows that everything her grandma did was for her. I will leave you all with this last thought. Make sure that Mercedes lets everyone know the entire truth. Everything she knows about Karisma and what she knows about her parents.*

*With all the love from my heart and soul - Janet.*

Janet laid the pen on the dresser and put the letter right next to it. She looked up in the mirror and noticed that her face was a wreck. She could never have someone see her looking at this. She went into the bathroom and washed all the makeup off her face. She began to apply her new makeup foundation and all. She went back into the room and picked the letter back up and kissed it so her lip print was on the letter. Janet had a strange smile on her face, sort of evil. She walked out the door and before she closed the door she remembered something. She walked back into the bathroom and picked up a pill bottle. She didn't even read what the prescription was for. She went back out the door and walked to the elevator. She took her key out and the elevator door opened, still having the strange smile on her face. When the elevator stopped at the main floor the door opened with Mercedes waiting outside. She immediately started playing 100 questions. Janet put her finger up and told her that she needed a drink first. She walked onto the floor and found the nearest waiter. She grabbed a glass, took several pills out, and swallowed every single one of them. She did it when Mercedes wasn't really paying attention to her. After she drank the glass of champagne she grabbed another one to make sure everything was washed down.

Janet grabbed Mercedes' hand and told her that they should hit the dance floor. Mercedes was puzzled. She asked Janet did she forget that Richard was out there somewhere or he has already somehow found a way to get off the premises and may have the baby with him. All the hard work we had been through would be for nothing. Janet told Mercedes to relax. She assured her that Jasmine and Imani were safe and they could check on the guards progress in a few minutes. Janet just kept saying dance with me for a little while. Mercedes couldn't even think straight. She grabbed a glass as the waiter walked by. She sipped on it as she didn't lose focus. There was a party to celebrate Karisma, and the guest of honor was nowhere to be found and there was no way she could have walked out of the room. Hell, she could not even walk. Mercedes continued to dance with Janet. It was just a little bit of time before she noticed that Janet was slowing down. She was kind of happy because maybe now they could really talk and get a plan together on what they were going to do next.

One of the guards came over to them and told them they had found something and they both should follow him. Mercedes grabbed Janet's hand and they followed the guard. They went into the stairwell where only the staff walked. The guard informed them that they believe this is the way that Richard was moving around. He easily could have gotten up and down the stairs without being seen. They located one of the guards that was missing for a while. He said that some man sucker punched him. Mercedes immediately said that the guard be fired immediately. He had no purpose here. Janet didn't even dispute it.

"So, do you know where he is now?" Mercedes asked.

"Unfortunately, no," the guard responded. "But we are working diligently to find him and the baby."

Mercedes told Janet it was getting late. Did she think that they should end the party soon? It doesn't appear that it would be a big announcement tonight. Janet thought about it and told Mercedes, "Maybe we should see how much food was left, because they didn't want to waste it."

Janet just asked her to please check. She would be on the dance floor waiting on her return. Janet wanted to make sure she was enjoying the last hours. She wanted it to be a night that she would enjoy until her last breath. She did everything she thought was right and made peace with it. It would now be Mercedes cross to bear. She had all the answers and could make everything right.

Janet danced until Mercedes came back and found her on the dance floor. Mercedes let Janet know that the food was almost all gone. Mercedes walked toward the DJ booth and was stopped by a few of the guests wondering what happened to the big announcement. Mercedes just smiled and replied, "you just have to wait and see." She really didn't know what else to say. She was mortified that shit got fucked up, but at this point the best thing was to end the party and she would get together with Janet in the morning with a new plan. She could only pray that if Richard did leave the house, he would not call the police. Technically, Janet was Karisma's grandmother and her immediate family. Mercedes updated the DJ and told him to make the statement right away. Before Mercedes could make it down the stairs, the DJ was giving the news that the party was going to be coming to an end in one hour. Mercedes watched as the partygoers grabbed the champagne glasses and one yelled out "To Janet! What a great hostess!" Everyone repeated the same thing and clicked their glasses. Janet put her glass up in the air and yelled to the crowd cheers. Mercedes raised her glass and repeated it.

# Chapter Fifteen

As Richard drove away from the house he felt an aching pain in his stomach. He knew that he had done the right thing, but he could not shake the feeling that he left Jasmine behind. Now what was he supposed to do with the precious baby girl? He had never taken care of an infant. He drove down the road thinking should he just go to the local precinct and let them know what was going on. He immediately thought better of that knowing that it appeared that everyone was in cahoots in that area with Janet and Mercedes. Richard continued driving in the direction of Westchester County. He had managed to get some of the bottles and a few outfits on his way out. As Richard was driving, he kept peaking back to make sure Karisma was okay. She was sound asleep. Richard kept thinking about how lucky he got to even get out of the house. One day he would have to thank the young man who gave him his waiter uniform and later caused a distraction to allow him to escape out of the house. But the pain was still real that Jasmine was still in that house and who knows what was going to happen to her. Richard was getting close to home and he needed to figure out what would be his next move. Could he get the police involved down there? Probably not because they would just call the sheriff dept up in the Catskills and he would be back in the same bad positions. Just as Richard was pulling into his driveway it dawned on him. Maybe he could use Karisma as bait. Maybe she could be his bargaining chip. Maybe he could use her to get Jasmine back. But would Jasmine want that? He felt he was out of options. He thought hard but came up to the same conclusion. He had to be smart and make sure the plan was well constructed. He could not fuck it up. He picked Karisma up and she barely squirmed. He just looked at her fat checks and her small lips. He thought about never really knowing Precious, but Karisma definitely had similar features. Jasmine would always tell him that.

Richard grabbed the bag of things he procured from the house and walked up the stairs and opened the door. He walked into the house and got Karisma situated, sure the bottles were ready. She was still sleeping so he decided to change her diaper while he had the chance. Karima began to squirm and Richard feared he would wake her up, but once he put the new diaper on her she fell right back to sleep. He went into the bathroom and washed his face and hands. Richard really felt he was on his own. He came out of the bathroom and went into the kitchen to see what he could munch on. Richard took a pause and thought *I am a PI. I can figure this out. I can make it right.* He went and quickly checked on Karisma. He smiled as she was still sleeping. He went and sat on the bed and pulled out a pen and paper. He felt that if it listed all his options, it would clarify everything to him. Richard noted the pros first. 1. he had Karisma, what everyone wanted. He kept thinking but he didn't have any other pro on his side. He thought maybe he could use the fact that he knew how to get back into the house without being detected.

Richard then thought about the cons -

    1.        Mercedes and Janet most likely knew that he had taken Karisma.

    2.        It wouldn't take long to figure out where he lived

    3.        He had Jasmine hidden

    4.        They had a dirty sheriff on their side

    5.        Apparently they had some extra cash

Richard looked at this list and came up to the same conclusion Karisma was his only bargaining chip. He had to contact Janet to see what she was willing to do to get her grandbaby back. Richard knew he was also running the risk that the cops may have been called, but he didn't feel like that was the option they were looking to explore. It was early in the morning and Richard watched the sun rise. It was a beautiful site and very soothing. Richard thought a nap would be great for him, but he was worried that if he fell asleep he would not hear Karisma crying when she woke up. He laid his head on the pillow and it didn't take more than five minutes and Richard was asleep.

# Chapter Sixteen

As soon as the sun light started to shine in the room, Imani was standing up looking out the windows. The windows had bars across them so there was no escape. Imani didn't want to wake Jasmine up but she really wanted to talk to her. Imani decided that she would go wash up and she hoped that when she came out of the bathroom Jasmine would be awake. It didn't take Imani long but when she came out of the bathroom, Jasmine was still asleep. How could she leap under these conditions? There were problems that were going on in the house last night. Was anyone else aware of this? She felt like something had to be wrong because nobody ever came back to get them. She thought that maybe Mercedes or Janet would have come upstairs before or even after the festivities had ended. Imani really wanted to know what happened. She continued to look out the window thinking about everything that had happened, the good and the bad.

A few minutes had passed and Jasmine was watching Imani as she stared out of the window. Jasmine asked, "Are you thinking about what I was dreaming about?"

Imani quickly turned her head and had a big Kool-Aid smile on her face. "Finally!" she exclaimed. "It seems like I have been sitting here for hours waiting for you to wake up."

Jasmine got out of the bed and walked into the bathroom. It seemed like she was in there for an entirety to Imani. Jasmine walked back into the bedroom and asked, "You wondering why nobody came back into this room last night?" Imani just nodded. "I'm guessing Jasmine said that we should be finding out more this morning."

Jasmine walked to the door and started to jiggle it to see if someone was careless last night and forgot to lock it, but it didn't budge. She looked back at Imani and shrugged her shoulder implying oh well. The only clothes they could put on were the clothes they came to the house with or the gowns they provided for them. They both decided to put back on their clothes. They sat in silence for over an hour before they even heard someone in the hallway. Finally, they heard keys rattling by the door. They thought finally they would get some explanation about yesterday. All of a sudden, they heard a fading sound of the keys jingling. Jasmine ran over to the door and started banging on it and screaming "You can't keep us in here forever!" There was no reply.

Jasmine looked over Imani and saw the tears rolling down her cheeks. She quickly made it back to the bed. She rubbed her back trying to assure her that everything would be okay.

"I am sure that whatever Richard did he caused some kinks in their plan. Do you see how they shuffled us out of the party? It was big, and I can only think it had to do with Karisma. What else could have made them so crazy?"

"Their plan, whatever it was, hit a roadblock. You know what I am happy about? The fact that Richard is not in this room with us. That is very encouraging, making me think that he was able to find his way out of this place."

Imani continued to wipe the tears off her face. Jasmine kept trying to reassure her that it would be okay. "We didn't get this far to not make it out of here, I have faith. Imani you always find the silver lining in every situation. I know u can find out here." That put a brief smile on Imani's face. "You hungry Imani?"

"Starving," she replied. "They would not let us go the entire day without feeding us." Jasmine went back to the door and started banging again. Still no response. Jasmine didn't have any ideas but she didn't want Imani to start to see that she was really concerned. "I might as well just go back to sleep in hopes that it would all be a dream."

# Chapter Seventeen

Mercedes was up early prepping the staff about what had taken place. They could see the difference between Mercedes' attitude last night and how she was acting this morning. One of the waiters asked if it was going to become public knowledge that Janet had passed away. Mercedes advised that the police and ambulance were on their way to the house now. She let them know she had not even digested the tragedy. She wasn't even sure what had happened. She was going to leave that up to the appropriate party. She concluded the conversation by stating the most important thing is not to make this a public discussion at this point. "Please do not make phone calls to your family and friends and spread the news. Please," she said again. She also advised them the JR. would be around shortly to let them know exactly what needed to be done around the house.

Mercedes went back upstairs and started making phone calls before the police and ambulance arrived. She thought how it would be so nice to be able to go and speak with her friends about what she was feeling, but how would they receive it? She was sure they felt as though she had turned her back on them. She had stabbed them in the back without an explanation. Mercedes could understand why they felt like that. She never gave them a reason to think anything else. She didn't even know how to make it right because without knowing where Karisma was, she could not began to explain anything. She knew they would have questions once they started to hear the sirens and saw the ambulance coming into the house.

Just as she completed her thought she heard the sirens get closer and closer. She felt the knot in her stomach get tighter and tighter. The pain had not gone away since last night and she knew it wasn't going to be going away anytime soon. Mercedes ran down the stairs to meet the police and the ambulance. She reached the door just as it was being opened. As Mercedes greeted them, Jr came down. One of the officers asked who was the owner of the residence. Jr. responded it was him. As Mercedes began to speak the officer dismissed her and asked Jr. to show him to the body. Mercedes took two deep breaths and remembered where she was and also who she was. She tried to let them know that she found a letter in the room with her but they would not listen. She followed behind them at a very slow pace, starting to get her senses back.

She snapped back into reality. Why did she ever think that this was supposed to be her lifestyle? A lifestyle that she would have even wanted to raise Karisma up in? That baby girl was supposed to have a life fit for a queen. She didn't have to have that life around people she most likely would identify with. This is what Janet wanted and Janet was no longer with her. She knew that it was time to come clean with her friends and she had to do it now. She had to let them know everything that she knew. She had been living in a fantasy land that was created by Janet who made it seem so great. Mercedes started to get upset with herself. She could not believe that she fell for the bullshit that Janet was spewing. She told herself over and over again that it was the right thing to do until she began to really believe it. Mercedes watched as they put Janet's body on the stretcher. The EMS worker told the police that she had been dead for some time. They both agreed that an autopsy should be done to confirm how she died and time of death. They needed to rule out homicide. "Homicide" Mercedes belted out. "That sounds crazy. We were having a celebration last night. Everything was fine when I left her." The officer looked at Mercedes and told her not to go too far because he may need a statement from her at a later time. They walked away with Janet's body and she just watched with tears running down her cheeks.

It took Mercedes about twenty minutes to get herself together. She sat on her bed just going over everything in her mind. How did this happen? How did they let someone take Karisma one day and the next Janet is dead. How did she betray her friends? She wiped her face and decided that it was time to face her demons. She walked to the elevator to go upstairs to see Imani and Jasmine. As the elevator went up one floor she felt like it was an eternity. What was this taking so long? She had no clue what she would be saying to her friends, but she knew it was going to start with I'm sorry. That is all she knew she was going to say. Mercedes got off the elevator and began her walk of shame. She pulled the key out of her pocket and stuck it in the door, took a deep breath, and opened up the door. Both Jasmine and Imani were sitting on the bed with a face that made Mercedes feel uncomfortable. Mercedes decided immediately that inside the room would not be a good place to talk. "Take a walk with me, please."

They got up off the bed and walked out of the door. Jasmine felt as if she was just released from jail, like a weight was lifted off of her shoulders. She was still very confused and angry but thankful. Imani had become overwhelmed with emotions and just fell on her knees and started to cry. She could not control her feelings. Mercedes tried to help her up but she twisted her body so that she could not touch her. Jasmine walked over to her and told her that she had all rights to be feeling what she was feeling but they needed to get to a place where we can talk and this wasn't the location. Jasmine put her hand out and Imani grabbed it and got up off the floor. She gave Jasmine a big hug and just shook her head at Mercedes. They got back into the elevator and arrived back on the first floor. Mercedes guided them to the back yard and they all took a seat on the bench.

Mercedes stood up and began speaking. "First I would like to apologize from the bottom of my heart about everything that I have done to you. I am not sure what I was thinking. Wait, I do. I was thinking about Karisma. Janet confused me. She made me think that she was going to get custody of her and that she was going to raise her up here in the hicks. She would be afforded the best education, but she needed to eliminate the competition. She made me feel special because she chose me as her partner. She made me feel that even though me and Precious didn't agree with everything, I was still worthy. I needed that, so I thought. I made a huge mistake and Janet knew how to play on my weakness. She got money from these hicks and gave it to me, which really helped since I wasn't working on a regular since Precious had passed away. My focus became Karisma. I knew that she was all of our focus but somehow I lost perspective.

Jasmine interrupted. "Why are you telling us this now? What has changed that the fog has been lifted from in front of your eyes. Why do you expect us to just forgive you?"

Mercedes explained she is not expecting them to forgive her right away but she just wanted them to know where her mind and heart was and is now. "Janet passed away sometime overnight. I'm pretty sure that you heard the sirens and saw the cop cars and ambulance out of the window. I found a letter in the bed next to her.

For the first time Imani spoke. "Are you sure?"

"Yes."

"I am not sure how I feel about that news. Janet was Karisma's grandmother. She had to love that girl to go through all bullshit she put us through. We won't even ever know what her real game plan was unless you tell us Mercedes."

"There are other issues going on right now. Hopefully, since Jasmine put Richard in our life, she can help us find Karisma. I believe he is the one who came in here last night and took her. Not sure how he even got out of this place, but I do applaud him. Do you think you could call him Jasmine and let him know that you are okay? Can you make sure our suspicions are correct and he has Karisma?"

Jasmine didn't hesitate. "Of course, I can but before I make any calls, I want to make sure there will be no repercussion for what he did. Can you guarantee this, because my trust level for you is at an all-time low."

"Yes, I can," Mercedes replied. She handed Jasmine the phone to call Richard. Jasmine warned Mercedes that he may not pick up the phone if he does not recognize the phone number. Mercedes told her that is a chance they are going to have to take. She can only pray that Richard is the one who took Karisma. He has to be. Jasmine began to dial Richards number praying that he'd answer the phone. The phone rang and rang. Finally, the answering machine cut on. Jasmine hung the phone up and started dialing again. Imani and Mercedes just stood in silence. The phone began ringing again. This time Richard answered the phone. He sounded like he was sleeping, which worried Jasmine because if he had the baby who was watching her?

"Richard are you up? It's Jasmine."

He took a moment to reply and he quickly woke up. "Jasmine is that really you? Are you okay? I have some much to tell you." Richard just started blurting everything out before Jasmine could even interrupt him. "I made it into the house when we got separated. I was searching for you thanks to a waiter who let me borrow his uniform. As I was searching for you, I found Karisma. I was shocked but grateful. I had to make a decision on what I was going to do. I couldn't locate you and I knew how important to you it was for Karisma to be safe. So, I made a decision to get myself and her out of the house. I would find a way to come back for you if I didn't hear from you. Thank God I did."

Jasmine was happy to hear what happened, but a little more excited because Richard stopped talking, giving her a minute to cut in. She asked him how it was last night for Karisma and how she slept. He let her know she was a very good baby. He had no issues at all. "Matter of fact," he started, "she is sleeping right next to me." There was a long pause and then a scream. Richard yelled that the baby was gone. Jasmine dropped the phone.

# About the Author

Joanne Monteiro grew up in Westchester County, New York. She is the youngest of three girls and as a child, used reading to escape. Her love for reading inspired her to write poetry and have her first poem published on Poetry.com. That achievement inspired Joanne to write a book about the one thing she learned about growing up; strong friendships.

When she is not working as a litigation insurance adjuster, she loves to read, play poker, and play with her dog.

# What Happened to Karisma?

Joanne Monteiro